Eddie's Boy

EDDIE'S BOY

THOMAS PERRY

THORNDIKE PRESS
A part of Gale, a Cengage Company

LIBRARY OF CONGRESS CIP DATA ON FILE.
CATALOGUING IN PUBLICATION FOR THIS BOOK
IS AVAILABLE FROM THE LIBRARY OF CONGRESS.

ISBN-13: 978-1-4328-8745-2 (hardcover alk. paper)

Published in 2021 by arrangement with The Mysterious Press, an
imprint of Grove/Atlantic, Inc.

Printed in Mexico
Print Number: 01   Print Year: 2021

For Jo, as always.

conversation with his wife, Meg.

Meg's family had kept a house near the
Royal Crescent in Bath for a couple of
centuries, and Bath was where she and Michael had met decades ago and still lived
for most of the year. Each spring, she would
pick a day when it was time for their retreat

1

Michael Schaeffer had not killed anyone in
years, and he was enraged at the fact that
he'd had to do it again tonight. He drove
the big black sedan along the deserted,
winding British lane toward the south under
the lightless sky, keeping his speed near the
limit of his ability to control the car.
Strapped upright with the seat belt in the
passenger seat beside him was a man with a
small, neat bullet hole through the side of
his head. In the rear seats two more men
with more pronounced firearm wounds
were strapped upright. In the trunk of the
car — he still thought *trunk* even though
everyone around him said *boot* — was
another corpse that had bled profusely and
was wrapped in a tarp. The sun would rise
in a few hours, and he would have to be rid
of this car and far away from it before then.
He went over his memory of the way this
had happened. It had started with a normal

7

conversation with his wife, Meg.

Meg's family had kept a house near the Royal Crescent in Bath for a couple of centuries, and Bath was where she and Michael had met decades ago and still lived for most of the year. Each spring, she would pick a day when it was time for their retreat from Bath. One day a few weeks ago, she'd had her laptop open on the big Regency desk in her study when he walked in.

Meg had already checked what she called "migration day" — the end of the spring semester in the academic schedules of American universities. She usually began with the ones in and around Boston. During the winter, Boston held over 250,000 students, and each summer a great many of them would be heading for England, most of them stopping in Bath, population 84,000. She used American students as bellwethers, because their movements were predictable, but there would also be hordes from other countries.

"I've checked the spring-semester exam schedules. It's off to Yorkshire no later than May fifth this year." She meant the family's historic home, the old estate a dozen miles outside the city of York. York was also a destination for tourists and students in the summer, but the house was off the main

8

routes and was not the best historical example of anything or the site of an important battle or a Roman ruin.

"Got it," said Michael. "I should be able to pack a razor and a toothbrush by then."

"Don't worry," she said. "You'll be reminded. Many times."

Whenever they stayed in the Yorkshire house, they slept in the second-floor bedroom remodeled in the 1650s for the earl of that generation and his wife and last modernized five years ago. It was one of eight large chambers for the family, but Meg and Michael were childless and the older members of her family had died years before. The lower level of the old house had been designed for public functions: a central dining hall, a big kitchen and pantry behind it, a drawing room, and a library — all modernized in the 1630s, over stone laid in the 1300s, and refurnished many times since then. The top two floors had contained an attic and the servants' rooms, but were long unoccupied. Meg had spent every day since they'd arrived planning and arranging her annual May party, and Michael helped with the practical work but stayed as unobtrusive as possible most of the time.

Then it was their tenth day back at the

Yorkshire house, the day of Meg's party. The party was important to her, because it was her way to issue greetings to her York friends and their families and the web of relatives and ancient connections who lived in the north. Her May party had gone on for enough years now that it was seen by many as the unofficial start to the part of the year when the island became less cold and wet.

Few if any of the minor aristocracy could afford to keep the garrisons of workers these houses had once employed. So once a year for her party, Meg would retain a gardening company and a crew of cleaners for ten days, a party rental company, a good caterer, and a group of parking attendants.

In her unabridged form Meg was the Honourable Margaret Susanna Moncrief Holroyd. Her family's holdings in York were first granted in the time of King Edmund in 941, after he had restored Anglo-Saxon control from the Scandinavians. In 946 he was murdered at age twenty-five by a robber in his royal hall at Pucklechurch, near Bath. In 1472 Edward IV granted the estate again to that generation's earl, his close drinking and whoring buddy. When Meg told Michael about it, he laughed, because it had cost the king nothing: it had already belonged to his friend's family for five hundred years.

The manor house had been given several major renovations over the centuries. The last large one was the result of the April 29, 1942, bombing raid that Hitler ordered after the RAF bombed Lübeck and Rostock. Ninety-two people were killed in York that night, none of them on the estate, but the central hall received a bomb through its roof, which needed to be repaired and restored.

Meg's party always began as soon as anyone appeared at the front gate and wouldn't end until she detected a diminution of gaiety late in the evening. In the morning there was a cricket match on the huge south lawn, where the party rental company had set up tables so that Meg could provide tea, pastries, and other refreshments for spectators. At one o'clock the caterers served lunch on the long tables of the great hall. In the afternoon a chamber orchestra performed and a church choir sang. Older adults played sedate outdoor games like croquet, lawn bowling, and lawn darts, and there were foot races and other sports for the young and the irrepressible. The caterers set out a buffet dinner at six, and at eight a rock DJ began playing music on the old pasture on the east side of the house.

That evening the party did not show signs of exhaustion until 11:00 p.m. Meg stopped the music at 11:30 and sent the parking attendants to direct traffic so that cars could get off the estate without hitting each other. She had drivers offer van rides to anyone who needed or wanted one.

Meg was triumphant. "It went smoothly this year, don't you think?" she asked.

Michael nodded. "Yep. You've outdone yourself again." Meg's party was one of his least favorite days of each year. Meg was not only an extrovert, but was also strikingly attractive, and had the money and taste to be glamorous. She was generous, witty, irreverent, and socially in demand even now, in her fifties. There were people from the North Sea to the English Channel at intervals of about a half mile who considered her one of their closest friends. Thirty years ago, when she first got romantically involved with an American who had typical American tastes and manners, there were some people in her social sphere who had been horrified, and others who simply shrugged and said that scandalizing snobs was her chief delight, but there was nobody who wasn't a little sick about it.

As soon as they met, Michael had realized that a man in his special circumstances had no way to survive except to become part of the background. The day he had flown to England, he had left many people in America who wanted him dead, people either burning for revenge or eager to collect on one of the contracts out on him, or whose job it was to put him in prison.

Once he was in England, he made an effort to avoid conversation when he could, and to cut it short if he couldn't. When Meg's friends asked what he did for a living, he said he was retired. When they wanted to know from what, he said he'd been in business. When they asked what business, he said it had been so dull that he had promised himself never to bore anybody else about it. He also maintained a lack of visible interest in most things other people said about themselves, and he had learned to keep Meg at the front, where she would attract all the attention.

Trouble had found him a couple of times anyway during their years together. The first time was just a chance sighting. A young American who had seen him once as a child in New York had been sent to serve an apprenticeship with casino operators in England and had spotted him at the horse races in Brighton with Meg and two of her friends. The next time was about ten years later, when an American boss named Frank Tosca had tried to inflate his reputation with the Mafia families by showing that his men could find and kill even the professional murderer who had been known as "the Butcher's Boy." Both times Michael had done the only thing he could — kept himself and Meg alive, and then made the person who had ordered his death realize, if only for a second, that he had made a terrible mistake.

Meg's Yorkshire party was one of the few times of the year when Michael could not be absent, hidden, or anonymous. He was Meg's husband, one of the hosts of the festivities that he dreaded. When Meg declared this year's party a success, he agreed, but what he meant was that he had not attracted much attention, had not had many personal conversations, and had not made himself memorable. There had also been no accidents, injuries, or illnesses at the party that would have forced him to deal with any authorities, now or later.

He and Meg stayed up that night until the caterers had cleaned the kitchen, packed their remaining supplies, and departed; the party rental people had loaded their trucks with all their furniture, appliances, tents, and decorations, and driven off safely; and all the extra helpers, parking attendants, and others had been paid and then cleared out. When Michael locked the doors and went up to bed with Meg, he felt a profound sense of relief. The damned Yorkshire party was over for another year.

But it wasn't. It was not until later that night, when Michael and Meg were asleep, that the final four visitors arrived.

Michael heard the sound from downstairs and identified it instantly. One of the leaded-glass panes of the windows along the side of the great hall had been pried out and slipped, and he heard it smash on the stone floor with a musical sound. He touched Meg's arm and whispered, "Wake up. Something's happening downstairs."

He stood up and remembered that he had locked the pistol he'd brought from Bath in the trunk of their Jaguar so that it wouldn't be where guests or temporary workers could stumble on it, and at the end of the evening he'd neglected to bring it upstairs.

He got out of bed, put on the clothes he'd taken off at bedtime, stepped into the old smoking room down the hallway, and went to the gun cabinet that had belonged to Meg's great-grandfather. The guns displayed

15

behind the glass doors were beautiful pieces of workmanship. His hand skipped past the three Purdey shotguns. They were each worth over £100,000. The two Holland and Hollands beside them were worth more. He had once used the Westley Richards with the single trigger and the barrel selector switch on top, so he chose it. This intruder was probably just an incompetent burglar who had cased the house during the party, and if so, Michael wouldn't have to fire the weapon anyway.

He slipped the gamekeeper's bag containing shotgun shells off its hook and over his shoulder and opened the gun to insert two shells. He moved down the hall away from the grand staircase and hurried to the back stairs, which had been used by the maids in the old days. He descended quietly, emerged in the kitchen, and stepped into the dining hall.

He saw two men at the window. They had already reached through the empty frame where they had removed the glass and had disengaged the latch. Now they were climbing in.

Schaeffer moved along the inner wall across from the windows until he was abreast of the one they had opened. One of the men looked up and saw him, so Michael said, "What are you doing here? Are you lost?"

The man crouched and aimed a pistol at him. Michael pulled the trigger of the antique shotgun. It roared, and the man was swept backward, as though swatted by an invisible hand.

The second man aimed his pistol at Michael, so Michael selected the other barrel. The shotgun roared again, and that man jerked backward and collapsed onto the floor in a lazy dive.

Michael heard the sound of running feet toward the open window. He ran to the first man's body, pulled off his hooded rain jacket, put it on himself, then laid the antique shotgun across the second man's chest. He lay down on his side with the man's watch cap tugged down on his head and checked the man's pistol by touch. It was a nine-millimeter semiautomatic, and the rectangular shape of its slide told him that it was a Glock. The safety was incorporated into the trigger mechanism, so he wouldn't have to search for a catch.

The third man ran to the open window and stepped to one side so he could see the three bodies in the moonlight. He quickly chose the man with the shotgun across his chest, assuming he was Michael, and fired a

17

round into the man's head.

In a single quick motion, Michael half turned, raised the Glock, and fired it upward into the underside of the man's jaw.

He stood up, picked up the second man's pistol, put it in the pocket of the coat he'd taken, and then climbed out the open window.

The grass beside the manor house was wet with dew, and in the moonlight he could see the three men's shoe prints on it. They clearly had come across the lawn from the direction of the woods on the south side of the estate near the gate.

He looked closely at the wet grass, and once he was in the open, he could see that the feet had not been walking. They had been trotting. It made him think there must have been a time issue. If they had just driven onto the estate, they should have been able to park and walk as slowly and quietly as they wished.

So time must be tight. That meant they must have concocted some sort of idiotic alibi that required them to come here and kill him while their alibi time was ticking. With beginners, the alibi was usually a ticket to a movie or a sports event, something that would not require an actual person to stand up in front of the cops and lie for him.

They had certainly been amateurish. They hadn't been difficult to kill, and their plan seemed to have been no more than to put themselves in his house while he was asleep and assume that made him practically dead to start. There had to be a car parked somewhere. No, it could be more than that. Anybody who wanted him dead would be an American, and Americans might have an English driver.

He supposed the three were the current generation of American bosses' idea of professionals. Someone had sent them to England to take him out after all these years. Somebody — maybe a British contact — should have realized that they were not the best choice for driving a long distance over the English countryside at high speed in the dark, getting themselves to Meg's Yorkshire house, and driving themselves back in time to save their alibi. So somewhere on the property would be a fast car and maybe an English driver. He hoped that if the driver existed, he hadn't heard the difference between the shotgun blasts and the pop of a pistol. But Schaeffer hadn't fired the shotgun outdoors, so the thick old stone walls might have muffled the sound a bit.

Michael broke into a trot. If the schedule

of the attackers required that they run to the manor house and back, surely it required that he run too. If the driver heard or saw a man trotting toward him instead of sneaking, he'd feel reassured. At least he would until Michael got there.

As he went farther toward the woods, he could smell the exhaust of the car in the night air, and then he could hear the engine, faintly. The car had to be in among the trees. Michael followed the sound and found the car parked just inside the edge of the woods, where the trees were far apart. It was a big black Bentley sedan. The car added to the evidence that these men had not simply been violent burglars. They had been sent to kill him. He approached the car in its blind spot to the right behind the driver's head.

When Michael was close behind him, the driver jumped and spun halfway around in his seat. He appeared to recognize the rain jacket Michael had taken. "You think that's funny?" An English accent, but not from Yorkshire. "I ought to leave you here."

Michael held one of the pistols to the man's head. The driver was frozen looking up at him, and Michael could tell he was thinking he would have been better off if he had backed into the woods and were still facing the windscreen. He might have stomped on the pedal and sped off.

Michael answered his thought. "You wouldn't have made it. I've killed a lot of men when they tried to drive away. But if you can tell me who sent the four of you after me and why, I'll let you go."

The driver seemed to feel cheated of his expectations. He obviously hadn't been paid yet. "Where are the others? Them three? This was their job, not mine. I was just hired to drive the car."

"I could tell. That's why I couldn't offer them the same deal."

"I heard shots. Are they dead?"

Michael nodded. "They weren't as good at this as they needed to be. Did they even know who I am?"

"Maybe they did," the driver said. His brain seemed to be working frantically. "I don't."

"Who do you work for?"

"Nobody. I drive customers on long-distance rides. They found me online."

Michael flung open the door, dragged him out onto the ground, and held the gun on him. "Somebody owns the Bentley, or owns you, and sent you to do a dangerous job. You wouldn't have sat waiting for them to finish a murder if they were strangers who hired you online. You shouldn't have lied. One more chance."

"I told you the truth."

Michael fired into his forehead and stepped back from the car and into the trees. He waited for any other man he hadn't seen to come toward the car, but after a few minutes, none had. He took the driver's wallet, got into the driver's seat, and backed the car onto the pressed-gravel drive to the manor house. Then he went inside and turned on the lights in the great hall to look at the bodies.

The first man, who had the shotgun lying across his chest, was dead. The third man, who'd shot from outside, had been fooled by the shotgun and put a bullet through his head. Michael had shot the third man from the floor as he leaned in the window; a bullet under his jaw had come out the top of his head. Michael had some hope for the remaining man. His only wound was the shotgun blast from the other side of the big room. In the dark Michael had guessed that the shells were probably number 7, because the only game anyone had shot here in modern times as far as he knew was pheasant.

He looked closely at the man and felt for the pulse in his neck, but found he had been optimistic. He opened the breach of the shotgun and saw that the shells were number 4, intended for deer and men. He closed the shotgun, set it carefully on the table beside him, and looked up. His eye caught movement at the top of the big staircase.

Standing there in an ankle-length white satin nightgown and a long, lightweight robe was his wife. Meg stood with perfect, erect posture looking down at him.

"Oh, hello," he said. "I'm sorry for all the noise and commotion."

"I assumed it must have happened again," she said. "Are you all right?"

"Yes."

"It looks as though you've got it under control."

"Yes, it's pretty much over."

"What sort of time have we got?" she said. "Should I be throwing on some clothes and running for the car, or do we have time to talk?"

"We'll make the time," he said. "I have these two men under the windows, one outside, and another in the wood on the way to the gate. I'll join you after I've cleaned up."

"You know, Michael, you're not thirty anymore. Maybe we could ask some men we trust to help out."

He shook his head. "I'd rather not. Even helping at this stage would make them guilty of serious crimes. That wouldn't be much reward for being worth trusting."

"I suppose not." She turned and walked away from the top of the stairs toward their bedroom.

Michael took a deep breath and knelt beside the two bodies. He searched for wallets, weapons, and other belongings and discovered they both had US passports. He got up, closed and latched the window, and set the broken piece of glass on the table with the shotgun.

He took off the first man's rain jacket, spread it on the floor, rolled its owner onto it, and dragged him to the door and out to the rear of the Bentley. Then he took the jacket back and used it to drag the second body out, and then used it a third time on the grass for the man he'd shot through the open window.

He had too many bodies to transport in a car trunk. They would have to be in the seats. He hoisted one of them to the rear seat and fastened the seat belt around him, and then another. He opened the trunk and managed to get the head, arms, and torso of the third man's body up over the edge of the trunk, and then one leg at a time, bending one knee and then the other. The final man was the most difficult. The whole process of loading the car had taken no more than ten minutes, but Michael's arms, back, and legs felt as strained as if it had taken several hours. He sat on the stone steps until his breathing returned to normal.

He heard Meg's voice. "I hope you didn't hurt yourself."

He glanced over his shoulder. "I'm fine. Do you remember what we did with that blue tarp we bought for the painting last summer but didn't use?"

"It's in the carriage house. They used it to shade the coolers for the cold drinks during the day and then put it in there."

"Thanks." He got up and walked to the carriage house to retrieve the tarp. When he came back, Meg was looking in the car window at the three killers he had propped up.

"It's not like you to look."

She shrugged. "This reminds me that you only get a certain number of days. If you spend any of them without paying attention, it's as though you weren't alive at all. Not just the pleasant parts either."

He opened the passports of the three Americans and was puzzled. They appeared to be genuine, but they said the men's names were Koslowski, O'Rourke, and Benson. The names of the people who had reasons to kill him were all Italian. These men must all have been hired shooters. He opened the glove box of the Bentley. The registration papers said the owner was a place called Luxury Rentals, with an address in London, but no name of a human being. Time was passing, and he had to move. He looked up at Meg. "Let's go talk."

2

They went upstairs to the master bedroom. Michael took some of the clothes he had brought to Yorkshire off the hangers and out of the drawers and laid them on the bed, then folded them quickly in neat stacks.

"What are you doing?"

He said, "I've got to drive their car away from here as soon as possible. We can't have four bodies lying around."

"I'll follow you in the Jaguar so you can park them somewhere, and then we'll go away."

He looked at her, her bright green eyes still astonishing to him after all the years. Her hair, a dark reddish brown when he met her, was still that color, kept that way by a visit to a salon once a month for years. She had begun noting the arrival of each wrinkle on her face when she was thirty, but had stopped talking about them because she believed the worst kind of narcissism was a person whining about time and her body's offenses against her.

He still loved to look at her, and he had every day. She'd told him she didn't mind. "You saw me when I was in my twenties, gorgeous and athletic, and partly for that reason I can bear to have you see me now. I know that who you see includes both then and now." It was true, like thousands of surprising things she'd said over the years.

He said, "We can't just go away together and hope this is over."

"This isn't the first time they've found you."

"No, it isn't."

"The first time it happened we were still young. You lied to me about it."

"Well."

"When you came home I didn't know any of the details, but I knew the gist of it. You made up a story that you thought would make me feel better, and I loved you even more for it. I still don't know what you actually did to make it stop."

"The truth wouldn't have made you like me any better."

"Don't be too sure." She paused. "And then we were happy for years and years, until the night when they came for you again. And that time the men were dead in fifteen minutes, and in twenty you had left me alone again."

"I'm sorry. I've never been somebody who was worth your attention, or your company, much less your love. The attempts to kill me were things I brought on myself that I earned before we met. You never had a reason to stay once the first time happened."

"The point being not to elicit a tardy apology but to note that tonight it happened — is happening — a third time. Twice in our lives you left me at home and went off to find enemies you had not anticipated would be coming for you. I will only remind you that I have lived with you and loved you for thirty years, thinking of you as Michael Schaeffer, even though I've known for at least that long that it was never your name. Now I want you to do me the favor of considering a suggestion."

"What?"

"I know that right now part of your mind is ranging ahead, thinking about how you get to America and leave me in some kind of storage so I'll be safe while you go off down some hole to kill whoever is after you. I'm begging you not to."

"What do you want me to do?"

"I want you to take me on a trip, but not

to America."

"Where, then?"

"I don't know or care. Not to kill some-body. Maybe Australia, where nobody knows you or the people who hate you."

He took his watch from the nightstand, slipped it on, and looked at it. Time was passing, and he needed to be on the road. He said, "I can't take you with me. I know that seems debatable, but it isn't. You have a million friends in England who will be delighted if you would visit them for a month or so. You'll be as safe as a person can be. I want you to pack up, put a suitcase in the Jaguar, drive yourself to one of their homes, and later, if necessary, another, and another. Stay out of sight for as long as this takes."

"Then please, just make me a deal. If we can't go to Australia together, you can go alone. It will buy you time, at least. You can use computers and phones to learn what you can from there. Just don't rush off to America. Since their first try failed, they'll be waiting for you there, expecting you." She hugged him. "Please, Michael. Just give me that much. I'll know you're safe for a while. If Australia is safe, I could even join you there."

He looked at her, then said reluctantly,

"I'll try it."

She hugged him harder. "Thank you, Michael. I know you've got to get going now. Do it. I'll be packed and off in the Jaguar in ten minutes or so."

"I'll try it."

She hugged him harder. "Thank you, Michael. I know you've got to get going now. Do it. I'll be packed and off in the Jaguar in ten minutes or so."

3

He put his leather carry-on bag in the trunk of the car on top of the blue tarp that was spread over the body of the driver, got into the Bentley, and began to drive. He drifted slowly as far as the front gate, watching for a glow of headlights, and then turned south onto the high road and accelerated. He looked at his phone and saw that the distance from York to Manchester Airport was 144 kilometers. He opened the case of the phone, took out the battery, and put the phone in his sport coat.

He could drive now with the three corpses strapped into the seats of the Bentley, but he knew he would have to get rid of the car before there was enough light to see that his passengers were dead. He had to put as much distance as he could behind him each minute of the next hour and a half.

As he drove south, he couldn't help thinking about how his life had narrowed down to this. He and Meg hadn't said it, but they both knew that it was unlikely he'd live to return home one more time. He'd had a long life for a man in his line of work. He had begun working at age fifteen and quit at age thirty-one, the week he had met Meg Holroyd. Yes, as she'd reminded him, a few years later he'd had to go back to the United States to kill some people, but not for money. Years after that, Frank Tosca's men had found him. He had survived his trip to solve that problem too. It had been a long haul. As of tonight, when he'd made the four corpses he had strapped in the seats and placed in the trunk, he had been killing people as needed for about forty-five years, the last thirty just to keep breathing.

Everything he knew about his early life he had heard from Eddie Mastrewski. He could practically hear him talking now as he drove through the night fifty years later. "Your parents just showed up in Pittsburgh, nobody knew from where. They were new and nobody knew much about them. They were in their mid-twenties, maybe twenty-three and twenty-four. This neighborhood — the Flats — was the way it is now, a nice place to live but not fancy. The only place anybody wore a necktie was to church or their funeral. Things looked the same as now — one-family to four-family houses. Your parents rented an upstairs apartment in a big house. They already had you, so they showed up with a lot of toys and books and kid-size furniture and stuff. They also had a bunch of books for grown-ups, but I don't know what kind.

"Most of the businesses were already here. The two grocery stores, the three barber shops — Mel's, the Barbery Coast, and the Hair House — and the four or five women's salons. There were already the two regular pharmacies, but the chain drugstore hadn't come in yet. Vincent the tailor has been there since the last ice age, and the same with the Heaven-Scent cleaners and Lana's Sewing Shop. The liquor stores, the pool hall, Dan's Shoe Repair, and the pawnshop were left over from when I was a kid. The churches were all around since the 1820s, I think — Catholic, Eastern Orthodox, and a few Protestant denominations. I started my butcher shop the year after I got out of the army.

"Your parents never told anybody much, not because they were the kind of people who kept secrets. They just hadn't been in town long enough to have many conversations before they were killed in the car wreck. In those days I was always in the

34

shop working during the day, and they weren't customers, so I never actually saw them."

Other short conversations had taken place at other times. He remembered Eddie saying, "Even the landlady didn't know much. She didn't have much to say, except that she thought they might be students because of the books and the fact that they lived a quiet life — no late nights, no boozing — but you could have said that about a lot of people."

Another time Eddie said, "You were kind of a challenge for the neighborhood. You were about three years old, or a little younger. The cops who came to investigate told somebody that you would probably have to be turned over to the county since they hadn't located any relatives."

"The county?" He remembered that he couldn't imagine what a county would do with him, or with anybody.

"It probably wouldn't have been so bad," Eddie said. "What they usually did was place a kid with a foster family, who would take care of him until some other family adopted him."

"How come they didn't do it to me?"

"We kind of headed it off. They called a neighborhood meeting one night at

Sidderly's restaurant. We — the grown-ups who sort of owned and operated the neighborhood — talked about it."

"Who was that?"

"There were three hairdressers, and Mr. and Mrs. Sidderly, since they were there anyway, and the owners of the two pharmacies, the managers who ran the grocery stores, a couple of teachers, some PTA mothers, a couple of ministers, a doctor named Birken who's since died, and I don't remember who else. None of us felt we wanted to just hand you to the cops, so we decided to find a way to handle your situation ourselves. After a lot of talk, one of the others said, 'Does anybody have a suggestion?'

"I've always hated long meetings, so I got up and said, 'You all know me, Eddie the Butcher. I haven't raised any kids, but I have a good business, a big house, and I can give him a good room, clean clothes, healthy food, and reasonable encouragement. I can also teach him a trade, if he turns out to be up to learning it.' People talked about it among themselves, and they decided to take me up on it." He added, "I want you to know I've never regretted it. Not for a second."

Now, looking back on it, Michael

Schaeffer had to admit that Eddie had more than lived up to his promise. He had taught him how to cut meat; weigh and wrap the cuts; make change for customers; run a spotlessly clean, sterile shop; pay suppliers, bills, and taxes; and keep up appearances. Eddie had also taught the boy his other profession, the one that the other shopkeepers and businessmen and their families never knew about.

He remembered being about ten when Eddie had begun teaching him that other profession — how to see the best way into a house, how to follow people. They would walk along, and Eddie would deliver muttered observations: "That guy up there? He's following that woman a hundred feet ahead of him. He's going too fast. She's about to go by a bunch of women's stores, and she'll slow down to look. Even if she doesn't go in, she'll pretend to look at the clothes, but really check her own reflection to see if she looks good. Since she does, she'll look longer. He should be able to see what's ahead as well as you and I can, but his brain is in neutral. He'll come right up on her, close enough for her to feel him. Then he won't want to pass, so he'll stop and light a cigarette or something. That will make him stand out even more and spook her."

"Why is he following her?"

Eddie shrugged. "Who knows? Maybe he's shy. Maybe he's a cop. Maybe she's cheating on him or a friend of his. Maybe he's nuts."

It seemed odd now that some of the biggest decisions in Schaeffer's life were ones he hadn't even made. They had just seemed to be the conditions for keeping life inside him, made before his mind began fitting sights, sounds, and thoughts into memory.

4

Schaeffer fought the forces of physics to keep the Bentley moving as fast as he could without hurtling off into a field or hitting something along the road. He hated that the British government kept adding new CCTV cameras from one end of the country to the other. He could be completely successful tonight, and there might be a video shot from the top of a pole in some out-of-the way-village, and there he would be, driving this opulent death wagon down the road.

He could only comfort himself with the articles he'd read saying that the cameras had not had any effect on crime statistics. None. Since they're no good at it, he told himself, he was probably safe. And in England, people who could afford cars like the Bentley often felt they had bought the right to drive them at full speed. Maybe that would keep the cops from assuming he was a criminal.

Schaeffer turned his head and used the rearview mirror to check his passengers. He had pulled their seat belts as tight as he could so that none of them toppled over, but as he hit bumps or made hard turns, their heads nodded or leaned slightly.

He wondered where Meg was driving now. Even thinking about her made him angrier. These killers had come all the way to England and then somehow figured out that this was the season when he and Meg went to the house in Yorkshire. They hadn't tried to find him out alone somewhere and pop him with a rifle or something. They had come to murder him in his bed, which meant killing Meg too, after she'd seen them killing him first.

He looked at the bodies again and resented them. But he was alive, and they were not. He told himself he should accept that fact as though it were a triumph. He didn't imagine there would be any other triumphs this trip. Before long, he would probably be cornered, and then dead too.

When he was still forty miles out from Manchester, he put the battery back in his phone and used it to make a reservation for the next flight to Sydney, which would leave at 8:00 a.m. He knew the Manchester Airport was south of the city center, but the details were fuzzy, so he used the map function, which showed him that he needed to get on the M56. He memorized the route, took the battery out again, and drove harder and faster.

It was a bit after 4:00 a.m. now, and at this hour there were no delays. Once he switched to the main highways, most of the traffic was fast-moving trucks heading for the city to deliver the thousands of products that would be unloaded into the stores that morning.

In less than an hour he was on the M56 passing signs that directed him to the big parking lots for the airport. He pulled onto the shoulder of the highway, put on the knitted watch cap he had taken from one of the dead men in the dining room at York, and tugged it down to his eyes. He patted the body beside him and found a pair of tinted sunglasses. The man behind him had a scarf in his pocket with no blood on it, so he took that too, wrapped it around the lower part of his face, then drove on. He picked the first airport lot he saw, pulled in, took a ticket from the machine, and then drove to a remote section of the lot, where he parked the Bentley with the grille aimed off toward an empty field. A sign said there was a shuttle to the airport every fifteen minutes.

He opened the trunk, and took his suitcase out, then spent a few minutes wiping down the car to get rid of his fingerprints. When he looked around him, there seemed to be nobody else waiting for the shuttle. Most of these cars must have been left here in the lot yesterday or even earlier. He walked away from the Bentley and its four dead passengers and toward the farthest sign for a shuttle stop.

5

If anyone was aware of where he'd driven from York, they hadn't caught up yet, but he had to be alert and keep his eyes open. First, he needed to get to the terminal without attracting any attention. The shuttle would probably not be full at this hour and would probably make the rounds of every lot on the way. He would have to be patient. Nothing raised suspicion among watchers like impatience. Fugitives, terrorists, and thieves all felt each second like the stab of a needle, and today he would too. He couldn't show it.

In America there were always at least three sets of watchers at major airports. The local police forces always had older retired police officers there to watch for criminals and their bosses. The Mafia watched for people they were interested in — each other or the up-and-coming types who were working to replace them. The third group were thieves.

They watched for women who set their purses or carry-on bags on seats around them, for people who didn't pick up their bags right away when they came out of the X-ray machines or lost track of a bag in the bathroom. They would sometimes pick suitcases off the carousels at baggage claim. If a traveler caught them, they'd say they worked for the airline. He hadn't flown out of the UK often, but he knew that British airports had the equivalent. He was eager to get past all those people and onto a plane.

Meg had bought his bag as a companion to one of hers. It was a leather carry-on, designed to take a few worries out of travel. It had several zippered pockets on the outside and a shoulder strap consisting of leather sewn around a steel cable, so a thief couldn't slash it and run off with the bag. This morning he carried it with the strap on his shoulder and kept his hands in his coat pockets as he waited.

Waiting to be taken to a place he hadn't wanted to go reminded him of working with Eddie Mastrewski. Eddie had told him, "If you're not sure what's there, don't make a mad dash for the city. You can always sneak up on it. Go most of the way there and then stop to look around. Go past the neighborhood where you're supposed to do the job.

If there are people hanging around like they're waiting for something, turn around and drive out of town. What they're waiting for is you."

Michael had an American passport in the name Paul Foster. It was a relic of his last trip to the United States seven years ago. He had used it only once, and it had been intended for only that single use, to get him out of the United States. It had been obtained at a risk by someone who had owed him a big favor. He had not intended to ever use it again, but he had kept it, aware that he couldn't predict the future.

The time was weighing on his nerves, so he forced himself to think about other things. He had found that since getting older, he had a surprising number of unexpected thoughts and feelings. He didn't like the prediction that in five billion years the earth would succumb to the sun's gravity, fall into it, and burn up. This was surprising because it raised the possibility that he cared about Man, not just a few people. It put him in the category of the ants, which did brave and strenuous things while in the process of dying to preserve not just some ants but Ant. He had lived a life without being aware of species loyalty, partly because at no time after he was fifteen had he been confident of living for long.

Sometimes it seemed to him that he had lived a long life — and done it with surprising success — without having learned anything about why things were as they were. He had met a beautiful and brilliant young Englishwoman by pure chance one day while he was trying to stay invisible in the ancient city of Bath. They had been attracted to each other in the first minutes, and became lovers just hours after that. Life-threatening circumstances that surprised even him — the attack at the Brighton races — had made the two of them cling to each other like drowning swimmers, and they had never relinquished each other since. He had experienced all those years with her and had never stopped being amazed and grateful that this woman, the Honourable Margaret Holroyd, now O.B.E., had given herself over to his keeping, allowed herself without visible hesitation to love him, and stayed faithful, loyal, and constant.

He was frustrated that after so much time he still didn't know much about women in general, or about Meg. She never overtly told him anything about her motives, her fantasies or desires, or what she really thought about him. All he knew was what had happened between them, and she seemed to think it was all he was entitled to know. He hoped that right now she was already safe in the house of one of her friends.

The sky was still dark as a misty rain began to fall, putting tiny droplets on the windows of the cars nearby and turning the lot into a vast wet black pavement.

After waiting about ten minutes, he assured himself that the shuttle would appear in another five. He knew that the shuttle had to enter at one of the entrances, and guessed it wouldn't drive past a man standing in the rain, so he decided to walk toward the entrance he could see.

He took a few steps toward the end of the aisle and heard an engine behind him.

The engine was too loud. Michael had lived a long time by not assuming that things weren't dangerous. He looked over his shoulder only once to locate the car and chart its speed and direction. He thought, *This might be nothing.* But the car had passed a number of open spaces and hadn't taken one. It hadn't moved toward a different part of the lot, or chosen one to begin with. It had turned to go up the same aisle as the only pedestrian in the lot.

Michael walked on, using the sound of

the car to gauge its distance. The car was closer now. He listened intently. If it sped up, it would be trying to hit him. If it slowed down, someone in it would be planning to shoot.

Four more strides and he sidestepped to the right to put himself between two vans.

There was the growl of the engine speeding up, then a loud squeal of tires as the driver braked, and then the tires spinning. There was the slam of a car door, then fast footsteps, leather-soled shoes dashing toward him.

Michael knelt on the ground, looked under the van beside him, and saw the feet of the running man. He went up on the balls of his feet and waited, then launched himself into the space between the van and the next car. Like a football tackler, he hit the man with his shoulder and slammed him into the car. The man's own speed, combined with the force of Michael's tackle, made the impact hard and damaging. The man was hurt, and he was down. In a second, Michael had his legs wrapped around the man's body like a wrestler would, and he was tightening the strap from his suitcase around the man's neck.

After a few more seconds of intense effort, Michael sensed a change and let go of the strap with his left hand. He pulled it, and it came off the man's neck and the man lay still. Michael rolled the man's body away from him and then knelt over it, rapidly patting its pockets and running his hands along the sides, the legs, the small of the back. He found a large folding knife, but no gun.

He looked up from the man and his eyes went straight across the aisle of cars where he heard the engine again.

He heard another car door slam, then more footsteps. This time he saw the reflection in a rearview mirror of a man moving from the direction of the car sounds to the opening between two cars where Michael had run.

The driver seemed to have assumed that Michael had been killed by his friend and that now it was his responsibility to help clean up. Michael slid under the van beside him and slithered toward the front. Then he heard leather-soled shoes again, running this time, making that *chuff, chuff* sound when the balls of the feet hit the pavement. He used it to tell where to look for the man's feet.

When he saw them, he slid out on the other side of the van. He stood still and waited until the man was near the back, then came around the front of the van to approach him from behind. Michael hooked his left forearm across the man's face at eye level, jerked his head backward, and brought the knife across the man's throat. Michael quickly withdrew his arm and pushed the man hard with his other hand. Blood spurted out in a stream from the man's open wound as he lay sprawled on the pavement between the cars, bleeding heavily.

Michael ran along the aisle, got into the car the two men had left there, and drove it between two white lines into a parking space. He pressed the key fob to lock it and then ran back to where the first body lay. He picked up his leather bag, reattached the strap to it, and began to walk.

His eyes caught headlights at a distance. It was the shuttle coming in the entrance. He trotted to the end of the aisle and stepped out to flag down the bus before it got close enough for the driver to see the two bodies lying between the cars.

6

Schaeffer checked in for his flight to Sydney as Paul Foster, received his boarding pass, and then used some of the waiting time in the airport shops buying clothes. He had gotten splashes of dirty water on the clothes he'd worn in the Long Stay Car Park. He was sure that he'd picked up some blood spray too, although he couldn't see it. He also wanted to change his appearance as much as possible.

He found a guidebook to Sydney in a tourist shop and looked up the weather. It was late autumn there now, with temperatures between 14.6 and 22.2 degrees Celsius — not much different from May temperatures in Manchester. He still automatically translated the numbers to Fahrenheit, even though he didn't need to anymore: it was about 58 to 72 degrees.

He replaced the clothes he'd been wearing and left those in the trash in the distant restroom where he got changed. He spent the rest of the wait near a gate far from the one where he would be departing. He approached his gate right as the plane was boarding, so he could minimize the time he spent standing still. As he approached the gate, he stared intently at each person, looking for watchers. He doubled back to be sure nobody was following him, then waited for his boarding group to be called and got in line. As soon as he had made it past the doorway into the boarding tunnel, he began to feel a bit better.

He made it down the aisle of the plane and pushed his bag into the overhead compartment. Soon the airplane's doors were closed, the plane pushed back onto the apron, and then it bumped along on the pavement, its wings vibrating slightly. It stopped, the engine noise swelled, and it roared off and upward into the sky.

The flight was enormously long — fifteen thousand kilometers — and his first stop would take place after twelve hours. He would wait in Singapore for two hours and then endure eleven more hours to Sydney. After that, he would find his way to a section of Sydney called "The Rocks." It produced no image at all in his imagination, but according to his guidebook, it was the right place to go.

It was incredibly far, and that was the idea. It was his attempt to do things the way Meg wanted. At one time that would not have occurred to him, but he wasn't just humoring her. For his whole working life and afterward, he had followed the strategy that Eddie Mastrewski had taught him: "If you learn there's a contract out on you, don't hesitate. Find out who it is and go after him. Don't bother wasting bodyguards or underlings. Go right to the one who pays them all. Find him and stop his heart any way you can. You don't get anything for giving his people an extra hour of open season on you."

In this situation he'd never done anything else. Maybe it was time to use Meg's idea instead. He was alive, the ones who had followed him were dead, and he was flying away at over six hundred miles an hour. Maybe this was going to be the end of the killing. If Australia turned out to be safe and pleasant, she would join him.

He lay back in his seat and thought about the start of his life as a killer. When he and Eddie had talked about it years later, they always called it "Opening Day."

The memory of that day nearly fifty years ago was clearer than the sight of it had been at the time. He could remember all that had led up to it, could see and feel the bright warm sunshine and the excitement and anticipation, and could hear the voices of the people around him that day. But this time through, he knew all the rest of it too. He knew what was going to happen, and he knew what it meant, and how the world was going to change, and how he was going to change. What would have surprised him at the time were the many ways in which he would be exactly the same. He would still be the boy, feeling and thinking and wondering the same at sixty as he did that day at fifteen.

He walked along the sidewalk with Eddie, aware of the difference in their sizes. Eddie Mastrewski was bulky and strong, not much taller than the boy was at fifteen, but broader, with a bull neck and big workman's arms and legs.

The boy wore a baseball cap that day with the letters *N* and *Y* superimposed on the crown, because it was New York and anything else would have seemed exotic, and he had a well-worn baseball glove folded under his arm as though he hoped to catch a foul ball. He was a walking story that day. Anybody who looked would have said, "This is a kid who loves baseball, and his dad is taking him to the opening home game." Eddie had set it up. "You take the hat off afterward and you're a different person. As soon as the gun goes off, that's who you're going to want to be."

It all happened fast, and even though he'd known it would, it was still faster than he'd expected. They came up on the man Eddie had agreed to kill, walking up from behind. Eddie stuck his hand out and the boy opened the glove to let him take the gun — a short-barreled .38 DA's Special. Eddie grasped it and took the shot — loud, bright like a hammer blow — and the man's head jerked forward and the rest of him snaked downward after it onto the concrete.

The boy accepted the gun back and folded the glove over it. People were already going, "What? What was that?" And Eddie did the rest of the pantomime. "Oh my God," he said. "He's bleeding," and bent to look so that other people would look down too.

The next seconds taught the boy a lot. The target was down and dead. But Eddie was not prepared for the man beside the victim to turn toward Eddie while digging a gun out of his coat. When Eddie had planned the hit, this man hadn't existed yet.

Eddie was too far away from the boy to snatch the gun back, and he knew it instantly. He stopped looking toward the man and looked at the boy — not a message, just a sad look, a goodbye look.

The boy's hand went to the glove, came out with the gun, and fired it into the second man's head. As the man fell, Eddie took the boy by the hand. They walked off together and stepped down into the next subway entrance. Eddie had already bought tokens that would get them back to the hotel. They pushed through the turnstile and made it onto a subway car that was unloading its baseball fans and was now nearly empty. They sat down. The boy sat stiffly, his heart pounding while the train filled. He was looking at people to see if they had followed him and Eddie down. When he saw that they were just regular riders, he silently urged them on, begged them to hurry. Finally the train's seats filled, the doors closed, and it moved ahead, picking up speed with that clacking and rattling noise that he knew was making them safe. Eddie looked up and saw two women standing above them, hanging onto a chrome-plated bar.

Eddie elbowed him and nodded, then smiled at the women. Eddie and the boy stood, and Eddie offered their seats to the two women. "Please have a seat," he said.

The more attractive of the two women, who was tall with long blond hair and about thirty years old, turned away as though she hadn't heard. Her companion slipped right in and slid over to the window.

Eddie leaned close to the blond woman. "Please. As a favor to me," he said. "I can only keep teaching my boy manners by trying to have them myself."

She looked at him and gave him a tentative smile. Then she said to the boy, "You should pay attention to your dad. I'll bet women all love him because he's so polite." She slid past Eddie and sat in the aisle seat beside her friend.

"Yes, ma'am," the boy said. Then he added what Eddie always wanted him to say in these situations. "But he's not my dad. He's my uncle."

"Oh," she said.

"It's been just us at home since I lost my parents."

The woman was pretty enough to have been the target of many lines, overtures, and impostures, so she sensed this might be another. But would it come by proxy from a teenager?

Eddie held on to the chromed bar and made sure the boy had a good grip too. Eddie was too wily to try to expand this interaction into a conversation. He stood straight, stared ahead, and waited.

After a few minutes, the woman's dark-haired companion half-stood. "My stop is coming up."

The boy and Eddie stepped backward to give the blond woman the space to let her friend out. She had to lean forward while her friend slid out. The back of the dark-haired woman brushed against the boy — a sensation the boy found much nicer than he had imagined. The woman half-turned to look at him quizzically, because she could not quite ignore the fact that she had pressed her backside against his body to get out. She could see that he'd had nowhere to go to avoid her. "Sorry," she said, and pushed the moment into her memory of the inconsequential events of the day, and not the outrages and offenses. She smiled at him and then said to her friend, "Bye, Brenda. See you tomorrow."

Brenda slid into the window seat and looked up at Eddie. "There's plenty of room."

Eddie smiled and said, "Thank you." Then he gently pushed the boy into the seat.

Brenda turned to the boy. "Is he always like this?" She glanced up at Eddie to be sure he'd heard.

"What do you mean?"

She leaned close to the boy, and he smelled her faint, sweet perfume. She whispered, "So nice."

The boy shrugged. "I guess so."

She kept her eyes on the boy. "What does your aunt think?"

"I don't have one. It's just us."

After about five minutes the boy said to Eddie, "I'll stand for a while."

Eddie said to the woman, "Do you mind?"

"Of course not."

Eddie took his place, and then the conversation was all Eddie and Brenda. When she got off at the next stop, Eddie and the boy got off too. Eddie explained that the boy was hungry. She told Eddie about a really nice restaurant not far from her stop. He seemed to have trouble understanding the directions, so she walked with them.

When they reached the restaurant, Eddie asked her to stay and have dinner with them. She refused. When he smiled in his friendliest way, she refused. But when he took her aside and, in a whisper, invented the story that the boy wanted her to because he missed having adult women around since his mother died, she said, "Oh, of course. I hadn't thought of that. I didn't mean to be insensitive."

The dinner was as good as she had promised. They walked her home and somehow ended up staying the night in her apartment. He had not heard how that had been arranged, or if by then a story had even been necessary. He fell asleep on Brenda's couch under a blanket. When he woke in darkness late at night, Eddie and Brenda were beyond the closed door on the other end of the living room.

The reality he woke to was that he had killed a man. He had not exactly forgotten it. Even during the long subway ride, the dinner, and the walk, he had seen flashes of it, but he hadn't had time to stop to think it through. There had been too many things happening, being said or done. There were too many words in the conversations between Eddie and the pretty woman, Brenda, that he wasn't supposed to hear, but did. For the next couple of hours in the dark living room, he revisited the whole day, step by step, seeing the sights, hearing the gunshots and the shouting, and then feeling the urgency of walking to the subway platform when his body wanted to run.

He heard the sounds of small, graceful footsteps and opened his eyes to see it was light. Brenda was making them breakfast before she had to get ready for work. She was wearing a short nightgown. When the food was ready, she went behind the door and woke Eddie so they could eat while she bathed and dressed.

As they ate, Eddie said, "Good, huh?"

"Yeah," the boy said. "She's a good cook."

"Then don't forget to tell her."

A few minutes later, she emerged to find Eddie washing the dishes. The boy said, "Thank you very much for breakfast. It was very good."

When they left, Brenda stopped them at the door and gave Eddie a long, serious kiss. Then she said, "Let me know next time you're back in New York." As they stepped through the door, she grabbed the boy, hugged him, and kissed his cheek. "You too."

They went out and walked toward the corner. Eddie looked at the boy for a few seconds as they walked. "You did great yesterday. Good nerves, giant balls. You okay?"

"Sure," the boy said.

Eddie waved a cab to pull over, and they took the cab to the lot on Staten Island where he had left his car. Then they drove home to Pittsburgh.

When Schaeffer remembered the visit to New York now, he knew that it wasn't just the first time he'd used Eddie's teaching and preparation to take a step into the secret profession. It was also the start of bad times. Within a few days, Eddie was bringing home newspapers from other cities and reading them with a frown on his face. The boy would say, "What's wrong?"

Eddie would answer, "A guy I knew died."

"Who?"

"Just a guy. You didn't know him."

They had this conversation at least four times, once while he was reading the *Chicago Tribune,* then the *New York Daily News,* then the *Buffalo Courier-Express,* and then the *Cleveland Plain Dealer.*

Finally, after a few months, after Eddie had tossed aside one of the papers and sat in silence, the boy said, "Another guy you knew?"

Eddie stared at him before saying, "Listen carefully. I'm going to tell you some things that will help you understand. The Mafia families were made up of southern Italians who immigrated around 1900 or so. Some had been criminals in Italy, and others were just desperate for a job. They established some ways of stealing money and got by. Then in 1920 the government made it illegal to sell whiskey or wine or beer. This was the best news they ever heard. If people couldn't buy alcohol in stores, they had to buy it from somebody. The crime families supplied it — made deals with people who knew how to produce it or smuggled it in from other countries — and earned a whole lot of money. Then in 1933, Prohibition was repealed. The Mafia came into 1934 rich and strong and heavily armed. They were also friendly with thousands of cops and public officials accustomed to getting bribed and expecting that to be the same in the future.

"Once anybody who wanted to could sell alcohol, the Mafia families had to rely on other ways to make money. They had learned how to run gambling joints and bookie operations because they'd been doing it all through Prohibition. They knew extortion because they'd been doing that since the Romans. They also knew prostitution and drugs. But at this point there was competition, and the families fought over territories with each other, and with the gangs of outsiders who competed. That brought public attention. In 1936, one of the most powerful bosses, Charles "Lucky" Luciano, got locked up in prison — though he still ran his businesses from there. But there were other big arrests too.

"In 1941 the Japanese attacked Pearl

Harbor in Hawaii and started World War II. For the next four years the fighting between the gangs was start-and-stop, because most of the mob guys who would have done the fighting were drafted and sent to battlefields all over the world to fight somebody besides their cousins. There was rationing. People were only allowed to buy a certain amount of anything needed for the war — butter, meat, car tires, gasoline. And so the Mafia started black markets to get those things and sell them secretly. Sometimes they stole them, or paid somebody to divert the trucks, or counterfeited rationing coupons.

"The war ended in 1945, and Lucky Luciano got taken out of prison and deported to Italy. The government must have thought that would get rid of him, but he could run his Italian operations and his American businesses even better from there. And other bosses found new ways to operate. Things stayed pretty stable for a while, and the Mafia expanded into a lot of businesses, some of them not even illegal.

"Things got more profitable. There were about twenty-five families in the United States with maybe five thousand 'made' men who were full members. To join, they each had to kill somebody, burn a saint's picture, and swear to follow omertà, which was a vow that they'd never talk. The whole shebang was run by a group called 'the Commission,' which was the heads of the five New York families and the heads of the Chicago family and the Buffalo family.

"In 1957 the cops stumbled on a big meeting on a little farm in upstate New York. They caught sixty-two bosses, including all seven members of the Commission, trying to run away through the fields in suits. No outsider really knows what the meeting was about, but probably it was about a lot of things. They were a worldwide conglomerate by then. They called the organization La Cosa Nostra — 'Our Thing.'

"But in 1962 Luciano was in the Naples airport and had a fatal heart attack. That took away an important force, a strong man at the top who liked things quiet. Right away in Palermo, the Sicilian boss Calcedonio Di Pisa was shot to death, apparently by the La Barbera brothers. His death set off what was called 'the First Mafia War,' a fight for control of Sicily. It was one of those fights that are like cats in a bag — no way out and everybody has claws.

"When the fighting moved to the United States, it was Frank Costello and Vito Genovese fighting over who would control Luciano's American holdings. Right about that time, 1962, was when a friend got in touch with me. It was a guy I knew from the army named DeSilvio. He told me that somebody he was related to needed some help in the fighting. He had been in Vietnam with me, and he wondered if I needed money. I had just started the butcher shop, but it wasn't paying for itself yet, so I was interested. I took a job, got paid for it, and then he called me again about a month later. That's how I got into the other business. Before long I was getting calls from his uncles. Things were okay for a long time. But now I think we've got trouble."

"What kind?" the boy had asked.

"That guy that I got hired to kill on opening day outside Yankee Stadium was involved in the argument over the Luciano family's holdings in the United States. The other guy, the one who was going to kill me if you hadn't gotten him first, was a visitor from Italy who was on the same side of things there. I didn't know anybody was going to be with the guy ahead of time, and I didn't know the target was that important. Maybe I would have done it different, or turned the job down. But what we did was help turn an argument into a war."

He gestured toward the newspaper he had thrown aside. "These people want to know

66

who did that. I hope they don't find out, but they're going to offer a lot of money for our names."

The boy understood that he and Eddie were in danger, but not much more. None of the names meant anything to him. The places seemed either impossibly distant or all around him and moving nearer. He listened closely, but knew instantly that there was nothing he could do about it. He and Eddie were not members of a Mafia family. They weren't even Italian. They had done a job, which was like an errand — do it, get paid, and go home. He thought that if Eddie didn't take on any other jobs, they might stay safe.

At first things went on just as they always had. The boy had to spend each day in school because he and Eddie couldn't afford to have a truant officer or cop come to ask questions about the boy.

During school hours, Eddie was devoted to his butcher shop. In the mornings he cut sides of beef into steaks and roasts, and lamb carcasses into racks of lamb. He sliced and weighed and wrapped hams, cut meat into pound packages, sliced bellies into bacon or pork belly, cut pork ribs. He butchered chickens and turkeys. His knife work was fast and surgical — clean, precise cuts that made meat into a fantasy portrait of a meal in a women's magazine. He always dealt in high-quality meat from special wholesalers in western Pennsylvania and charged his customers only slightly more than the big markets did, weighing everything in plain sight with accurate scales.

The only exceptions to Eddie's policies were his special-delivery customers. There were very elderly customers, some in wheelchairs, who couldn't come to the store. There were also a few neighborhood housewives whose orders he would personally deliver to their houses while their husbands were away at work. He would often charge them special-friend prices. If one of them was having an important dinner party, Eddie would make sure that everything was just right.

Eddie was not the sort of man women looked after wistfully as he passed. His features were regular and straight but not remarkable. What he had were three things. One was a presence that exuded physical strength. He spent his days lifting, carrying, and cutting, on his feet for many hours. The second was his genial affability — a happy disposition. The third was a respect for technique. The reason he was a great butcher and the reason he was a great killer were the same: his concern for mastery.

While the boy was growing up, Eddie lectured him on the importance of technique in every endeavor, and if the boy failed to cut, weigh, or wrap the customer's order right, Eddie made him do it again. If he missed a spot in cleaning the shop floor, Eddie made him start over and mop the whole floor again.

During this period, Eddie's special home-delivery customers included four or five of the most attractive married women in the district. During the hours when these deliveries took place, the boy had to take over the shop. There were also occasions when one of Eddie's special customers would come to the shop to pick up her order. Eddie would go with her into the office at the back of the building. There was plenty of meat in the case at the front of the store, and there were thousands of pounds of it in the refrigerator room. There was nothing for sale in the back office, and nothing there of interest except, possibly, technique.

Eddie took his role as a teacher seriously. While he was teaching the boy to be a skilled meat cutter, he was encouraging but watchful. Once, after a particularly long and successful day at the shop, Eddie told him, "You're a smart, hardworking kid, and you've learned what I taught you, so you'll always be able to support yourself as a butcher. And you're learning the other trade too. There's not much you don't notice."

"Where did you learn?"

"The army taught me both my trades. They trained me to cut meat and sent me to a war, where I learned how to be the one who came home."

Eddie had a friend who owned a farm about forty-five miles northwest of Pittsburgh near Kittaning. On Sundays, when the shop was closed, he and the boy would sometimes drive out there and take the key placed atop one of the struts that held up the porch roof. They would use the bath-room, write a note to the friend to say they'd been there, and then go out to the back hundred acres to shoot.

Eddie taught the boy special lessons about the physical act of killing. Every lesson was clear and practical, and now, all these years later, Michael was sure that every lesson had come back during some moment when he needed it. One was about knives: "Guys get into knife fights without having any idea what they're doing or how to do it. They have an excuse. You won't."

"What's their excuse?"

"That nobody wants or expects to be in a knife fight. It's hard, and shooting some-body from a distance is easy, so they think that's all that can happen. It isn't. The real reason they don't prepare is that they're just on their way to being killed, only they don't know it yet. You're not the loser, so you don't get an excuse. You were raised to use knives. You know them from working in the shop, and you have years of muscle memory for how they feel, how to get the deepest cut, how to hold one to keep your hand from slipping down to the blade, even when the handle is wet with blood."

Eddie had a roll of red electrical tape. He cut strips of it and put them on his own

71

shirt and pants and around his neck to remind the boy where the vital blood vessels were. Then they fought, using knives with the blades wrapped in several layers of black electrical tape.

From time to time Eddie would cheer him on. "Come on, kid. I've seen you cut a hundred ribs in a day. Control the blade."

"I am."

"What do you do now?"

"Put the blade through the rib cage."

"What are you going for?"

"The heart and lungs."

"Where's my heart?"

"Between the fourth and fifth ribs. Here."

"What if there's no opening to reach that?"

"Neck. Front of the elbow, back of the knee, inner sides of the thighs."

After their first few lessons, the shooting was always done with moving targets. Eddie said, "Most of the guys you'll collect on are the kind who have always walked right up to somebody and stuck a gun in his face. They'll be about as close to you as twenty feet and then can't hit you if you're moving. You're not going to be like that."

Eddie made him practice with a pistol, first trying to hit a small Hula-Hoop covered with butcher paper that Eddie propelled at different speeds. Then it was a set of kids' rubber balls six inches in diameter that Eddie bought in bulk. Eddie would roll them, bounce them, or throw them. Only when the boy could hit the ball nearly every time did Eddie move on to the next lesson.

Eddie started his rifle training with paper targets, but later the same day changed it to hitting something in motion. He would tie a length of chalk line to a tree limb, tie the other end to an object, push it hard so that it swung like a pendulum, and retreat to stand near the boy as he fired at it. Eddie explained, "The point of shooting is to hit somebody who is alive. If he's not moving, he's probably dead, so shooting him is a waste of time and ammo."

At the end of each shooting session, Eddie taught him to break down each weapon, clean it, and reassemble it quickly. It wasn't too long before the boy could step into a room, pick up a firearm he hadn't seen before, and handle it safely and knowledgeably enough to be able to load and fire it in seconds, or take it apart and reassemble it.

Almost a half century later, as Schaeffer sat in the airplane on the flight to Singapore, he knew that what Eddie had been teaching him was about living. It was an attitude, a willingness to put in the work to become an expert. People who didn't do that would only live if they didn't meet someone who had. Michael's life had been dangerous, and he owed the fact that he still had it to Eddie.

So much time had passed. There were many aspects of getting older that Schaeffer did not like. There was a new uncertainty that his muscles would operate as they once had. Because of Eddie, he had always stayed fit and strong through exercise. He had lifted weights, run, and walked. In later years, he added tai chi and yoga so that he could stretch and bend. He had a thin, sinewy body. He knew it must be in the process of wearing out, but it still worked well enough. He had lived to look in a mirror and see gray hair.

Eddie had made his old age possible when he was young. The secrets were not complicated. "Eyes open. Hit first. Move fast. Stop when he's dead."

There were variations and extra practice. "Everything you do in a gunfight has to be automatic, done as a habit, a reflex you've programmed into your brain. Do it without taking the time to think. Always carry your pistol with a round in the chamber. Put your hand on it as soon as you know you're going to need it. When he's close enough, you raise it, aim, and fire exactly as you've been taught, exactly as you've practiced. It's unlikely that you're going to hit any organ that will kill him with your first couple of shots. Aim at his high center mass and keep firing rapidly until he dies or your pistol's slide stays back and the chamber stays open. When it does, you'd better be moving. You reload quickly and automatically on the run. Eject the empty magazine, slip in the spare one, pull back and release the slide to chamber a round, and fire. You practice these movements until you can't forget or fumble because your body knows them." Eddie had taught him how to be the one who survived.

Now he was being hunted again. The four men who had been sent after him in York hadn't been up to the job, and they had died for it. Their arrival had not been a complete surprise, because people had come after him before. But their passports had worried him. They didn't have names that were familiar to him from the old days. They weren't sons of men who had fought him before.

The ones in the parking lot at the Manchester Airport had been even more of a shock to him. There must have been a transponder hidden in the Bentley so that the owner could keep track of where it was.

Certainly somebody had sent the two men to the lot at Manchester. The two men weren't carrying passports, but their driver's licenses showed they were English, not Italian American or any other kind of American. This time the threat was different. It was good to be as far away as possible.

8

The captain made his announcement, the cabin-crew chief issued her instructions, and the plane descended slowly from above the few wispy clouds into golden unimpeded light, bumped and rattled over the runway until its momentum was expended, and then rolled along sedately toward the terminal.

Schaeffer had slept most of the twelve hours from Singapore to Sydney. He remembered flying when he was young, out on a job. He had learned to lean back in the seat and be asleep before the plane reached cruising altitude. He would get off the plane feeling as strong and flexible as a big cat. He still had the knack, but this time his joints were stiff and his spine felt as though it were missing a couple of vertebrae. Age levied a tax to be paid in small discomforts. A few had come from memorable injuries, but most were just time and wear.

It took him a minute to loosen up, and he felt like a thawing snake uncoiling to get out of the seat. Standing straight was a pleasure, and he stood there letting his muscles loosen while he waited for his turn to leave. He watched the passengers ahead of him retrieving their bags from the over- head compartments, then slowly making their way toward the open hatch on the left side of the plane. They went, and then he went. As he walked up the aisle with his bag, his mind was fully on the question of who was trying to have him killed.

There were plenty of suspects. During his last trip to the United States seven years ago, after Frank Tosca had sent Mafia soldiers after him, there had been collateral damage. He had needed to take out a young man who had been guarding the trail above the resort in the Arizona mountains so that he could reach Tosca's cabin. Whoever the man was, he'd been at a highly sensitive gathering, which meant he had relatives high in the hierarchy. Dozens of powerful bosses had been there, and because of Schaeffer, they'd all been rounded up by the FBI, booked as persons of interest in Tosca's murder, and photographed. Some were old enough to have known him. He could think of about twenty men who would like to kill him, but could think of no reason to suspect or eliminate any of them now.

He had bought a few guidebooks to Sydney in the Manchester terminal and read parts of them on the plane to Singapore. He had also downloaded a version onto his cell phone and read more on his flight to Sydney. Now that he'd finally landed at the Sydney airport, what was most attractive was that there was a train from the airport into the center of Sydney. Trains were designed to pack large numbers of people aboard quickly and speed them to a destination, and that seemed to be what he needed now.

As he stepped off the plane, he began scanning faces. He looked for people who showed signs of recognizing him. He saw nobody he could identify as a threat, but his whole situation was a threat. One of the things that bothered him was that neither of the groups of men who had attacked him included people he'd ever seen before. That could mean that somebody had a picture of him. A picture in a telephone's memory could have been sent ahead to any destination in seconds. If someone in Manchester had found out his destination was Sydney, they could have sent his photo to someone in Australia a whole day ago. There could easily be people here waiting for him, and his photo could be forwarded from one to another without limit. Hiding half a world away from danger had become hiding a half second away.

He went through customs easily with his Paul Foster passport. He was carrying enough money but not too much, had no weapons or contraband, and looked like a respectable, well-dressed older man. He moved quickly from customs, as Eddie had taught him. "Never miss a chance to help the enemy make a stupid mistake. Start with anything you've got that's misleading. Once you're chasing or being chased, all the decisions have to be made fast, with no warning."

A person had to choose every time a crossroad came up, or he hit a fork in the road, or there were two means of transportation, and keep reversing himself, appearing to do one thing but then doing another.

He saw the sign over the escalator that said "Trains," walked toward it most of the way, then veered away from it in the direction of the exits. He quickly turned around, stepped on the escalator, and rode it down, looking back to see if he had drawn anyone else off course. He hadn't.

The escalator took him to the train station

under the international terminal. At the foot of the escalator were vending machines. He had read about this in the guidebook. The machines sold Opal cards and single tickets, and he knew it was best to buy the card.

He looked at the escalator again, but saw no stand-outs. He spotted a couple of Australian officials in uniforms and emergency reflector vests, with sidearms on their belts. He decided cops made good company for this trip.

He looked up at the signs and chose Platform 1. The train for the place everyone wanted to go was always Platform 1.

He needed to wait for only about four minutes before a train swept in and stopped, the doors huffing open all at once to let out the arrivals. When they had passed, he stepped in with the rest of the people waiting on the platform. The train was clean and new-looking and had mostly empty seats, all of them upholstered in a blue-patterned fabric that made them look like airline seats.

He noticed the two cops he'd seen earlier striding ahead on the platform to a car at the front of the train. A few seconds later, several passengers came back along the aisle, as though they'd been displaced.

He looked at the guide on his phone. The

train to the city took thirteen minutes. The train ride was the last chance for anyone who knew he was here to begin trailing him. After these thirteen minutes, he could climb into a taxi and disappear into a city of five million people. The city center was only six miles away now. The sound of the doors sliding shut while the last people hurried past to get into seats made him feel calmer.

As soon as the train began to move forward, Schaeffer felt his seat tugged back from the top as someone big grasped the back and held it to lower himself into the seat behind. Schaeffer glanced over his shoulder and saw two men had come forward from another car and sat down. When he looked ahead again, his mind carried an image.

They were both bigger than he was. One was tall and lanky with squared shoulders, large hands, and knees that were visible in front of his lap as though his tibia and fibula were overly long. His head was shaved, with only a hint of blond peach fuzz within the hairline. The other man was slightly shorter, but much thicker, with arms that looked as wide as the other man's legs. Both wore raincoats.

Maybe it was raining outside at ground level, or had rained. It was winter in Sydney, but to Schaeffer it looked as though the coats were meant to cover something. He knew nothing about Australian organized crime, but he'd seen men like these a thousand times in the United States — an expression in the eyes that seemed to say, "You weren't expecting a nightmare like me, were you?" and a strange mobility of the mouth. Some, like the tall one, would begin to make chewing motions, as though they were aching to say something.

Schaeffer felt a sudden jolt when the thin man hit the seatback with his knee as he stood. Nobody had followed these two men into the car, and the ones who had entered before them had gone on to the next car forward, so Schaeffer was alone with these two. The tall man walked up the aisle, stepped up on a seat, and took out a spray can to spray white paint over the bulb covering the security camera above him. He used his long legs to step over into the next row to spray the next one, and then the next.

Schaeffer used the thin man's distance to slip out of his seat while facing the big man, and move up the aisle to the front of the car.

By now the two men were both out of their seats. The heavy man, who was supposed to be the strongman, didn't worry

Schaeffer as much as the long one, who put his spray can in his overcoat pocket and was now gripping the overhead bars and stepping on the tops of the seats to propel himself toward the front. As he neared Schaeffer, he swung toward him like an ape.

Schaeffer sensed the man was trying to occupy Schaeffer's attention so his friend, the strong man, could charge up the aisle to take him down from behind.

Instead, Schaeffer lunged toward the tall man and punched him hard while his arms were above him and his ribs exposed. When the man dropped from the bars, bent over, Schaeffer snatched the paint can that was protruding from the man's coat pocket and sprayed his face with white paint.

The big man charged forward up the aisle toward Schaeffer, but Schaeffer turned the spray can on him, covering his face too, half blinding him. While the big man was trying to wipe his eyes, Schaeffer threw the can so that it hit his face hard, which bought him time to slip out the sliding door to the next car.

Schaeffer dragged the door shut, unhooked the leather strap from his carry-on bag, wrapped it around the door handle and the safety bar on the wall near it, and fastened the two clasps to hold it. He glanced at his watch. Only two minutes were gone. Eleven more minutes to the station, where there would be more cops. He looked ahead in the car he'd entered, but nobody seemed to have noticed anything going on behind them; they were all facing forward.

Schaeffer turned to face the door he'd strapped shut. The two men, both with faces painted white, were on the other side, pulling hard to open it. The cable in the strap would almost certainly resist, but the leather and the brass clasps were more questionable.

The two white faces grimaced and bared their teeth as they strained against the door. They were big, strong men, and the strap wasn't made for this kind of use. Schaeffer was comforted by the observation that for the moment, at least, they were going about it the wrong way. The thick, strong man was exerting constant pressure, and his long-limbed companion stood beside him, using his reach to exert the same steady pressure.

As Schaeffer watched, he saw the tall man get frustrated with the first method. He shoved the door hard, then took a step backward and prepared to hurl his shoulder against it again.

The strong man seemed to notice that the

sudden jolts when the tall man hurled his weight against the handle were making the door give a little each time. The force must be stretching the leather a bit, or bending the clasps.

Schaeffer guessed that the two attackers were going to succeed at some point. There was no question it was better to keep the pair beyond the door instead of letting them break in. Now they began to work together. They threw themselves against the door handle over and over, stretching the leather a little more. Schaeffer tried neutralizing their efforts by timing their thrusts and pushing the opposite way each time.

He knew he was not as strong as either of them, let alone both. They were about half his age, and the big man was twice his size. He tried to raise his spirits with the theory that these men had been hired only because they looked scary to competitors and debtors, but when he felt the force as the men gave a few more tries, he began to fear that they were as strong as they looked.

Schaeffer kept trying to soften the force of the combined pushes the men exerted, but he was wearing himself out and time was going too slowly. He couldn't hold them indefinitely.

He saw the moment when the lanky man

realized how to win. His eyes focused on the strap as he seemed to realize that if it stretched only a little bit more, there would be enough space between the door and the frame to let a blade through.

Schaeffer looked at the hands of the two men gripping the door. The big man wore a watch with a face about an inch and a half in diameter. Only four minutes had elapsed. There were still nine to go. He braced his back against the wall of the train car and his feet against the door handle, and sapped the next few attacks of their force. Meanwhile he watched the men's faces. The tall man strained harder. He grimaced so that his spray-painted face looked like a bleached skull gritting yellowed teeth.

The knife came out fast, the man's right hand appearing from somewhere behind his thigh, shielded from sight at first by the overcoat. It arrived at the crack between the door and the frame and jabbed through, the long blade protruding as it came down, sharpened side first.

Schaeffer dropped his leg to get it away from the opening just as the blade slid downward. The skull-face's snarl changed to a smile, and the man strained harder as his partner pushed the door. The blade was long — about eight inches — and it almost reached the strap this time.

Schaeffer shifted his weight to the armrest of the aisle seat and kicked the blade from the side on the chance that it might be thin enough to bend, but it wasn't. He turned, took his leather bag by its handle, and hurried forward along the aisle toward the next door.

As he slid the next door aside, he studied the mechanism to see if there was a more effective mechanical way to block it — a built-in lock or something, but if one was present, he didn't see it. He shut the door, used the belt from his pants to wrap the handle and the nearest bar, and buckled it in place. Then he went on to the next car and the next.

Many passengers were in the car he'd just left and the one he'd entered, and a few of them became aware that he was engaged in some kind of struggle but didn't seem able to interpret it. A couple of the men half stood, then sat back down. A few seemed to think that since he was moving quickly, he must be the problem, but then they looked behind them, saw his two pursuers, and changed their minds. For one reason or another, all seemed paralyzed.

He had thought that the two cops he'd seen in the airport station had boarded the train somewhere near the front. He might be able to talk them into arresting his two pursuers, or at least calling for reinforcements to be waiting at the city station. If he couldn't persuade them, then staying close to the cops would probably keep him alive for a few minutes.

He moved ahead through the next car and saw them. They were inside the very front car, visible through the windows set into the two doors. He stopped at the first door. As he watched, they both took their pistols out of their holsters. One pulled back his pistol's slide to let a round into the chamber. That was more than odd. Uniformed cops usually carried their weapons in holsters that had some sort of clasp to prevent a criminal from grabbing one without disengaging it, but they carried their pistols ready to fire. And why had they drawn their guns now? There appeared to be no passengers in the front car with them, in the car with Schaeffer, or in the two cars behind him that would warrant that kind of treatment. Only the two men in the fourth car did.

Understanding came to him instantly. They didn't act like cops because they weren't cops. They were the shooters who were supposed to kill him. They hadn't been able to predict which car Schaeffer would choose, so they'd hurried to station themselves in the front car and kept it empty of other passengers. The two big, ugly guys had boarded the last car on the train and come forward to chase him from car to car into the front car, where he'd be alone with the shooters. He looked at his watch. In four minutes the train would be at the station in the city, and there might be a few real cops there.

He reached into his carry-on bag. He needed a way to block the sliding door to the car in front to delay the two fake cops. Could Meg have thrown in something else he could use, like another belt? No. But he had grabbed some neckties, and if he put them together, the silk might be strong enough to delay them a minute or two. He looked deeper into the bag and saw something shiny. It was a cigarette lighter. He had thrown away the wallets and identification of the men in the Manchester lot. But the lighter must have slipped between things to the bottom of his bag, so he'd missed it. He put it into his pants pocket, braided the neckties into a single rope, and tied them to the door handle and the safety bar near the door to prevent the fake cops from opening it. For the moment he was alive, but he was trapped with the other passengers between the two temporarily blocked doors. He rushed away from the forward door toward the back of the car.

He could see the two men still struggling at the second door, trying to get the knife blade to reach the belt he'd buckled there. As he hurried toward them, he saw a man with a shopping bag at his feet from Heinemann's Tax and Duty Free Shop. He stopped and glanced down into the bag, then took out a packet of Australian hundred-dollar bills he'd bought at the Singapore airport. He knelt down to speak to the man and pointed at the bag. "Three hundred for that bottle of Pincer vodka?"

The man grinned. "You must be a thirsty fella." He reached into the bag, and Schaeffer made the exchange.

Schaeffer slipped the bottle into his carry-on, said, "Thank you," and then moved on. When he was twenty paces from the spot where the two men were struggling with the door into the car, he saw first the knife blade and then the tall, thin man's arm protrude into the car. They'd stretched the belt and were about to cut it. He ran at them.

The two white-painted men looked mad with rage. As the arm brought the knife down over the belt to cut it, Schaeffer swung the bottle into the arm and followed through to smash it against the door frame. The bottle shattered and the quart of vodka splashed over the man's arm, shoulder, and chest.

Schaeffer opened the lighter and flicked the wheel against the flint. The high-proof vodka made a *poof* sound, and blue and orange ghostly flames enveloped the man's hand and arm.

The man dropped the knife and Schaeffer squatted to pick it up while the man withdrew his arm and danced backward, tearing off his overcoat and stamping on it to extinguish the flames.

The strong man didn't react quickly enough to stop what he was doing. He slid the door open. For a second he stood with one hand on the door handle and the other on the frame, with his body open and unprotected. Schaeffer slashed at his carotid artery with the big knife and charged past him, moving into the aft car toward the tall, thin man, who was now holding his wrist where the bottle had cut it. When the injured man saw his companion drop to his knees on the floor holding his throat and Schaeffer coming for him with the knife, he ran toward the rear of the train.

Schaeffer glanced out the window. The train was now in an area with tall office buildings and crowded streets beneath them. His watch said that eleven minutes had elapsed. Two minutes to go.

He turned and hurried up the aisle toward the front of the train. When he reached the entrance to the second car, he looked and saw that the two fake policemen were aware that the time was nearly up too. They had holstered their guns and were now trying some of the same methods the two leg-breakers had tried, throwing themselves against the immobilized door, trying to make it slide out of their way. They were not oversize and muscled like the first two, but Schaeffer was sure the neckties would not last.

Schaeffer could see they were standing still and arguing now. He could tell they were feeling panicky. Their prey hadn't come to them, and they couldn't open the door to get to the prey.

One of the men reached for his pistol and fired four shots at the door's window. The safety glass took on the look of hammered ice, and the two men began to kick the damaged glass out of its frame. But the shooting had already caused panic in the second car.

People screamed, stood, and stampeded in the aisle, the first ones running away from the shooting toward the rear of the train. As they passed others who were seated, they caused more panic, and those people got up too. The two fake police officers had managed to bring the passengers in the second and third cars to their feet, where they all tightly jammed the aisles while the train slowed to pull into the station.

When the train doors opened, people poured out, scrambling toward the escalators and running along the platform toward the stairs. Schaeffer moved into the thickest crowds and went up to the street. Taxicabs were lined up, and people got into them quickly, and the cabs moved off. Schaeffer saw an empty one and slid in.

As the cab pulled away, the driver said, "Why is everybody running?"

Schaeffer said, "I don't know. I think there was a fight."

"Where would you like to go?"

"The Four Seasons Hotel."

9

When the cab reached the Four Seasons Hotel, Schaeffer got out, paid the fare, and went into the lobby. As soon as the cab had pulled away, he went out another exit and took another cab. He said, "I'd like to go to the Adelaide Southern, please." In a moment he was gone, just another American who had come to the hotel and was probably going sightseeing for the day.

At the Adelaide Southern, the clerk found his reservation easily, could tell that he was very tired, and so gave him his key card and sent him off quickly with few preliminaries.

He went directly up to his room on the twentieth floor, locked all the locks, flopped on the bed, and stared at the ceiling. He was not pleased with his decision to take a detour to Australia. It had sounded like a good idea at 2:30 a.m. in Yorkshire surrounded by bodies.

He reviewed everything that had happened since he'd landed in Australia. It had been a disastrous decision to come here. Somebody in Manchester must have traced him to the Sydney flight and made a phone call to an Australian criminal group. The two sets of killers had been waiting for him, probably had received photos of him twenty-four hours before his plane touched down.

He was hungry but knew he needed to clean up before he ate. He went into the bathroom and took a shower, shaved, brushed his teeth, and combed his hair. Then he came out and dressed in clean clothes. He thought about whether to go to the restaurant downstairs or order room service.

Room service was dangerous. Years ago, when he had been hunting for people who didn't want to be found, he had often bribed a room service waiter. The people at the front desk would be trained never to divulge information about a guest even for a huge tip, but a room service waiter operated on his own far from his supervisors.

He decided on going out to a restaurant. He looked through the leather-bound book of hotel information left on the coffee table and saw that there was a fancy restaurant on the top floor. A restaurant on a ground floor could be watched by anyone who walked in from the street or just looked in a window. It was easier for a customer in an upper-floor restaurant to keep an eye on the new arrivals.

He went to the top-floor restaurant and was pleased to see it was busy but had a few empty tables. He had a good lunch among guests from a wide variety of countries and remained aware of each person who came in. Nobody showed any interest in him. When he finished eating, he went back downstairs and lay on the bed, intending to sleep.

Sleep was impossible. His mind kept going back to one odd incident that had taken place when he was fifteen, a few months after he and Eddie had killed the two men outside Yankee Stadium. His memory started with the preparations.

Eddie had said, "Shooting this guy outside Yankee Stadium has got to be easy. It's the first home game of the season, and every seat will be sold. People will be milling around out there, waiting to get in, and others will be in a big rush to get there. It'll be a crowd, but a moving crowd. That's the best. And there will be a lot of ticket takers, ushers, and security guys doing their first day on the job. They won't know where the john is, let alone what to do in an emergency."

Schaeffer remembered that the Yankees had been away during the first week of the season in Washington and Detroit. Their first home game was on Tuesday, April 15, against the Senators. The weather was perfect, and he and Eddie had only one target. Somehow Eddie knew in advance that the target had a ticket to the game. Years later Eddie told him that with so many certainties, it had seemed to be a perfect job to start the boy in the business and to test him.

The boy said, "Test me? For what?"

Eddie said, "What can I tell you? Not every male human being is a killer. Some guys are too eager, some too cautious, and some have faces that just about anybody can read. When some guys get scared, they freeze. Some guys who can do the work have something about them that makes people remember them. You don't have those problems. But the only way to know you're right for it was to test."

A few days after they got home from the killing, the rest of the money for their fee arrived in the mail. It was in a box about the size of a book. Eddie took a small stack of bills, read the label on it, laughed, and showed it to him. "See this?" he said. "They gave us a bonus for shooting the second guy. You earned this." He flipped the bills with his thumb so that the boy could see the bills were all hundreds. Then he put the stack in the safe with the rest of the money and spun the dial. "I'm proud of you, kid. You've got a great life ahead of you."

One day two months later, Eddie came back from a trip to Philadelphia looking thoughtful. He said, "I just heard there's a contract out for the two who shot those guys outside Yankee Stadium on opening day."

The boy said, "Really? Do they know who did it?"

"The only people who know are the guys who hired us for the hit, and they're in Detroit. I don't think they'll ever talk about it. The people who put out the contract stay in New York."

Then the articles about shootings began to appear in the newspapers. It seemed to the boy that what he and Eddie had done had somehow sparked a dozen attacks and reprisals.

At first Eddie simply waited for the talk to go away. He told the boy that when acquaintances asked if he had heard about the killing outside Yankee Stadium, he denied having any knowledge of it. He listened to the rumors instead of talking. He spent more time working at the butcher shop and left the other job to other people.

But the boy noticed Eddie made a few changes during those days. He placed an eight-shot semiautomatic 12-gauge shotgun loaded with Winchester rifled slugs under the counter where he waited on customers. He tested the accuracy of the slugs at fifty yards and then walked the fifty yards and put his big thumb through each of the holes in the wooden target. He could put the eight slugs into a five-inch pattern at that distance. He also began to keep two pistols attached to the underside of his cutting table. Every morning he reminded the boy where the guns were.

During the next few months, bodies started to be found in fields and in rivers all over the eastern states, but Eddie kept trying to wait out the disturbance. He said to the boy, "We're not in the Mafia, and we don't give a flying fuck who runs it, or if anybody does. That's between them. We can wait forever for them to settle it."

Then the day came that the boy had been sure would come. Eddie was offered a job, and the money was so tempting, he took it. They went by car again. In those days nobody at an airport checked passengers' identification on domestic flights or searched luggage for guns, but a car was cheaper, easier, and more anonymous than an airplane. Eddie and the boy were supposed to check into a particular hotel in Chicago and wait for a phone call to tell them when and where to move on their target. Their victim was a member of the Castiglione crime family who had grown ambitious and begun plotting against his bosses. One of them, an underboss named Taddio, was the one who had hired Eddie to get rid of him.

The boy didn't know if Eddie had been told more than that, and it didn't matter. The constant competitions and short-term alliances and tiny wars over territories or insults were impossible for him to follow. They were also issues that he and Eddie could never know from inside. What was at stake for them was only money.

Eddie and the boy arrived in Chicago at night and stopped outside the hotel where Eddie had been told to stay. Eddie had the boy wait in the car. If there was trouble, he was to start the engine and drive to Eddie, who would be running toward the corner of the hotel, and pick him up where the hotel wall gave them cover.

Eddie went into the hotel, stayed for about

five minutes, and came out walking. When he reached the car, the boy slid over to the passenger seat to let Eddie drive. As he pulled forward he said, "It doesn't feel right."

The boy watched and listened, but asked no questions. Asking questions would only have distracted Eddie while he was identifying his feeling. Finally Eddie said, "It's not the way things go. There were four guys in the room with Taddio. I didn't know any of them. Why would they need five guys to tell me where and when to find one man? Taddio said they can't do it themselves or it'll cause hard feelings in the family, but" — he ended the sentence with a shrug.

The boy waited. Apparently he was not expected to answer. Eddie said, "Well, they all got a good look at me. They'll know me if they see me again. And you know what else? Taddio comped a room for us to sleep in at a motel on the south end outside of town. That means they'll know exactly where we're going to be."

When they reached the motel where they were supposed to stay, Eddie turned into the parking lot and said, "Motor running, gun in your hand, eyes on every door." He got out while the boy moved over to the driver's seat and rolled down the window.

The boy watched Eddie go and then studied the motel. It was the old-fashioned kind that consisted of two long, low wings, with two rows of identical doors to identical rooms, like arms embracing the parking lot. Where the two long wings met was the lighted office and lobby, so the whole place was V-shaped. The boy paid close attention to the doors with cars parked in front of them.

He saw Eddie step into the lighted lobby. He and the clerk looked like the crafted figures in a diorama on display in a museum. The boy turned his attention to the two long rows of doors where somebody could be hiding, waiting for Eddie to get out into the open again.

None of the doors opened and Eddie returned. The boy moved over and Eddie backed up to a door numbered 208 and parked. He said, "This whole thing is still bothering me, kid. Keep your eyes open."

They both got out and Eddie went to the back, opened the trunk, took his suitcase out, and let the boy carry his own. The boy knew this was so each could keep his gun hand free. He followed Eddie to the door marked 212. It seemed odd to him that Eddie hadn't parked in front of 212 if that was their room. Eddie opened the door so that he wasn't standing in front of it, and that told the boy an ambush wasn't out of the question. Eddie went in and then looked outward from the doorway while the boy came into the dark room. Only when the door was closed did the light come on.

Eddie spoke quietly as he looked in the bathroom, in the closet, and under the bed. "I think we might get a late visit from the four men I met at the hotel uptown."

"Are we going home or to another hotel?" asked the boy.

"Neither." He opened the front curtains an inch. "Look. This is 212. The one across is 112. The fourth door from the end."

"Okay."

Eddie stepped to the door of the bathroom and pointed. "See the window?"

"Sure."

"Can you fit through it?"

"I think so."

Eddie unlatched the window and pulled it to the side. The boy closed the toilet and stood on the lid, lifted himself up, and put his head and shoulders, then his waist, through the window sideways. Then he reached up to brace against the inner wall while he pulled one leg outside, then the other. He hung there.

"Good," Eddie said. "You got a knife on you?"

"Sure."

"Then go around the back behind room 112 and climb in the bathroom window. It'll be just like this one. Then come to the door on the other side and unlock it. I'll be over in a few minutes."

The boy extended his arms, let go of the window frame, and dropped the last two feet to the long grass behind the row of rooms. He walked away from the lighted part of the motel where the office was. The open end of the horseshoe was a field with bushes and shrubs, so he had no trouble walking farther out, where no light would reach him, and hooking back. He confirmed that the fourth door was room 112. In a minute he was behind the fourth bathroom window of the other wing. There was a garbage can a few yards away with some grass cuttings in it, so he dragged it over, inverted it, and climbed up to the window.

The window consisted of two sheets of smoked, tempered glass. He used his knife to bend the frame a little and slip it in between the glass and the frame to reach the latch. He completed the maneuver, used the blade as a lever, and depressed the latch to slide the window aside.

He hoisted himself up, slithered in sideways to his waist, rested his weight on his hip, dragged himself in until he could press one hand on the wall above the toilet tank, and then braced himself to pull one leg in. He pulled in the other, tentatively rested his weight on the sink, and then stepped down into the nearly dark bathroom. He slid the window shut. Then he walked through the sleeping area, between the twin beds, and unlocked the door. He opened it a crack and then closed it again.

A few minutes later Eddie slipped in the door and closed it. He was carrying something in the duffel bag they used for their laundry. "Good job, kid," he said. "We'll spend the night here."

"Are our suitcases in the other room?"

"Everything is back in the car except what we'll need here. I used the pillows and extra blankets and towels to make it look like we're in the beds."

"Won't they notice?"

"Only after it's too late. I took the bulbs out of the lamps."

The men arrived around three in the morning, during the boy's turn to watch. A big sedan rolled into the lot with its lights off and stopped. The car doors all opened, but the dome lights were turned off, so the car didn't emit light except for the faint glow of the dashboard dials. The driver stayed behind the wheel while four men got out and left the doors open so there would be no slamming sounds.

The boy stepped to Eddie's bed and nudged him. "They're here."

Eddie got up and picked up his shotgun. "Stay down." He went to the window and watched.

The boy didn't stay down, but he stayed back in the darkest part of the room. He watched the four men kick in the door of room 212, step inside, and fire. There were bright orange flashes and showers of sparks as burning powder followed the bullets out the muzzles of the guns.

Eddie's first shotgun slug blasted through the side window of the big car and pounded into the head of the driver waiting behind the steering wheel. The far window of the car and the left part of the windshield looked as though a bucket of red paint had been splashed against it.

Eddie charged. He sprinted from the doorway of room 112 to the attackers' car, leaned on the hood so the engine block would shield him, and fired four more slugs into the open doorway of room 212. Someone in the darkened room pushed the door shut, but Eddie fired two more shots through the door at belt level, ducked down to reload, then retreated from the car to the end of the 200 wing of the building, keeping his eye on the door.

The boy ran along the other wing to the lighted windows of the lobby. He appeared on the outer side of the glass near the front desk just as the clerk was coming out from behind it with a rifle in his hands. The boy waited until the man came out the door and then killed him with a pistol shot to the head.

As the boy started back toward Eddie, the damaged door of room 212 swung open. Two men had evaded Eddie's shotgun slugs, and now they ran from room 212 toward the big car. They saw that the driver had been killed behind the wheel, so they each took one of his arms and began to drag him out of the seat so that one of them could get in and drive. Eddie and the boy each shot one, and they fell beside the driver.

Then Eddie stepped over the driver and the two fresh bodies, leaned in, and put the car in gear. Very slowly, the car moved forward toward the field at the end of the lot. The boy went to the door of 208, where they had left their car facing outward. Eddie went into room 212 and collected two men's wallets, then came out and got the other three wallets.

As they both got into Eddie's car, he tossed all five wallets in the boy's lap, and some of them fell in front of the passenger seat. Eddie started the engine. "Nobody woke up, which means they kept the motel empty for this. But the whole town can't be deaf, so cops will be on their way." He drove off, heading back north, the way they had come. "Take out the money and the driver's licenses, and toss the rest out the window."

10

Schaeffer woke up and it took a second before he remembered he was in Australia now, not Chicago. He had been lying on top of the bedcover fully dressed. He looked at the bedside table, where the electric clock read 8:45 p.m. He sat up and looked around him at the hotel room. It was beautifully furnished and comfortable. The sun had set already, but he could see through the window that his room was very high, even with the tops of many buildings. It occurred to him that nobody was likely to use the stairway to or from the twentieth floor except in an emergency.

His memory of the night in Chicago stayed with him now that he was awake. It seemed to him that the memory had floated into his consciousness for a reason. Something about this situation was similar, and it felt like a warning. What had saved him and Eddie that night was sleeping where they weren't expected to.

He stood up, went to the closet, and took the spare blanket from the shelf. He picked up one of the pillows off the bed. He made sure he had his wallet, his room key, and his phone. He picked up his leather carry-on bag, walked quietly to the door, opened it, crossed the hall, and entered the stairwell. It was cool and, at this level, quiet. He partially unfolded the blanket, set the pillow on the floor above the steps, and then stretched out to wait.

Schaeffer heard the sound of the elevator doors opening and then the rattle of china as a serving cart rolled out and came along the hall. The cart stopped, and Schaeffer looked out the small window set into the stairwell door.

It was a room service cart, and it had stopped in front of the door to his room. There were two men. The one pushing the cart wore a waiter's white coat; the other, a suit.

The men knocked on the door of Schaeffer's room. They waited. The man in the suit leaned close to the door and listened. Then he rapped on the door harder. The man in the waiter's coat called out, "Room service."

The man in the suit removed something from under a white linen tablecloth on top of the cart. Schaeffer recognized a Steyr bullpup rifle with a short barrel. He knew that some countries issued the Steyr to their military, and supposed Australia might be one. The man shouldered the short rifle and aimed it at the door while he waited a few seconds for an occupant to open it.

The waiter used a key card to unlock the door, turned the handle, and pushed it open. The man with the rifle slipped in past him, staying low. The waiter stepped aside and leaned his back against the wall in the hallway. About thirty seconds passed.

The man in the suit emerged, looking angry. He set the rifle on the cart and the waiter covered it again with the cloth. The man in the suit closed the door of the room and wiped the door handle with a handkerchief. The two returned to the elevator, rolled the cart into it, and then disappeared behind its closing metal doors.

Michael Schaeffer sat in the stairwell and began the process of repacking his clothes and other belongings more neatly in the leather carry-on. Australia had been a terrible idea. He had been trailed right off his plane onto the train into the city, and it had taken only a few hours after he'd lost his trackers to be found in his hotel. His chances of not being found again were poor.

Probably the Americans who wanted him dead had hired fixers to put out a contract on him in many countries, sending his photo ahead. They must have realized he'd go as far as possible from York after the first attack, and would have guessed he would go under the surface in a place where people looked like him and spoke the same language, more or less — the UK had been used up, so it would have had to be Australia, New Zealand, Canada, Ireland, or South Africa. There were probably freelance shooters in all those countries with a photo of his face in their phones.

Why now? He hadn't bothered anybody in years, so it seemed insane that someone was afraid of him. The other two times he'd been attacked since he had gone to England there had been an element of accident. Somebody had happened to spot him in a public place and known he was a chance to make money. This was bigger. They were hunting him on the other side of the world. Something important must have happened, and the place where it had happened must be the United States. He had stayed unobtrusive in England and used the Internet to keep abreast of major events involving people in organized crime. And he had seen nothing that could prompt this sudden manhunt. He would have to go back to America to find out what it was.

11

The best method he could find to get to the United States was a flight to Melbourne to throw off any pursuers and then a fifteen-hour flight to Los Angeles. He had lasted less than one day in Australia, and he knew he was lucky to have made it that long. He hoped that since he had just gotten there, the hunters had stopped looking for him in airports.

It was still dark when his plane took off for Melbourne. Before he went to the gate for his flight from Melbourne to Los Angeles, he stopped in one of the airport stores and bought the three American newspapers that were for sale: the *New York Times, Los Angeles Times,* and *Washington Post.* As soon as he was in the airplane aisle, he studied the people on the plane to make sure there was nobody he'd seen before and nobody who showed an unusual interest in him. He sat in his seat and watched the rest of the passengers board.

He spent the first two hours studying the newspapers for signs that the American organized-crime families were in some kind of upheaval or under special pressure. No police organization had announced big arrests, and there was no mention of the deaths or disappearances of any bosses. Gambling, prostitution, drugs, extortion, stock fraud, and money laundering were in no danger of going out of style.

While he was searching, he kept thinking about Meg. He couldn't help worrying about her. He couldn't quite feel sure she was safe. By now she should be in the private home of some friend or relative of hers somewhere in England, Scotland, or Wales. A few of them actually lived in houses that had withstood medieval warfare. She was probably safer than he was, but he still worried. American criminals had turned their attention on him once more. Whatever was going on in that world now was something big and frightening, and had come to England for him. He searched his memory and his imagination to figure out what could have prompted someone to start a world-wide search for him after all this time.

He awoke as his plane swung around and came in over the dry, jagged landscape east of Los Angeles and landed facing into the west wind off the ocean. When the plane was on the ground, he walked to the Southwest Airlines terminal and bought a ticket to Manchester, New Hampshire, with a stop in Charlotte.

He had decided not to fly into New York, Boston, Philadelphia, Miami, or any of the other airports where the watchers from the police and the Mafia stared at one another all day long, and the watchers from Homeland Security watched everyone else. He'd never had much trouble with the police, because he had never been arrested. But he knew there might be something that the police or FBI knew about him now that could make them interested. He purchased a ticket using a passport with the name Charles Ackerman, and the airline employees didn't see anything on their computer screens that disturbed them.

When he reached New Hampshire, he stayed at a hotel close to the airport to keep things simple. He was back in America now, so he would do what Americans did — get a car and then go shopping for guns.

He knew it was not prudent for him to rent a car. It was easy for the companies to trace their rental cars. Leasing a car was worse, because it required a serious credit

117

check and a bank's approval. What he needed was to find a used car being offered for sale by its owner. The normal way to buy a car like that was cash, since nobody would take a check for that much money from a stranger.

He slept the night in the hotel, went down to the dining room for breakfast, and stopped to buy a copy of the *New Hampshire Union Leader.* He searched the ads placed by private owners. He could see that there wasn't much variety or supply. Had that end of car sales moved online since he'd left the country? He set aside his newspaper to use his cell phone to look for ads, and found more online.

He called a couple of the phone numbers, got names and addresses, and made arrangements to look at the cars in the right price range. The third car he saw was a six-year-old Toyota Camry. He offered $4,000, settled for $4,500, and paid for it in cash. After less than an hour of pink-slip signing and counting and lying, he drove the car away, already on his way to his next errand.

One reason he had chosen New Hampshire was that it had virtually no meaningful gun laws. He visited several gun shops and bought two .45 pistols modeled on the M1911, with threaded barrels and caps for silencers. After buying his last plane ticket, he knew there was nothing about the Charles Ackerman identification that would alarm the authorities, so he used it for the federal background check, which was completed while he waited.

Schaeffer drove to another gun shop and picked up a rifle, an AR-15 clone with one hundred rounds of ammunition, a flash suppressor, and a scope. He had seldom used a rifle in the days when he was working, but he had no idea what he would be facing this time, and when he found out, it might be too late to go shopping.

He went to the trunk of his car, stowed the rifle, loaded the two pistols and put them in his coat pockets, closed the trunk, and began to drive. When he could, he turned south. As he drove, the weight of the two pistols in his coat made him think about the old days again.

He remembered the night he and Eddie had survived the ambush at the motel outside Chicago when he was sixteen. Eddie had driven away from the motel, and the boy had turned around so his knees were on his seat and his chin and hands were on top of the backrest as he stared out the back window of Eddie's car.

The men he could see were all dead, some

lying in the entrance to room 212 where they had fallen and the driver a few feet off, where he had been dragged from the car. He could see the man from the front desk who had come running with a rifle.

Eddie turned as the car bumped down off the lot into the street. He didn't look into the rearview mirror, but he seemed anxious.

"They're all dead," said the boy.

"I know, but the police aren't. The manager kept the rooms empty, but the rest of the town can't be deaf. We all made a lot of noise back there."

"Are we going home?"

"Not for a while," Eddie said. "We have to make things right with the people who run the place."

"What place? The motel?"

"No. Chicago."

It was already daylight when they reached the middle of the city. Eddie parked and called a number on a pay phone in a drugstore. The boy heard a bit of what he said. "This is Eddie Mastrewski. Do you know who I am? I would like to have a moment of Mr. Castiglione's time. Anytime he can spare it. I'm going to be waiting at the restaurant of the Brewster Hotel with my boy. I'll wait for word from him as long as I can. But if he won't talk to me, I'd appreciate it if you would call the hotel and let me know. Thank you."

They drove to Michigan Avenue, where the hotel was. The building was tall, like some Pittsburgh buildings, but it was bigger and fancier than the ones he'd seen in Pittsburgh. He and Eddie went in the front door of the building, through a giant lobby, and into the restaurant.

Eddie selected a table near the back of the room, away from the front windows and the entrance. When the boy looked at Eddie, he said, "I know, kid. I like a window too, but we're going to be here for a while, and there will be people around who won't like us. We want a thick, hard wall behind us and clear paths to a couple of doors."

"Should we be afraid?"

Eddie's lips gave a quick twitch that the boy knew was a smile he had smothered. His face turned serious again. "Fear isn't always bad. If it keeps you thinking, it can't hurt. When we're working, we don't have any friends. All our friends are regular people back in Pittsburgh. The man I asked to meet with us is very powerful and important. He hires hundreds of people to do things for him. They make him more money and protect him and so on."

"Is that why we're meeting him in such a

fancy hotel?"

"Not exactly. I suggested this hotel because he owns it. Everybody you've seen, from the parking guy to the waiter, the cooks, the desk clerks, and the chambermaids, all work for him. Even the hookers in the bar work for him. Our coming here is a gesture to show I mean him no harm."

They ordered fried chicken and mashed potatoes for lunch. After they had finished eating, and Eddie was drinking coffee and the boy cola, two young men in suits and shiny shoes with dark, slicked-back hair came through the double door across the room from them. They closed the doors behind them, looked at each person in the room, and then walked toward the table where Eddie and the boy sat. The boy straightened in his seat, but Eddie seemed to be concentrating on moving as little as possible.

Just as the two men reached the table, the kitchen door at the back of the room swung open. A tall, thin man wearing a black suit with a red tie came out, walked to their table, and sat across from Eddie and the boy. He seemed to the boy to be very old. One of the men stepped toward Eddie as though to search him, but the old man said, "Not necessary. I know Eddie. You guys can get a coffee at the bar. Just keep an eye on the door." As the men walked to the bar, the old man said, "Hello, Eddie. And who is this?"

"This is my boy."

"I heard about you, kid. *Un uomo forte,* eh? You know what that means?"

"No, sir."

"It means I heard good things about you." He turned and focused on Eddie. "What's on your mind, Eddie?"

"Well, Mr. Castiglione, I came to you because I have a problem. Last night five men came to our motel after us. We had to kill them and the hotel desk clerk who helped set us up." He reached into his breast pocket and took out five driver's licenses. He laid them out on the table.

The old man's eyes were like the shining black eyes of a crow, taking in the licenses instantly and then flicking back up to Eddie's face.

Eddie said, "Taddio got in touch with me and said he was calling on your orders. He wanted me to take out a man who had been plotting to replace you. He said it was important that an outsider do the work to avoid hard feelings. He told me to check into the Starlite Motel and wait by the phone while they located the guy. Instead of calling, he and his four friends came in the night and fired into our room."

"What did he offer you for the hit?"

"Thirty grand. I guess it doesn't matter, because he was never going to pay."

"Taddio knew something you apparently didn't. There's a contract on you, both of you. He was trying to collect. He shouldn't have. You did the right thing to come see me, Eddie. It's going to keep you alive — for a while anyway. You can go home when you want. I've hired you before, and I have a feeling I may need you again before long. All the old stuff is coming out again."

The boy saw the old man a few more times after that, when he was grown up and working on his own. There was one day after he had killed a man named Harrow for old Victor Castiglione. He went to the house on Lake Shore Drive that they called "the Castle." The old man had him brought to the living room to get paid, but caught his thirteen-year-old grandson, young Salvatore, around a corner trying to eavesdrop. The old man had one of his soldiers bring him into the living room to stand there for the meeting.

"That's right," the old man said. "Take a good look. That's the scariest man you're ever going to see. Doesn't look scary, does he?"

"No."

"Well, he is. Look in his eyes. You see now?"

"I don't know."

"Does he like you, or does he hate you?"

"I can't tell."

"That's because the answer is 'neither.' He looks at you the way you look at a fish. It's alive now, maybe not tomorrow, but it doesn't matter which."

"I get it."

"Good. You see another one like him, make sure he's on your side."

Tonight Schaeffer was traveling again with the two guns weighing down his pockets. He had tried all the easy ways of learning what was going on in the world of organized crime, and now he had to try one of the harder ways. He had a pretty good car for the trip, meaning that the engine was sound and that nothing about the vehicle would attract attention or make it memorable, like prominent dents or scratches.

His phone told him he had 473 miles to go, which would be around nine hours of driving. He would stop for the night at a hotel along the way, just as Eddie would

have. This was not a fight to charge into
with no sleep.

126

12

He drove past the house in McLean, Virginia, late at night, long after all the commuters had come home, parked their cars, and locked their doors. He had no proof that Elizabeth Waring — E. V. Waring in her Justice Department life — still lived there, but it was a place to start.

The neighborhood was essentially the same as it had been when he'd first seen it in 1992. He'd seen it again in 2011, when he had sent E. V. Waring a personalized gift and followed the gift from the Justice Department to her home.

His impression of the area then was that the two-story houses were built in the 1950s for upscale families. They had started out being nearly the same size and shape, but modifications and additions had made them increasingly different. One thing that made them even more different was the landscaping. In a few years the trees had grown much taller and wider. A row of scraggly bushes had become a high, impenetrable hedge.

He parked a block away from her house and walked to it, then cut behind it to the tall window he had used to enter it the last time. He had known that the contact between the magnet and the alarm system's sensor was only on the lower frame where the window met the sill. He had been able to lower the upper section and climb in over the two frames, then raise the upper section again without moving the lower section, breaking the contact, and setting off the alarm.

This time, as he came around the house, he looked for cameras along the eaves but saw none. The windows were the size and shape he had remembered, but they were different. He stepped closer and used his phone to illuminate the corner of the window. The window was now double-pane tempered glass, the kind designed to withstand a flying two-by-four in a hurricane. The frame was steel coated with baked-on metal flake. He could not tell whether it was connected to the current alarm system or not, so he continued on.

He had not kept up with all the technology and advances in American home security and didn't know whether she had either. He had never expected to be back in McLean, Virginia, trying to get into her house again. In the light from his phone he looked in the window and spotted a painting on the wall that he recognized from seven years ago. It was an English-style landscape with trees and cows.

He put his phone away and continued along the outer wall, trying to find a way in. When he had last seen Elizabeth Waring, she was already the highest-ranking non-political official in the Justice Department's Organized Crime Section. She'd advanced to the corner office by outlasting and outperforming any rivals. During that time she must have been pulling in a good salary, and probably received some raises, but she hadn't moved to a fancier house. He supposed the kids were gone by now, moved out and maybe married.

He tried to remember the exact look of the windows and doors so he could spot any more ominous changes since he'd last broken in. There had been a couple of times when he'd needed to talk to her and walk away free afterward, so he had simply shown up in her bedroom, spoken to wake her, and asked a few questions. The last time he had arrived this way, seven years ago, they'd had a conversation in which they agreed to trade information. She knew what was going on in the Mafia in the present because she got reports from field agents and investigators about it as soon as it happened. He had been living on another continent, so he knew very little about the things members of the Mafia had done recently, but he knew a great deal about murders they had committed twenty years earlier. He hoped she hadn't retired.

He walked close to the walls of the house. Its brick facade went from the foundation to the roof, something he admired because it made it impossible for a drive-by shooter to fire through the wall. Elizabeth Waring would have to be standing in the front window to take a hit. Brick was something he had looked for when he'd bought his own house in Bath years ago. Where his house didn't have it, he'd added it.

He stepped to the front door and stood still. Her husband had been an FBI agent. She had been a young widow when he'd seen her the first time, and a widow in middle age the next time. He remembered thinking that she was attractive. That was bad. It had been risky enough to deal with her when she was alone, but she could easily have married another FBI agent by now, or a marine colonel, or some other unpleasant sort. If Schaeffer made noise, there could be two people coming to see what the commotion was, both of them armed, trained, and in practice.

Her bedroom — the master suite — was on the second floor in the center of the back wall. He went into the back garden, which he had used twice as an escape route. In those days, there had been a big brick barbecue with a chimney back here. It was gone, replaced by a stainless-steel model with a gas hookup. He supposed that was an upgrade. She had undoubtedly not wanted her children to breathe and swallow the carcinogens from charcoal.

The path was now paved with flagstones and surrounded by decorative bushes — another reason not to want an open fireplace. He noticed that she had added a second entrance to the kitchen, apparently a door just for carrying things to and from the new grill. He examined the new door and wondered if she'd had it wired into the alarm system. The floor below it was polished concrete, and the frame was steel. He didn't see any wires or contacts, so he took out his pocketknife, opened the blade, and jimmied the lock. He pushed it inward and no alarm sounded.

He slipped in and closed the door, then made his way through the kitchen, which had been enlarged. It occurred to him that people did that as soon as they were cooking for fewer people and there was no point. The dining room looked the same, but he couldn't tell for sure because he couldn't see the paint color, and the furniture looked like lumps in the dark.

He made his way up the staircase to the second floor, walking up the wooden steps as Eddie had taught him fifty years ago: holding the rail and placing his feet at the inner edge of each stair, where the nails held the board to the under-structure and prevented bending or creaking. At the top he stood still for a long time, listening for the sounds of the house to tell him what he needed to know.

In a mid-century house like this one, there were messages. The night was calm and warm, so there weren't shifting sounds as the boards held up to the wind. He heard no sounds from humans — no radio or television, no voices or footsteps. When the central air conditioner's thermostat reached its high setting, the compressor and fan went on, and he stepped forward, letting the normal, reassuring sound mask his steps up the hall toward the master bedroom.

At the doorway he heard a sudden swish of sheets and saw a figure sit up in bed. The figure was in front of a row of windows at the other side of the room. It was a female shape — her. She was naked. She stood, snatched up a thick bathrobe from the chair near the bed, and threw it over her shoulders so that she could get her arms into the sleeves as she hurried through the doorway into the hall.

She grasped Schaeffer's arm tightly, pulled him with her into a spare room, and whispered, "Sit tight. Ten minutes."

He heard her bare feet making small sliding sounds as she walked back along the hall to her room. Then she clicked on a small bedside lamp. She said in a normal, calm voice, "Okay, David. I just got an alert from the office. I need to get ready. They're sending a car. When I looked at the clock, I saw that it's time for you to get up and out anyway. Remember, you've got a plane to catch."

Schaeffer heard a male voice muttering something.

She said, "Yes, it was lovely. Now pull yourself together and go."

There were lights being turned on, and then a toilet flushing, and the shower running, and a lot of walking around. Their talk was loud enough for Schaeffer to hear but not loud enough for him to understand. Then there was the clomp of a big man in dress shoes going down the hall past the room where he sat and to the stairs, and then the sound of her smaller feet, this time in slippers. She was still talking, so she must be escorting him out. Schaeffer heard the front door close and then a bolt sliding into its receptacle.

After about thirty seconds, Elizabeth Waring appeared in the doorway of the guest room in the dark.

Schaeffer said, "Who was that?"

"Just a guy I know. Don't you approve?"

"He's not good enough for you."

She laughed and shook her head. "Why are you here?"

"I think you were expecting me. That's why you got up and came out to head me off."

"I expected you sometime. Not tonight. I'm not clairvoyant. I wouldn't have risked David's life if I thought it was tonight."

"Why did you expect me?"

"I'm sure you know that we have informants who tell us what they hear, and we also tap the phones of certain people. We've been doing that forever — before I was part of "we." We've heard there was a new contract out for you, and it occurred to me that you might have heard it too. People have been saying that there's a lot of money being offered."

"Why take out a contract on me now? Who's offering it?"

"I don't know yet, because nobody has said the name where we could hear it."

"Has something else happened — like somebody important getting killed? Or even a near miss? People could be blaming me for the hit."

"I don't think so. The biggest news going around is that Carlo Balacontano has a parole hearing scheduled for August 1."

Schaeffer stared at her. "The last time I heard, he was in a federal prison. You can't get paroled from federal prison."

"Not under current law. Congress passed a law to end federal parole in 1984, and it went into effect in 1987. But Carlo Balacontano was convicted in 1982, and so he's one of the remaining criminals the system has to treat under the old law. He gets a hearing just as though this were 1982."

"I can't believe he's still up to that. When I was here seven years ago, everybody expected him to die in a year or two."

She said, "More like a wish. I went to see him in prison then. He looked like a very healthy man to me. He was sixty and he'd been in prison for twenty years because of you. He told me a lot about you, and I'm sure you could supply most of the monologue. He was in there on a mandatory work schedule. That day, he was cleaning the small building that the prison used for conjugal visits with wives. I caught him goofing off, but he still had to get that much cleaning work done in a morning. Every morning. He's had a diet with no alcohol, no creamy or buttery sauces, no sweets, no pastries. It's all plain, healthy food. He's probably in better shape than either of us."

Schaeffer shook his head. "I still have to take care of myself because of people like him." He paused. "And I noticed that you do too."

Her face turned weary. "That's by way of reminding me that you just saw me naked?"

"I did, but I wasn't. And it doesn't matter."

"It does to me. I knew that you wouldn't be expecting a man here. I couldn't take the chance that you'd get startled and kill him. He's a fine, decent person."

"I'm not here to harm you or anyone, or make you feel uncomfortable. I just didn't have any other way to reach you except to show up when nobody would see me. I shouldn't have assumed you were alone, and I apologize."

"Okay, okay." She looked away from him. "I don't want to keep talking about it. What, exactly, do you want?"

"I was living in a place I thought was safe. A few days ago I got attacked by four men and had to kill them. I went to an airport where nobody should have expected me, but I guess some others must have put a transponder in the car I was driving. I was attacked in the airport parking lot and had to kill two men there. I flew to another country and was attacked there. Twice. I haven't been doing anything since I lived here, so all of this has to be coming from here, from the past. If somebody is offering a contract, it has to be someone from the past."

"I told you, the biggest current news I've heard is that Carlo Balacontano is having a parole hearing."

"Which means he's still in prison now. Who is doing this stuff?"

"I would guess there are people who want to kill you because they think you'll supply information that sinks his chance for a parole. And there are probably others who think you'll make a deal with the Balacontano family to give them proof that you

137

framed him for the murder of Arthur Fieldston, so he'll go free. There must be lots of other people who have their own reasons to kill you, and think that once you know there's a parole hearing, you'll be drawn to it. The one who would know most about them is you."

He stared at her unmoving silhouette in the dim light. "Seven years ago we helped each other by telling each other a few secrets. I came here to see if I could make a deal to do that again."

"What you're talking about was a terrible risk I took to get you to come in as a protected witness. My superiors at Justice refused to approve it, and you wouldn't do it. So I was the only one in the deal."

"I gave you evidence of an old murder."

"And then killed the murderer before we could arrest him. Isn't that what happened? Nobody ever determined why, when the FBI found Frank Tosca at that resort in Arizona, his throat was cut. That was you, right?"

He took a deep breath and let it out in a sigh.

Her sigh was just as frustrated. "You told the truth just to get me to trust you and think we had a deal."

He said, "This time it's different."

"That's nice. Here's how things are. Nobody will approve a deal that saves you. Get it out of your head. When you came here before, the people who ran Justice were all too idealistic and naive to favor a killer over the creeps who were after him. Now the executive branch is run by people who aren't troubled much by ethics. Everybody in the Organized Crime Section is barely hanging on and doing whatever semblance of our jobs we can."

"Give me a way to talk to you. It'll be light soon, and I can't be here."

She went to the table beside the bed and opened a drawer. She took out a pen and pad and wrote a number. "That's a phone that's private and isn't from work."

He took it. "Is this the phone David calls?"

"It is."

"Then it'll do."

"If they start to be curious about me, it will be bugged as quickly as any other phone."

"Then make sure they don't suspect you of anything." He paused. "I'm sorry I came here like this."

"Forget it. Now go away."

He stood and seemed to glide through the door. She heard him moving to the staircase, then listened for the front door opening, but heard nothing more.

13

He got into his car and drove out of McLean. She had surprised him. The big news, the only events that people were talking about, were that somebody wanted him dead badly enough to be offering a huge payoff, and that Carl Bala was up for parole. It had not occurred to him that Bala would ever get out of prison, or that there was any mechanism left for him to be released other than death.

In 1982 Balacontano had hired him to do a couple of very risky, high-paying jobs. Bala protected himself by hiring Schaeffer through a Las Vegas go-between lawyer named Harry Orloff. After doing the jobs, Schaeffer was walking down an alley in Denver and got jumped by a pair of muggers. He killed them, but not before getting marked up and hurt. One of them had hit him with a rock the size of a brick.

He went to Las Vegas a few days before

the prearranged pay date, partly to recover from his injuries and give his bruises and cuts time to heal. Being there with his face looking that way made him a liability, and maybe made him seem weak too. It had also given Balacontano time to do some thinking. Balacontano had not been foolish enough to openly refuse to pay a professional killer, even one who knew only the go-between. But he had calculated that it would save him a great deal of money to pay some less expensive men to kill the expensive killer.

When Schaeffer broke into Orloff's house, he found Orloff had been killed, probably to keep secret the name of his employer. But Schaeffer had found a living man there named Arthur Fieldston, who was the legitimate-looking front man for some of the businesses owned by Carlo Balacontano.

Schaeffer killed Fieldston, cut off his head and hands, put them in a cooler, and drove it across the country to Balacontano's horse farm outside Saratoga Springs, New York. He buried the head and hands about two hundred feet from the main house and called in a tip to the New York State police.

As he drove, he thought about Elizabeth Waring. He was reasonably sure she was telling him the truth. Carl Bala really had been scheduled for a parole hearing, probably the most unexpected news that she could have told Schaeffer. And while she didn't know who was trying to kill Schaeffer, her guess that it had to do with Balacontano's possible release was probably right. What Schaeffer needed to know now was whether the hunters were people who wanted Balacontano to stay in prison, people who were working for Balacontano to ensure his parole wasn't sabotaged, or people who simply wanted Schaeffer dead for their own reasons and thought he'd show up if Balacontano was about to be released.

She could have been lying about it, he knew. She was certainly not a friend of his, but they had forged a kind of truce. It was a tested legal practice in America that the police were allowed to tell a suspect all the lies they could think of and then charge him with whatever they wanted to without penalty. But his experience with Waring over time had been that she didn't use that tool, at least not with him. Lying wouldn't accomplish what she wanted, which seemed to be to convert him into an informant.

He thought about the glimpse of her personal life he'd just gotten. He shouldn't have been surprised. Of course she must

143

have had some kind of love life over the years. Her husband had died when she was very young. He should have been prepared for another person to be in that room with her, but he had been thoughtless. He was lucky it wasn't a homicide cop.

Everybody had a right to a personal life, and everybody had a right to keep it personal. He had come to learn that while growing up in Eddie's butcher shop. Eddie always had a few special customers. Often a lady would call while the boy was in school to place her order and arrange the best time for Eddie to deliver it to her house that day. He would be gone about an hour, come back as cheerful as always, and go right back to work. He would come and go by the back door, so most customers would assume he had never left and was simply doing some cutting, weighing, and wrapping in the back of the shop.

One afternoon about a month after the boy had turned sixteen and had his driver's license, Eddie was waiting on customers when the boy came home from school. The boy headed straight for the back of the store to get rid of his books and coat and put on his apron, but Eddie stopped him. "I've got a delivery order ready to go out."

The boy said, "No problem. I'm here."

Eddie said, "She asked me to send you. It's Mrs. Whittaker. Do you know where they live?"

The boy was confused. "I don't think so."

Eddie took the black pen from his apron pocket. "Here. I'll write it on the wrapper." He scribbled the address on the white butcher paper. "You can take the car."

This was a big moment for the boy. Eddie had taught him to drive, and he had passed the road test and gotten his license. Eddie let him drive the car whenever he wanted, but this was different. It was using the car the way grown-ups did — to do business, make deliveries, serve customers.

It was the sort of winter day that people in Pittsburgh learned to expect from January to March, a world of dirty snow that never melted, the leafless trees looking skeletal under an iron-gray sky. He arrived at the address on the package just before four o'clock. He parked Eddie's car along the curb, around the corner where the snowplow had already pushed the snow into a ridge and where he could walk without stepping into snow higher than his shoes. The house was large, a survivor from the nineteenth century, with a big porch and a steep, high roof above the second story.

When he climbed the steps to the front

porch with the package, the door swung open. Mrs. Whittaker was inside holding the door open for him. As soon as he was past the threshold, she shut the door and locked the bolt. She was wearing a thin blue dress with a flower pattern. She gave a shiver and hugged herself. "So cold already," she said. He saw her perked nipples under the dress. She took the package of meat, walked quickly up the narrow hall to the kitchen, and put it in the refrigerator. Then she walked back, her eyes mostly turned downward toward the hardwood floor but looking up a couple of times to glance at the boy.

She seemed shy. She was only twenty-three, something he knew because she had been a senior when Ray Politz's older brother Dick was. He'd seen her a few times. He and Ray had been almost twelve. He had forgotten how pretty she was, or maybe never really been aware of it because she was so much older than he was. She was thin, about five feet four inches tall, with blond hair that looked like corn silk, and light skin that showed pink blushes, at least at that moment.

He watched her coming back and saw her notice it and smile, showing her perfect white teeth. The boy remembered that her father was a dentist. She reached him and leaned against the wall. "What do I owe you?"

The boy was shocked. He had come unprepared. He had no idea. "I'm sorry," he said. "Eddie just told me to deliver the meat. I forgot to ask."

"That's okay. Maybe you can tell me next time."

"Eddie will open a charge account. In fact, I'll do it myself when I get back," he said. He was trying to impress her.

"Thank you," she said, and smiled that beautiful smile for him again. She seemed young, with her thin, graceful shape and the kind of blond hair that seemed to belong to a child. But she also seemed older, more grown up and sophisticated.

She said, "You know, I have a little problem, and my husband doesn't get home from work until eight-thirty on Thursdays. I wonder if you would take a look at it."

If she had asked him to walk through fire, he would have agreed. "Sure," he said.

She started up the stairs, and he couldn't help looking at her as she climbed the steps. He watched her hips sway as she climbed. She stopped at the top of the stairs, looked over her shoulder, and must have noticed he was looking at her bottom, but she ignored it. "It's this door that keeps getting stuck so I can't pull it open. Could you open it?"

She pointed at a door a few feet to the right of the landing. He went to the door and pushed it with his shoulder. It budged and then swung inward to reveal a small, neat spare bedroom. "Do you have any sandpaper? I could sand it so it won't stick."

She moved in behind him so closely that they were touching, and snaked her arms around his waist. Her lips were close to his ear. "Next time. You know, Michael, having you look at me like that makes me feel all warm and confused."

"I'm sorry."

"It's all right. I like it. And all men like to look at women." She stepped back, and he turned to face her. She said, "Go ahead. Touch me."

He let his hands go to her waist. It felt impossibly tiny. She took his wrists and lifted his hands to her breasts and then down along her sides to her hips. "I know you like me." She released his wrists. "I like you too. I think you want me to take off my clothes. Do you?"

"I do want that. Yes, please."

She laughed, and then went ahead. When she was naked, she stood in front of him for about five seconds, watching him look, and then undid his belt and helped him out of his clothes. After a few minutes of embracing, kissing, and touching, she went to the bed, pulled back the covers, reached under the pillow, and produced a condom. She tore open the package and rolled it onto him.

He made love to her, shyly and clumsily at first, but with curiosity and wonder and interest. He saw her turn her head occasionally and squint to consult the electric alarm clock on the nightstand. At a certain point during their second time, she said, "Finish now. It's okay. I'm happy now. Give in to it."

He did. She lay still and embraced him, ran her fingers through his hair and kissed him gently. "That was really nice," she said. "But we have to get dressed and send you back to work now."

He didn't resist. He was still amazed at his great good fortune and didn't want to risk it. They both dressed quickly and efficiently and found themselves facing each other. They kissed once more, and then she placed both hands on his chest to push him a foot from her so she could look into his eyes. "Did you have a nice time?" Her eyes were blue, like a summer sky.

"Yes. This is the best day of —"

"Okay. I did too. I'll call the shop the next time I have the chance, and you can do the delivery again."

He smiled. "Thank you."

She laughed. "You're funny." She gave him a gentle push to get him to start down the stairs. "Is Eddie the Butcher your father?"

"No, why?"

"I've been watching you for a while. I always wondered. I know we're going to be close. We already are. I can't help being curious about you."

When they got to the front door, she unlocked it and held it open. "Drive carefully. It's been getting really cold this time of day, and the roads are probably slippery."

"I will."

She said, "One more thing. This is a secret between us. Please don't ever tell anyone else that we did this."

"I won't." He never did. When he got back to the shop, Eddie was already mopping the tile floor in the meat-cutting room, the smell of the steaming soapy water and Lysol filling the air. The bell rang when the boy opened the front door, and Eddie appeared at the doorway to the cutting room. "Hi, kid. Delivery go okay?"

"Yes," said the boy. "But I wasn't thinking. I didn't ask for the price or bring change or anything. I told her I'd start an account for her."

"Good thinking," Eddie said. "Make your customer feel trusted." The boy stepped closer to the counter. "What should I be doing now?"

"Just start the card for Mrs. Whittaker. The charge for today was fourteen dollars and sixty-seven cents. Then clear the register and lock the cash in the safe. Where's the car?"

"Right outside at the curb."

"Great. We won't have to freeze our asses off walking home."

Eddie went back to finish the floor. He never gave the boy a knowing smile or asked any questions, either then or during the years while Mrs. Whittaker kept her account active. The boy had occasionally revisited this day in memory over the next decades.

Michael Schaeffer thought again about Elizabeth Waring. What she had done was give him a little information but not enough to identify his enemy. He needed to know who was sending people to kill him. There were probably twenty bosses who had reason to hate him. In order to create enough chaos to escape the manhunts when he was young, he had killed some important men and tried to make it look as though another family had done it. Some of the current bosses were probably the sons or nephews of the men he had killed. They might see the release of Carlo Balacontano as simple bait to bring Schaeffer in front of a gun sight. But he had studied Carlo Balacontano, and he was sure they had too. If Balacontano was freed, many of those bosses had reason to be afraid. Bala had been powerful, ruthless, and smart when he'd gone to prison. There had been no limit to his greed or his need for power. During all those years in prison, he had been ruling his crime family through a series of puppets and stand-in bosses. If he was a threat in the old days, would he be different now, or just smarter and angrier and richer?

And Elizabeth Waring could be manipulating Schaeffer. It was easy to forget that she was the most dangerous person in the world to him. She had been trying to trap him for about thirty years, just as some of the crime bosses had. And she was better educated and smarter than any of the men who were after him. Every time she turned her attention to him, she remembered everything from before, and she demonstrated that, in the meantime, she had learned something new. He was a murderer who had never been to jail, and she was in the business of taking people like him off the street. Maybe she had arranged the parole hearing for Carlo Balacontano just to lure Schaeffer back from where he'd been living.

She would have been justified. He was guilty of a lot of murders. It occurred to him that she was one of the people who would have said it was terrible of Eddie to make him into a killer, if she had known. Maybe it was true. But what Eddie had taught him wasn't just the killing. He'd also taught him how to live through it.

14

He drove the hundred miles to Richmond, Virginia, keeping his eyes moving to check the traffic behind him. What he looked for were crude methods that Mafia soldiers might use — changing a driver's appearance with hats or coats, falling far behind and turning on the high-beam headlights so they could still see him but didn't look the same to him, or having two cars follow and switch off at intervals so they didn't get too familiar.

He assumed that the methods Elizabeth Waring would use if she wanted his location were more sophisticated. He had removed the battery from his cell phone so his GPS signal wouldn't give him away. The Justice Department would probably check the license plate–reader networks of the local police forces. She knew the time — a few minutes after 3:00 a.m. — and knew he was heading away from her house in McLean.

Traffic was sparse, so her people might be able to narrow the list down to a few thousand license numbers, possibly only a few hundred. She could get somebody to find out if any of these cars had changed hands in the past month. He had used electrical tape to alter some of the numbers on his plates, but he was going to have to register the car in another state soon, possibly New York or Pennsylvania,. A nonexistent license plate number would move his car to the top of their list.

He knew he was likely up against killers who hadn't been born when he'd left the United States the first time. He didn't ask himself why they wanted to kill him. They did it for the same reason he had in the old days: somebody was offering them money. The ones he'd seen in the past few days were more overconfident than he had been. They assumed that because they were younger, they would prevail. When he was a teenager, he had known more about how to do the job than they did the day they died. Eddie had made sure at the beginning.

After he had learned to load, fire, and care for each of Eddie's pistols during the spring and summer when he was twelve, Eddie said he was happy with his progress but added,

"I need to take you to a guy. We'll leave Sunday when the shop is closed. Pack enough clothes for three weeks."

The guy was named Don Sarkassian. He lived on a farm out in the sticks. It took Eddie an hour and a half to drive out there. Don had about a hundred acres of flat land that he never planted, and at least five times that many acres that were rolling hills and second-growth forest.

He had converted a hill like a barrow at the edge of a flat field, dug a gaping scoop out of the hill with a backhoe, and poured sand into the depression so that when a bullet went through a target, it burrowed into the sand a few inches. He would occasionally start up the backhoe to sift the sand through a screen. Then he'd recycle the bullets and reload them into brass casings.

Sarkassian was a former pistol champion who had won so many medals, trophies, and commemorative guns that he had grown bored with competition. Eddie let the boy know that Sarkassian had, on occasion, taken on some wet work, but a man who could flip a quarter into the air and hit it with a .45 pistol didn't see men as challenging targets.

The morning they met, Sarkassian led him and Eddie out to the range to take some target practice. When they'd each emptied a magazine, Sarkassian stopped and studied the boy for a minute and then talked to Eddie some more. Suddenly he tossed a .45 pistol at the boy, who caught it with both hands and then held it out to Sarkassian, handgrips first. Sarkassian said, "Thanks." To Eddie he said, "It'll cost you about two grand for ammunition. I'll teach him for free."

"Thanks a lot, Don," Eddie said. "But you don't have to do that. We've got plenty of money."

"This one won't take much of my time. When he's fired five hundred rounds, he'll be better than you are. When he's fired a thousand, he'll be scary good."

After lunch Don took the boy through the living room of his house to the gun room. It had a combination lock on its steel door like a safe. He opened it, and the boy walked in behind him and looked at his collection. He had military rifles and pistols from a variety of manufacturers, configured for the armies of a number of countries. He had at least a hundred pistols on the racks, a dozen sniper rifles, and five shotguns.

At the end of the gun room tour, he opened a drawer with seven pistols in it. "Which one of these is worth the most money? Look at them carefully. You can pick them up."

The boy picked up each one, examined it, then put it back. There was a Glock, a Sig Sauer, a Makarov, an antique Webley from World War I, a Walther, a Beretta. He picked up the Ruger LC9, and said, "This one."

"Why?"

"It's got its serial number drilled off. If I had to drop it, I wouldn't have to worry about it or take any risks to get it back."

Sarkassian said, "You're Eddie's boy, all right. Let's go shoot."

They spent the first afternoon with nine-millimeter Glock 17 pistols, firing at paper targets at fifteen yards. Sarkassian could put all seventeen rounds into the three-inch bull's-eye every time. When the boy fired, Sarkassian stared at him hard, looking at every muscle, watching his hands, his breathing, his eyes, legs, feet.

He adjusted the boy's grip. "Like this. The part of your finger that touches the trigger is the last bone, where your fingerprint is. Using any other part tugs your weapon to the side, off the target." He adjusted the boy's right arm. "You want the force of the recoil to push your shoulder back, like a piston, not make the barrel rise."

All afternoon the adjustments that were

made got smaller and smaller until they would have been hard for an observer to see. And by the time the sun was behind the barrow, the boy could fire seventeen rounds into the bull's-eye every time.

As they walked back toward the house for dinner, Sarkassian said, "You did well. That's the paper target that police academies use at nine yards, not fifteen. If you were a cop, you'd be getting a few bucks in your next paycheck for qualifying at that level." Two steps later he said, "That's not good enough, of course."

That evening they cleaned the pistols, and Sarkassian tested him on reassembling them blindfolded.

Sarkassian was as firm as Eddie in the belief that the only kind of shooting that mattered was hitting moving targets. The next day the target was a steel disk swinging back and forth. The day after that it was a volleyball bouncing across the boy's field of vision; the next day a softball, and then a tennis ball. Two days later the softball was simply thrown, either bouncing or flying straight across or up in the air, with no warning.

Whenever the boy had trouble with the next stage, Don would repeat, "There's no magic, no talent, no trick. All there is, is practice."

There might not be magic, but there were skills. These were mostly ways to control the mind, forcing all his concentration and his will to think of nothing except placing that round where it would pierce the ball.

The first day of the second week, Sarkassian greeted him at breakfast and said, "Today we're left-handed." They began with the same exercises and firing sequences, except holding the pistols in their left hands. During a few breaks they fired different pistols — a .44 magnum revolver, a .380 pistol. But the main work of the day was applying each of the initial lessons to the boy's left side.

Day after day the practice continued while there was sunlight, and they disassembled and cleaned the guns in the evening.

After the second week of shooting lessons, Sarkassian said, "Today I want to try something I don't usually teach anybody, because for most people it's just a stupid parlor trick. For you, it might be different. It might be what saves your life one day."

When they reached the range, Sarkassian opened his backpack, where he usually carried the guns and ammunition. This time there were the two Glock 17s again. He said, "You're going to learn to use two pistols at once. There are moments when it's worth directing a double barrage of fire at a single target, and there are times when having the ability to direct fire into targets in two different directions would be useful."

At the end of ten days, the boy had learned to do both. After that, he practiced firing over his shoulder with either hand. Sarkassian taught him to use a wide selection of weapons, and spent a few days on using sniper rifles and shotguns.

Then Sarkassian and the boy worked on making some improvements to the firing range. Sarkassian even taught the boy how to drive and operate the backhoe to lift big scoops of sand into the sifter he'd made of wood and reinforced screen to recover bullets the two had fired for the past two weeks. They increased the width of the backstop, added more sand, and put together some wooden tables at various distances for holding ammunition and sighting in rifles.

On the last day of the boy's time with Sarkassian, Eddie's car pulled up in front of the farmhouse around noon. At the end of an afternoon of shooting, they all came in to make dinner.

Eddie said, "I've never seen anything like that. He's twelve years old. And that took a hell of a lot more than a couple thousand bucks' worth of ammo."

Sarkassian shrugged. "The more he learned, the more curious I got to see what else he could do. Now I'll have two good friends who can shoot and owe me a favor. You have any idea what that could be worth?"

Three years later, Eddie and the boy shot the two men in front of Yankee Stadium. In mid-summer they lived through the ambush at the motel in Chicago. Then fall had come, and the world was already getting cold when the next group of men came after them.

What had alarmed Eddie about the ambush in Chicago was that he'd fallen for the bait. And there were still people in Chicago who knew that Eddie and the boy had shot the two men in New York. Victor Castiglione knew. Eddie was pretty sure that nobody in the center of the country who knew would pass that information on to the New York people — the heirs of the late Mr. Luciano and their enemies. He told the boy that if trouble came, it would be people from the Midwest who got tempted by the money. Eddie was violating his own rule, which was not to think he knew more than he did.

They attacked on an ordinary Thursday.

The boy had just come in the front door of the butcher shop, carrying his books in a backpack to keep them dry. He remembered even now how quiet it was in the shop, as though someone had kept customers from coming in. The streets near the shop seemed empty.

He saw a car pull up outside the front door. In the front seats and the right rear, he could see three men, all wearing over-coats and the brimmed hats that some grown-up men still wore in those days. After a second, he caught sight of a fourth man in the left rear seat. "Eddie!" the boy said.

As soon as Eddie saw the car, he said to the boy in a quiet voice, "They're here for us."

The boy had been trained and drilled for this moment. He ducked beneath the counter and crawled to the far end, took out the 12-gauge shotgun that was kept on the shelf below the scale, pressed the safety off, and then stuck the pistol from under the counter in his belt. He knew that Eddie was doing something similar, because there were a series of clicks and the whispery sound of metal against metal coming from his end of the counter.

Eddie didn't wait to tell the men to put their hands up. There was only the door swinging open, the bell above it tinkling, and the deafening *blam* of Eddie's first shot. The boy popped up, saw the first man in the door topple backward, and fired his shotgun into the man coming in behind him. Eddie pumped his shotgun and got the third, who had been blocked and kept immobile by his two companions jammed in the front door.

Eddie launched himself toward the back rooms and ran hard to come out the parking lot door and reappear at the front. He fired as the car rolled off from the curb, blowing out the rear window. His next shot peppered the back of the driver, blowing his hat forward off his head, but the car kept going. A shotgun was usually lethal at five yards, but by forty yards the pellets had spread and lost much of their velocity.

Eddie turned and ran for his car. The boy, who was faster than the big man, caught up, but Eddie said, "Stay here."

The boy turned and ran back into the shop, stepping over the dead men. He heard a sound coming from the back of the shop, past the meat-cutting room and the walk-in refrigerator. He recognized the squeak of the back door. There were footsteps.

He squatted beside the front of the counter. He knew that when these newcomers arrived, they would first gape at the three bodies in the doorway for a second before they could get their eyes to move on and search for him.

He waited until the first man had cleared the doorway behind the counter and he could see the second man before firing the shotgun. He pumped it as the man fell, and got the second man too. He knew they must have come from a car parked in the small back lot where the delivery trucks parked. He stepped on one of the dead men to get through the front door and run around the building.

He saw the car where he expected it to be. This was a cold afternoon, so he could see the steamy smoke puffing out of the tailpipe. He could see that the car had a Pennsylvania license plate held by twisted wire over another plate. He lifted it and saw that the one beneath was a New York plate. Since it was running, why wasn't there a man in the driver's seat? He didn't see a third man anywhere. Had the two men just arrived in the car together and left the engine running?

He heard a voice behind him. "Drop the shotgun." The boy dropped it into the snow. Even now, he could still see how quickly the snow around the barrel melted because of the heat from his shots. "Now step back from it."

The third man had been hiding behind the wooden fence. The man stepped around it and picked up the shotgun with his free hand. As he did, the boy's hand slipped under his butcher apron, freed the pistol from his belt, and fired it through the apron into the man's face. Then he took it out and fired another round through his forehead.

As the boy started to walk toward the back door, he saw Eddie push open the door and stick out his head. When he spotted the boy, Eddie came out the rest of the way and craned his neck to see if he recognized the man on the ground. Then he looked at the boy. "Going to be a big clean-up tonight." He picked up the shotgun from the snow. He saw the boy's head tilt back. "What are you doing?"

"Listening for sirens. We fired seven shotgun shells and two pistol rounds."

"Most people who hear shots can convince themselves they didn't if it's over quick and they're safe indoors on a cold day. They don't want to get involved with police unless the shots were aimed at them. But we'd better get started."

They dragged the bodies to the two cars that had brought them. Eddie drove them away, one at a time, with the boy following each time in Eddie's car. They pushed the one with the broken back window into the Ohio River with four men's bodies in it and watched it sink. The other they drove into the city with three men's bodies in it and left it at the back of a weedy vacant lot.

Eddie and the boy drove home and spent the night cleaning the shop. They shoveled the blood-soaked snow into the storm drain and dragged the hose from the meat-cutting room through the front of the shop to hose the blood off the tile and sidewalk. They cleaned everything — walls, counters, floors. Then Eddie hung his sign in the shop door that said "Closed until" and set the hands of the sign's clock for two in the afternoon. In the morning, while the boy was sleeping, Eddie called the school to say he had the flu but should be well by Monday.

15

Schaeffer left his hotel to drive to a mall. He parked in the middle of a row of cars and walked to the big pharmacy, the nearest store. He bought a pair of throwaway cell phones and a couple of hours of talking time. Then he went to the aisle that was just one long selection of hair dyes. He walked along the aisle, looking at the picture of a woman on each box, trying to find exactly the right shade. He picked a couple of boxes that seemed close to correct, and then went to a display of sunglasses that had a mirror. He held the boxes up beside his head, studied his reflection, and then chose a shade. He also bought two pairs of sunglasses, one very dark and one with a faint brownish tint.

He paid for his purchases and went in search of a computer store, where he bought an iPad. He made a final stop at a department store, where he bought some new clothes. He knew that when people were searching for him, it was best to wear new or freshly pressed clothing in darker shades, so he replenished his supply.

When he returned to his hotel, he felt a strong urge to call Meg's phone. He wanted to know for certain that she had made it to the home of some friend or relative and settled in where she would be hard to find. He stifled the urge. All he could possibly accomplish with an international call would be to endanger her.

He took the hair dye into the bathroom and went through the process of dying his gray hair. The color he had selected was as close as he could find to his natural shade, a light, sandy brown. He had dyed his hair a few times in the past, and he was efficient and competent. In a couple of hours he had changed his appearance significantly. He spent a few minutes studying his reflection while wearing the sunglasses he had bought, and decided they brought him another few degrees of difference from his original appearance. The very dark pair covered a large part of his face, and the tinted ones projected a personality that was alien to his.

He went directly from disguising himself to getting used to his iPad, signing onto the hotel's Wi-Fi network and searching the

Internet for familiar names like Balacontano, Tosca, Scarpi, and Castiglione. In items about those important names he picked up names of their associates who were new to him. He read stories that were out of date and archived, and others that gave him information about recent crimes and arrests. There were far more books about the Mafia than there had been in the old days, when an interview with a reporter would get a man killed, and the government's ability to intercept conversations was more limited.

Easiest to find were the articles about established history. Carlo Balacontano was the third generation of his family to be in La Cosa Nostra. He had been born, like Joe Marsala and Salvatore Maranzano, in Castellammare del Golfo, Sicily, but two generations later. By the time he arrived in the United States at age eighteen, all the living generation from Castellammare del Golfo — Joe Bonano, Vincent Magaddino, Joseph Profaci, Joe Aiello — were near the end of their careers.

Balacontano never had any interest in joining or rallying Castellammare natives as a faction. What he wanted was to be the head of an American crime family, and someday *capo di tutti capi,* the boss of bosses, a title nobody had claimed since 1931, when claiming it was enough to get Maranzano killed by Luciano's hit men.

By the time the boy was growing up in Eddie's butcher shop in Pittsburgh, Carl Bala had become the boss of one of the five New York families.

The next part was extremely familiar to Schaeffer. Carlo Balacontano was convicted in 1983 of murdering Arthur Fieldston, owner of a Nevada investment and real estate firm called Fieldston Growth Enterprises. The real owner was Balacontano, but Fieldston made a good front for him. One night, after a mysterious phone call told them where to look, New York State Police found Fieldston's severed head and hands buried on Carl Bala's horse-breeding farm in Saratoga, New York. And on August 1, he would have his first parole hearing.

Outsiders, like the writer of the article and the law enforcement agencies called in at the time, had no idea that this event had anything to do with an earlier disturbance in Las Vegas, when a professional killer known as the Butcher's Boy had been ambushed on the Strip by a contingent of armed men, had killed them and escaped. But the two events had everything to do with each other.

The savagery of the details had, in the opinion of at least one of the reporters whose accounts had survived, helped persuade the jury and the judge that Bala's personal involvement in the physical crime didn't need to be established. Balacontano was a New York crime boss, and bosses didn't cut off people's heads themselves. The partial remains had been found on his land two hundred feet from the main house. How could this not have been done with his knowledge and on his orders?

Bala's men would have caught him if he hadn't jumped onto the back of a thoroughbred horse in the stable and unlatched the gate on its stall. The horse went wide-eyed and tried to kick its way out. It saw the gate swinging open as a divine act of liberation and ran through it. The horse galloped across a broad pasture, jumped a fence, ran even harder, and got scared by the next, higher fence, built to keep people off the property. It stopped long enough for Schaeffer to roll off its back and run through the darkness to the place on the next farm where he'd hidden his car. Later that night, Schaeffer had called in the tip to the state police telling them where to dig. The next morning he'd left for England.

The writer noted that Balacontano had

been in a federal prison for a very long time. He had been suspected of crimes, including many counts of extortion, robbery, assault, human trafficking, smuggling, selling drugs, bribery, tax evasion, racketeering, and theft. But when he had been convicted of murder all those years ago, the authorities had let everything else drop. Maybe they thought it was a waste of money to convict a murderer of fifty other things too. Now the statute of limitations had run out on all the incidental crimes that were part of his business life, and all but a few of the witnesses to the murders had died or been killed themselves.

There was one notable exception that Schaeffer knew of — himself. He had killed people, including a union leader and a US senator from Colorado, in exchange for money from Carl Bala. He remembered every detail of the few jobs Bala had hired him to do.

But the reporter was sure that the federal prosecutors were long out of new things to charge Balacontano with. He had been locked up too long. If his hearing determined, as it might, that he had done nothing to forfeit his eligibility for parole, he could theoretically be let out at the discretion of a hearing officer and one parole commissioner.

Bala himself, Schaeffer was sure, must still be interested in killing the man who had framed him for the one crime he had not committed, the murder of Arthur Fieldston. But could he be the one trying to kill Schaeffer now? Bala had gone to prison on a phone tip. Every one of his appeals had been exhausted decades ago, but he had one more chance to go free — to take advantage of a federal parole system that had been abolished so many years ago that most lawyers currently practicing in New York probably had never seen a federal parole hearing. Bala certainly knew he had a chance that was almost miraculous. Would he risk it by trying to get somebody killed now?

16

Schaeffer thought about sleep, but it was impossible at the moment. He had activated the part of his memory that had been there since the first time of trouble when he was in high school.

After the "Big Cleanup," which was what Eddie called the massacre at his butcher shop, there was another period when they seemed to be forgotten in the chaos of a war they'd started. Schaeffer remembered sitting in the kitchen eating breakfast while Eddie would read from the newspaper. "Here's another one. 'Angelo De Pinto, a reputed crime boss, was assassinated on the steps of a church in Palermo, Italy, last month.' What the hell kind of reporting is that? A month ago? 'Palermo police say this is the fifth such murder in the past two months.' "

Another time Eddie read aloud, " 'A boy who was walking his dog in a field on the south side of Niagara Falls, New York, found the body of a Buffalo man yesterday afternoon. Police identified the victim as Michael Floria, thirty-eight. The body showed signs of torture, but the probable cause of death was three bullet wounds to the chest and head. He had not been reported missing, although the police believe the body had been there for about three days.' Jesus. I knew that guy."

The boy remembered Eddie reading items just like that several times over the next year. He remembered that Eddie had remained watchful and didn't take on any contracts that year while the warfare went on. The boy went to school, and Eddie devoted most of his efforts to making the butcher shop more competitive and entrenched in the neighborhood than it had been. His only break from the shop during those months was when he would leave for an hour or two for one of his special home deliveries.

On those days, the boy would run the shop by himself after school until Eddie returned. But by then he was making his own home deliveries to Mrs. Whittaker, and then also to her best friend, Mrs. Casey.

The boy met Mrs. Casey, his second delivery customer, one day while he was ending one of his usual deliveries to Diane Whittaker. They were still upstairs in the spare bedroom where she liked to take him, and she began kissing and caressing him while he was putting on his clothes. He noticed that she glanced out the window a couple of times. At one point she reached down and touched him and said, "Oh. That's interesting."

He laughed. "You just did that because you knew that would happen."

A moment later the doorbell rang.

She wasn't alarmed. She looked out the window, smiled, and said, "Don't worry. It's only a friend of mine. Do you remember Linda McCutcheon from school? She was on the cheerleading squad with me. Long, dark-brown hair?"

"Yeah, I think so."

"She's Mrs. Casey now. She's here, so just sit tight for a few minutes."

He looked at his watch. He had just finished buttoning his shirt.

"You have to be back right now?"

"No," he said. "Not really."

She closed the door on him and went to the staircase. He heard the sound of her shoes going down quickly. He heard the front door open and shut, and then the bolt sliding into place. He sat on the bed to tie his shoes and waited for Diane to get rid of her friend.

After a few minutes he heard flat shoes coming up the staircase. The door opened, and there stood Linda Casey.

"Hi," she said. "Diane told me about your home deliveries. I hope you won't be mad at her. She said she promised you not to say anything to anybody."

"I don't know what you mean," he said. He meant that she had been the one to make him promise to keep the secret.

She slowly shook her head from side to side, and pulled her sweater over her head. "I think you'll figure it out though, won't you?" She unhooked her bra. "She said she thought you wouldn't mind once I was here." She had very light skin that contrasted with her long, dark hair. He had not forgotten her large breasts from high school. As she freed them, he saw the small, pink nipples. She waited for a few seconds, letting him look. "No?"

"Yes," he said. "If you want to."

"It's really why I came." She unzipped the back of her skirt, stepped out of it, and moved toward the bed, where he was still sitting. He put his hands on her white, silky underpants and pulled them down to the floor.

She pretended to be surprised by his audacity. "Oh!"

He quickly shed his clothes and put his arms around her, feeling the shape of her body and the softness of her skin. "Oh," she said again as she lay back on the bed and the encounter went on. She said it over and over.

There was something especially erotic about his afternoon with Linda Casey. She was very pretty — as pretty as Diane Whittaker. And she was clearly taken with the idea of this secret tryst with a man a few years younger than she was. She loved that he took charge, touching her with undisguised lust, as though he had a right to, and letting her do the same to him.

At the end of it, she lay on her back and stared at the ceiling. "That was nice," she said. "Thank you. Can I be your other home-delivery customer?"

"I, uh," he began. "Yeah. Just call in an order to the shop and tell Eddie you want me to deliver it."

After that, he usually made two deliveries a week at each of the two houses. A few times he would go to one house and find them both waiting. He didn't mind; it limited the number of times Eddie's car would be parked at either house, and made them all a bit safer — them from gossip, and him from the next set of shooters who learned that killing him and Eddie would be worth a trip from New York.

The men who would come for him and Eddie were sure to be men he didn't recognize. They would not recognize him either, but they would know about the butcher shop and might have seen Eddie's car.

When, at about age twelve, he had first seen Diane and Linda, they had seemed like celebrities, superior and unattainable. But now, whenever they were bored or feeling neglected or resentful of their husbands, they would call in an order for him to deliver. He knew that part of the attraction was that with him they felt the same superiority they'd always felt. They loved being with him because they could control him. He didn't bully them or look down on them or fail to appreciate them, the way their husbands did.

They adored him because he would do what they wanted and stop when they wanted him to stop. And because he was pliable and agreeable but inexperienced, they taught him. They said to him, "Women aren't really interested in that, but we all love it when you do this. Touch me here." They would guide his hands, his lips, his tongue, and then let him know with little cries when he had done something right.

He knew he was risking his life those four afternoons a week, but it never occurred to him to stop. It was better than anything else that existed in the world.

The home deliveries continued through his high school years and beyond. One day when he brought Diane Whittaker's order of sliced turkey breast and sausages, she took the package, walked down the hall to the kitchen, and placed it in the refrigerator as usual. Then she beckoned to him, handed him a Coke, and sat down at the kitchen table across from him. She reached across and held his hand, looking at him seriously. "I've got to stop ordering special delivery."

"Why?"

"I'm pregnant. Don't worry. It's not yours. It's Dan's. His and mine." She took his hand in both of hers. "It's funny, I never minded cheating on Dan, even though I love him. But I can't take that chance for my baby. Do you understand?"

"Are you happy?"

"About the baby? I'm so happy I can hardly stand it."

"Then congratulations. You'll be a great mother."

She looked at him with a kind of hopeless

exasperation, as though they both knew that couldn't be true. "I mean it," he said. "That's going to be a lucky baby. Its mother already loves it." He drank down most of his Coke and turned away to hide the inevitable burp. Then he said, "I guess I should probably go, huh?"

She nodded. "That would make it easier."

They stood up, and she came around the table to give him a long kiss. Then they separated, and he said, "Goodbye." On the way out, she stopped and kissed him one more time. He knew that she was doing it because she wanted to remember what he felt like.

About four months later, he found himself in the same conversation with Linda Casey. He had been expecting it because Diane and Linda were such close friends, and he imagined they wanted their children to be in school together.

By the time the two friends had opted out of his home-delivery service, the girls his own age had grown into adult women and more curious about boys, and particularly this boy.

Schaeffer looked at the clock beside the bed. It was after 1:00 a.m., late enough to walk the perimeter outside his hotel and make sure that none of the people he'd been reading about on his iPad had found out he'd checked in. If someone had, there would be people coming at night, maybe to hide a transponder under his car, maybe to set up an ambush for tomorrow, and maybe to get into his room to kill him tonight. He had learned that it was best to start out in the deep darkness, outside the glow of the parking-lot lights, and then move inward toward the building.

17

Elizabeth Waring stood in front of the big bathroom mirror and tried to move every hair into place and then apply a layer of delicate concealer that would hide the dark circles under her eyes. The lips came next, a subtle shade chosen for these occasions when she had to radiate substance. This meeting had been called at her request, and she had been thinking hard about the facts that she would present, the questions that would be asked, and how she would reply, so she was feeling as though it had already begun.

She reminded herself that she was a ranking official, no longer an adviser or a specialist. When she'd begun working at the Justice Department at age twenty-two, they still treated Organized Crime as a task force, as though any day they might make a few dozen arrests and then disband the group and reassign them where they were really needed. She had worked in a basement with a dozen or so other data analysts searching those long-lined printouts with accordion folds to determine which deaths might be the work of gangs, syndicates, or other criminal organizations.

She had seen all the changes and developments since then. Now she was one of the veterans. She occupied a corner office on the fourth floor, which was high enough to show she had status, but low enough to show she was still actively engaged in the work of the department. Some female agents coming up now would not have let an office like hers stay the way her male predecessors had left it — with a heavy dark-wood desk, chairs, and table that matched the chair rails and wainscoting. She had been smart enough to present herself as solid and familiar. "How's the new boss? Same as the old boss." That was what she'd wanted.

She had never personalized her office. She thought of it as a piece of staging to remind people that they were in a government agency that conducted serious criminal investigations. She had never put framed photographs of her son or daughter in her office. Her job was to be the enemy of some of the worst people in the world. Why would she have photos of her biggest vulnerability — her children — where suspects' attorneys, compromised politicians, or organized-crime witnesses might see them? Having a photo of her late husband, Jim Hart, in the office would have been too depressing at first, but now it would also be confusing. He had died almost twenty-five years ago, so all his photos were of a man too young to be her husband. People who actually cared about her knew that she was the widow of an FBI agent. Nobody else needed to know anything.

She took another look at her image in the mirror. Her face was the face of a woman her age, the black business suit was tasteful and fit her nicely, her shoes and purse matched. Time to go.

When she looked out the front window, the sky was the color of disappointment, and she could see rain streaming down her car's windows. She opened her umbrella to walk to the car, drove to the Justice Department, then took the elevator to her corridor. She spent a few minutes sitting at her desk, checking her messages for anything urgent, and then walked up the hall.

The people above Elizabeth in the hierarchy were all political appointees. That, even in the best of times, made her an outsider, and these were far from the best of times. There were many more women in responsible positions than there had been when she'd started, but most were not notable improvements over the men they'd replaced.

She stepped into the doorway of the deputy assistant attorney general's office at the end of the hall and presented herself at the receptionist's desk. The receptionist was young and pretty, as they always were and always had been. The men who hired them were susceptible to the stupid pleasure of looking at them, even the men for whom a connection with them was the farthest thing from their minds, and who knew that a wrong word or an accidental touch actually imperiled careers.

This receptionist was new. She looked at Elizabeth and said, "Good morning, Ms. Waring." She was alert. She'd had to tell quite a few others over the years that there was no Mrs. Waring. She was Mrs. Hart only at home, and Ms. Waring only at work.

The deputy assistant attorney general, Criminal Division, was the most powerful person at this meeting. He was in charge of the Computer Crime and Intellectual Property Section, the Human Rights and Special Prosecution Section, and the Organized Crime and Gang Section. There were four other deputy assistants who oversaw other things.

When she saw Deputy Assistant Holstra appear in the doorway of his private office, she could tell he was impatient for the meeting to begin. She went into the conference room and sat in the chair at the table that he seemed to indicate to her with his eyes.

When the others didn't come in immediately, he cleared his throat. That brought two more. Then he said, "John. Bill. Let's get started."

When all were seated along the sides of the big table, they were bunched at the high-status end, near Deputy Assistant Holstra.

She surveyed the faces. Mark Holstra was a political appointee, but he had experience working for the US attorney in Houston about twenty years ago and had then gone into a private firm as a litigator. He seemed to Elizabeth to have returned on some kind of mission that he had not yet revealed. Maybe he felt he'd wasted his talent and intelligence getting rich, or he had been feeling guilty about not having done much to help the country. Maybe he had simply felt he owed a service to Edward Benton, the attorney general, who was an old friend.

The others were all of a type that she had seen come and go at Justice for decades.

They were smart graduates of great law schools who expected to rise in government service, rid the nation of crime, become famous, win elective office, and get very rich within a few years. They were creatures dedicated to struggling toward the light and fresh air above them.

Holstra said, "Elizabeth has an important matter to discuss today. I've heard the bare bones of it. I should remind you that we're in a soundproof room. No recordings are being made, and no transcripts. The only people who will be discussing this meeting are the six people present. To make the situation clear, if this leaks, I will expect the four people other than Ms. Waring and me to resign instantly and without being reminded. Elizabeth?"

Elizabeth said, "The night before last I had a visit from a man in the middle of the night. I recognized him because I've seen and spoken with him before. In the course of my first case with the department, I only ran across his work, but never caught up with him and never saw him. He was a highly regarded professional hit man in those days, and people referred to him as 'the Butcher's Boy.' "

"Heartwarming name," said Bill.

"He had committed various murders for

189

several different LCN families beginning when he was about fifteen. At the time of my first case, he was about thirty. My first assignment was to go to Denver to take part in the investigation of the murder of Senator McKinley Claremont, who had gone back to his home district while Congress was in recess. The senator was planning, once Congress returned, to hold hearings on a lot of corporations that had made large profits but paid little or no tax during the preceding few years. Although the senator didn't know it, one of these corporations was partially or wholly owned by Carlo Balacontano, the head of one of the five New York crime families. This professional killer murdered the senator in his hotel room. He also murdered a troublesome member of a machinists' union in Ventura, California, who had been raising questions about why his company's pension fund hadn't grown in tandem with the stock and bond markets. Apparently that was Balacontano's work too.

"A few days after that, this hit man went to Las Vegas, where he was expecting to be paid for these jobs, and possibly others. The man he was to contact was a Las Vegas attorney named Harry Orloff, who often served as a middleman for the Balacontano family's western interests. There are several versions of what happened next. The version I've found most likely is that when Orloff asked for the money to pay the killer, his employer, Carlo Balacontano, decided that he could save a great deal of that money by having a group of thugs ambush this high-end killer instead of paying him.

"That was a mistake. The hit man killed several run-of-the-mill shooters on the Las Vegas Strip, and then he was both scared and angry. He had to get away somehow, and decided that the best way was to cause as much trouble and confusion as he could for his enemies, who, as far as he knew, included the entire La Cosa Nostra. He committed what we would probably label now as a series of acts of terrorism.

"He would arrive in a city and murder the head of the local Mafia family and one or two members of a nearby rival family or a tributary or splinter group. He moved so quickly that the LCN, the local and state police, the FBI, and the task force, which was what we were back then, had no idea what was going on. We would show up at a crime scene a few hours after the fact — often with the body still on the ground and the police technicians bagging evidence — and learn that another important gangster had also just been found dead five states away.

"Our leading theory was that some factions of the organized crime world had attacked some others, and now a war was rapidly heating up. Some people even called it the Second Mafia War. It wasn't exactly an exaggeration. Bosses who thought they might be next on somebody's list went after their favorite enemy to head off a surprise. Others who had people in their organizations they didn't entirely trust saw this as a time when cleaning house might be imperative.

"The angry hit man stayed angry. He kept searching. He found the man who had been fronting the Las Vegas company that Carlo Balacontano owned. He had been hiding in the house of Harry Orloff, the go-between lawyer, and his name was Arthur Fieldston. The killer also learned that the man who had ordered his death was Carl Bala himself."

Elizabeth could see that some of the faces along the table looked dazed and might have lost the thread, but she was nearly done. "The killer murdered Arthur Fieldston and buried his head and hands on Carlo Balacontano's horse farm in Saratoga Springs, New York. Then he called in a tip to the state police, telling them where to dig."

John's eyes widened. "Oh my God."

Bill said, "That's the case. Our case." He held his head in his hands.

Delia said, "You've known Balacontano was innocent all this time? He's been in jail for a quarter of a century."

Elizabeth said, "Actually, about thirty years. I didn't believe he'd done it at the time, but I was the only one, and they thought I needed to get out of the way."

Holstra said, "When Elizabeth told me about this yesterday, I ordered all the existing department records. They show that she was ordered at that time to take a leave of absence, which lasted through the run-up and the trial. She also filed memos asking the department to push to reopen the case. All requests were denied."

John said, "But now Balacontano is up for parole. We've prepared to oppose it, of course. But what now? What do we do?"

Holstra said, "We'll get to all that. It's a question, but not *the* question. Elizabeth, please go on."

She said, "I had no evidence, only my common sense, to suggest that Carlo Balacontano would not have buried the head and hands of a victim on his own farm. And he certainly didn't call the New York State

Police to tell them he had. Somebody else did both. But the federal court in New York, which tried him, and the appeals court were immune to an argument that made a mob boss into a victim."

"I can understand that," said Bill. "While we've been preparing to oppose his parole, we've been studying his record. Even if he didn't kill his own front man to keep him from talking to law enforcement, he certainly ordered dozens of other killings for years before that. He was known for avoiding trials by having witnesses killed. He also killed rival bosses and suspected turncoats."

Elizabeth nodded. "And after he was in prison, he was still doing that sort of thing. He was still the head of a major family. He had stand-ins on the outside pass on his orders."

"How did we get to where we are now?" asked Bill.

"The man who framed him — the one they call the Butcher's Boy — did a very effective disappearing act. After about ten years, somebody in the criminal world found him.

"From what I can piece together, mostly from things he's said, he had been living somewhere remote — apparently overseas, where he had been left alone for years. But a young man named Talarese spotted him. He and two others attacked. The Butcher's Boy killed them and then flew to New York, where he killed a Mafia soldier named Tony Talarese, the father of the young man who had recognized him. Then he launched himself on a second wave of killings, much like the one that got him out of the country the first time. He killed at least ten important gangsters and kept the police, the FBI, and the LCN confused long enough to disappear."

"How did he get away?"

"I have a theory," she said. "He introduced himself as a new neighbor of mine. He helped me get my car started on a winter day, so I invited him to dinner. He was a reasonably pleasant guest, helped with the dishes and so on, and then went home. I didn't run into him again. About a year later, I happened to be looking at some photographs and things that I had shown him that night after dinner — pictures from a trip to Europe — and I noticed that my late husband's passport, which had been in the box with the photos, was missing. I suspect he stole it to get out of the country.

"His second visit came about ten years after that. He appeared in the middle of the night at my bedside and told me he had been hunted down and attacked again. He said he had lost track of the day-to-day changes in the Mafia — who was moving up, who was taking over what, which leaders were too old to fight or too young to know how. He said he needed an update, a briefing. In return he would give me information about murders he had known about or witnessed in the past, in which living gangsters had taken part. He said he had evidence or witnesses enough to convict them."

"So you were to give him the present and he would give you the past."

"Yes. Murder, of course, is the crime that has no statute of limitations, so we would be able to prosecute all the cases he could give us. There were also hidden benefits that I couldn't accurately predict. He would have to tell us some very detailed stories. The stories would include information about people other than the victim and the perpetrator. And there would be information about illegal activities that might still be going on. Once a man like him begins to tell a story, it might go anywhere."

Holstra said, "And what did you decide?"

Elizabeth said, "I decided to keep him interested long enough to go to my superiors in the department for permission to pursue his offer. I held his interest with a tidbit. The man who was working hardest to get Carlo Balacontano's blessing to take over as surrogate boss of the family was Frank Tosca. I also asked the FBI to keep an eye on Tosca, to keep him safe for the moment."

"How did that work out?"

"When I went to Deputy Assistant Attorney General Dale Hunsecker the next day, he ordered me to end the operation and close the door to further talks with the killer. To him, it seemed immoral to deal with a professional killer. He also felt that by starting an investigation of Tosca, I was helping the killer get an enemy arrested."

"Did you disagree?"

"Strenuously. The problem with investigating organized crime is that all the people who know about it are criminals. The worse they are, the more they know. The man I had talking to me knew a lot."

"And the final outcome of the operation?"

"Largely because of our prospective informant, the FBI was able to surround and intervene in a Mafia meeting at a mountain resort in Arizona. Agents arrested and photographed over two hundred LCN members, including the leaders of the twenty-five families. I participated in many of the interviews. The problem was that because the Organized Crime Section was not allowed to work closely enough with the informant to keep an eye on him, he got to the conference first. When the FBI found Frank Tosca, he'd already had his throat cut. The hit man also killed a Mafia soldier who had been posted to guard the back way into the resort."

"Is he in prison? I thought you said you visited him this week."

"He visited me. He's not in prison. He left no evidence that he had ever been in Arizona. And he was not caught, taken into custody, or even seen by any official but me."

Elizabeth's memory of the last times she'd seen him flashed through her mind. She couldn't tell her colleagues any of it. He came to her house to see her two more times on that trip. The first time he came because the LCN bosses could not help knowing that she was the one who had made the raid on the Arizona resort happen. The bosses sent three murderers of their own to Elizabeth's house to kill her and her teenage kids, Jim and Amanda.

The Butcher's Boy — she still had no other name for him — had entered her house on the first floor and silently killed the leader of the group, who at that moment was trying to rape and murder Elizabeth. Then he and Elizabeth had sneaked upstairs with pistols ready, flung open the doors to both her children's rooms at once, and fired. The second and third men died at her children's feet.

She told the FBI that the man who had burst in and saved her and her family was a handyman named Pete Stohler, who worked for her. With their help, she manipulated WITSEC, the protection program, to get the killer out of Virginia by passing him off as her heroic handyman. The FBI and State Department got Stohler two passports in the names David Parker and Paul Foster.

She had paused for only a second or two, before Holstra prompted her. "What do you think he wants this time?"

"Somebody has found him again after all this time. It's probably because Carl Bala's fate is in play. What he wants is to keep on living. My question is, what do we want?"

18

Schaeffer had made some progress. He knew that the attempts on his life had been prompted by the fact that Carlo Balacontano was due for a parole hearing on August 1. But Schaeffer didn't know who was sending men out to kill him — a boss who wanted Balacontano out of prison, a boss who wanted him to stay in prison, or a boss who hated Schaeffer and thought the hearing would bring him within reach. It was possible that Elizabeth Waring had found out something that would help him by now, but if he wanted any favors from Elizabeth Waring, he would have to give her something. He needed to search his memory for an organized crime figure he could give her as a present, somebody big and important she could convict of murder.

He lay on the bed and closed his eyes, letting himself wander in his memories. It was late winter of the boy's senior year in high school. The smart girls in his class were already accepted into teaching, nursing, or liberal arts programs at colleges. The smart boys were mostly going to attend engineering schools; the ones who weren't smart or weren't interested in school planned to join the Marines. But Michael planned to stay where he was.

It was during this period that Rocco "Big Rock" Paglia in Newark, New Jersey, hired Eddie to kidnap a man named Boccio. It was an unusual request because Eddie was a killer. He wasn't a private detective or some low-ranking gang guy who did errands. Usually a customer would make Eddie an offer — the name of a man and a sum of money. If Eddie liked the offer, he would take half in advance, go make the man die, and then collect the other half.

This time, because Rocco Paglia was a cousin and protégé of Victor Castiglione's, Eddie had decided to take the unusual job. Castiglione had shielded Eddie and the boy after they had killed Taddio and his friends about three years before. At the time, Taddio had been preparing to unseat Castiglione, so the relationship wasn't one-sided, and that made it stronger and more important to Eddie.

Rocco Paglia said that Boccio was the

chief of a minor crew. He was suspected of cheating Paglia on his share of Boccio's take for a couple of years. He would get money and say he'd taken in less than he had, or he would give Paglia's collectors a long count of the cash they picked up from him. Now he had a score involving a truck hijacking and had suddenly walked away without paying anything. None of his crew had been paid either. Paglia needed to bring him back to maintain the belief that nobody could steal from his boss and hide for long.

Eddie and the boy drove to New Jersey to look for Boccio's trail. Eddie went to a lot of bars and asked if anybody had seen Boccio. Eventually he found a bartender who described a woman Boccio had brought in a couple of times. She had been there with some girl friends around a table on a night when a picture had been taken. Eddie bought the group photo from the bartender and spent the next couple of evenings in various bars watching for any of the women in the picture. One of them showed up and said Boccio's girl was somebody's cousin from New York. Eventually Eddie tracked down the girlfriend's address.

Eddie parked on the street outside the apartment and watched. At around five in the morning, the door opened and Boccio came out. The boy approached him as he was walking to his car and asked for directions, while Eddie stepped up behind him, clicked handcuffs onto his wrists, pulled a cloth bag over his head, and locked him in their car trunk.

Later that morning Eddie called Paglia, who told him to deliver Boccio to the back door of the restaurant where Paglia's crew spent time. When the boy, Eddie, and their captive entered, more than twenty men were sitting at tables in the restaurant drinking. The boy felt a vague uneasiness. What were they all there for?

Paglia came around to the front of the bar, handed Eddie a briefcase, and then took the bag off Boccio's head and stared at him. He made a face that was supposed to be uncertainty and then called out to the men in the restaurant. "Is this him? Is this Boccio, the man who was robbing me for years and then moved to New York City to work with people who want us all dead?"

The men in the room answered, calling out, "That's him. Hi, Boccio. Where you been? Nice to see you."

Then Paglia shocked everyone. He reached under his sport coat and brought out a semiautomatic pistol. The boy could tell from the way that he was waving the weapon around that he didn't have much experience using one. He had his finger inside the trigger guard, and he let the barrel sweep the room at about the eye level of his men.

Boccio said, "Rocco, I didn't do any of that. I've got a girlfriend in New York and I didn't want my wife to find out, so I've been going there. I haven't been making a lot of money lately. It's just a bad time. People in my neighborhood are out of work since the bearing factory closed down this year."

If Paglia had any doubts, he clearly knew his reputation would not be improved by accepting denials or excuses. He raised the pistol, and Boccio, who was no longer restrained, dodged and ducked as Paglia opened fire. The first round tore a hole in the shoulder of Boccio's suit but didn't appear to have hit flesh. The second bullet missed him and struck a man across the room, who slumped and collapsed at his table. Two others crouched beside him and tried to minister to his wound, but to the boy he looked dead.

Paglia didn't stop. His next two shots hit Boccio, who fell to the floor. It seemed to the boy that Paglia had expected Boccio to take one hit and die, but he was alive. Paglia fired again and again, but Boccio would roll to the side so that even if he were hit, it wouldn't be where Paglia was aiming. Once he even tried to get up. Paglia gave in to panic. He kept firing, and whenever he did, the bullet's impact would spray blood onto the tables and the men sitting at them, who held up napkins and tablecloths to protect their clothes and faces. Finally Paglia realized he had to shoot Boccio in the head or he would run out of ammunition. He stepped within a foot of him, aimed, and fired. He was too close, and the shot produced so much blowback that his own face and clothes were red with droplets.

Then Eddie was pulling the boy out the back door of the place. As soon as he was in the sunlight, the boy wanted to run to get into the passenger seat, but Eddie said, "You drive," so he did. Eddie opened the briefcase and made a rough count, then closed the case and put it on the floor between his feet.

The boy said, "Where do you want me to go?"

"Toward home. Look for I-78 west. I'll take a turn in a little while."

Schaeffer opened his eyes and sat up in the bed. Rocco Paglia was still alive. Schaeffer had seen an article on the Internet about him only last night. It was amazing that a moron like Paglia could be alive when people like Eddie Mastrewski were long dead. But he was. And it was highly likely that some of the men who had been there that night were alive too. He would go online to see if he could locate a few. If he wanted Elizabeth Waring's help, he was going to have to carve things out of the past and serve them up to her in slices.

19

The second half of the meeting with Deputy Assistant Holstra stretched past its allotted time the next day, as Elizabeth had known it would. Important people were always overscheduled. They had assistants who looked for ways to cut things short, pull the boss out early, and keep people waiting in case an opening appeared.

Elizabeth decided to get to the serious decisions before Holstra got called to his next appointment. "I believe he'll try to get in touch with me again. I think he'll want current information about an organized crime figure or two, and that he'll offer up an important gangster for prosecution, almost certainly for murder. I'd like a consensus on how far to play him."

She glanced at the others, taking the least time with her eyes on Delia. She was aware that Delia was the enemy. It was too bad, but Delia had already staked out the strict ethical position and could hardly relinquish it now.

Holstra said, "Would his information be good?"

"Yes," Elizabeth said. "He knows that practically nothing can be prosecuted this far out except murder. He only worked for the most important mobsters, so it will be somebody important. And he knows he'd have to supply evidence."

"Okay," Holstra said. "Let the opinions fly."

Bill said, "As much as I like the idea of this kind of informant, his fate is a side issue. If we can get him to talk, fine. But we can't forget Carlo Balacontano is the main issue. We've already got him. He's one of the old men, the bosses, and he's in prison, where he belongs. I haven't heard any evidence that he doesn't still belong there. He's never shown remorse, never provided testimony against anyone, and never met any of the other criteria for parole."

Delia had been waiting. "But you just heard that he was framed with at least the tacit connivance of our predecessors in Justice."

John's voice was bored. "Connivance isn't 'tacit.' It has to be active."

"You know what I mean," Delia said.

"Some people must have been active if they convicted him in a federal court. Everybody who worked here then must have known."

"I'm sure they acted in good faith," said John. "Bala's innocence seems to have been a minority opinion. If there was real evidence of innocence, it's not for a parole hearing anyway. In order to do this right, we would have to move for a new trial of Carlo Balacontano, and that's the last thing we want."

Bill shook his head. "Elizabeth, is this even a practical question? Is there any way that this killer could be brought to swear that Balacontano is innocent because this man did the killing himself?"

"I haven't thought of a way," said Elizabeth. "Why would he? It might be possible to get him into an incriminating conversation. But he's smart, and very wary. And I'm not sure that getting a parole or a pardon for Balacontano would be anything more than correcting a procedural error. To make anything the hit man says even admissible, it would have to be firsthand, not hearsay. We would have to reveal the reason they knew each other at all — that Balacontano had hired him to kill a couple of people."

John said, "We've collected a lot of indications that Balacontano has not been a model prisoner. There are recordings that imply he was directing the crime family's policies, appointing and removing people who ran certain operations, and so on. He's even suspected of ordering several killings in the prisons where he's served time."

"Any evidence of that?" Delia asked.

"We've got a nice display of parallels," Bill said. "There are recordings of things he said ought to happen in the prison, and then a line beside it about what actually did happen in the prison. They match up."

"Courtroom antics," said Delia. "Any long-term inmate was there when a lot of bad things happened."

"But it speaks to what kind of prisoner he's been," John said. "That's what parole decisions depend on."

Delia smiled. "A point and a question: The point is that it's dangerous to say what a federal parole hearing will depend on, since they've become so rare. The question is, are any of the things Bala said should happen good enough to take to court as independent new cases?"

"That's not required."

"I guess that means no," she said.

Bill said, "Here's another possibility. What if we set up the killer so that when he

210

contacts you, there's an FBI SWAT team to take him into custody?"

Elizabeth frowned. "I've thought of that of course. In honesty, I could only predict that he would be killed in a shoot-out and we would lose everything he knows. We would also lose two to five FBI agents."

"You think so?"

Elizabeth said, "He's been in dozens of armed confrontations. They produced a lot of dead people, certainly well over a hundred by now. He's not one of them. I don't like the risk."

John said, "I think we should go on as before. Balacontano has a parole hearing because of a historical accident. He and a very small number of other old prisoners are grandfathered in. We should keep our minds on the fact that he's a very bad man and that it's our duty to remind the hearing officer and the board of that, not retry a thirty-year-old case after he's already served most of his sentence."

Bill said, "Of course I agree on pragmatic grounds. Aside from the work we've put in, no public good would be served by freeing an old-fashioned Mafia don into the modern world."

Delia sat up very straight. Elizabeth envied her posture almost as much as her young body and smooth, unlined complexion. "I'm afraid that I agree with the former deputy assistant AG, Mr. Hunsecker, who seems to have been offended by the idea of helping a serial killer triumph over his enemies. On the practical side, I think we can get by without his rendition of who did what to whom in the days when cars all had stick shifts. If the Department of Justice knowingly withheld the fact that a man has been kept in federal prison for more than a generation for a crime he didn't commit, we're already down the rabbit hole. It's not administering justice; it's suppressing undesirables."

"Undesirables who have committed murder and been convicted," said Bill.

Deputy Assistant Holstra slapped both his palms on the surface of the conference table and pushed himself to his feet. "Invigorating, but I'm out of time. It seems that the issue isn't that we've got the wrong man in prison, but that we should have the other one in prison too. That means, John and Bill, keep up the opposition to the Balacontano parole. Elizabeth, you remain open to the opportunity that your informant offers us. Dale Hunsecker is a fine man and an honest one. But he isn't the man I would want with me in a fight. Everybody clear?"

212

Elizabeth watched the others nod in silence, all except Delia. She felt a little guilty for letting Delia strand herself in the ethical position. Delia was the only one Holstra had not given an assignment. Elizabeth wanted to reassure her that it was because he had respected her argument and would not order her to do anything against her conscience. That was true, but Delia was beginning to see that what she'd done was eliminate herself from the rest of the discussion, something a desperately ambitious person should avoid. Elizabeth wasn't going to give a potential rival a lesson in tactics, so she remained silent as the meeting broke up.

Elizabeth returned to her office and picked up her phone to invite her assistants to come in.

She said, "Now we do what we do best — keep track of the bad guys. What we need to know is which people in La Cosa Nostra are trying to find this retired shooter and kill him. If there are any factions that are more interested in harming Carl Bala than the shooter, we'd like to know about them too. We probably won't get a clear picture right away, but start with the usual: Who is on the move? Who is showing up in distant places? Are there any small conferences between just a couple of important men? Any sudden deaths? Have the FBI or other federal agencies noticed people watching airports, train stations, or places like that? Have they stopped and frisked any of them to find out who they were? You all know what to do. Go do it."

Schaeffer took out the second phone that he had bought. He called Elizabeth Waring's office phone. When the person who answered asked who was calling, he said, "Pete Stohler." That was the name of the imaginary handyman she had invented to explain who had saved her and her kids years ago.

It took only a few seconds for her voice to respond. "Hi, Pete," she said. "What's up?"

"Have you found out who has been sending people out to kill me? I also want to know if there are photos of me out there. People have attacked me who've never seen me before. Some of them wouldn't have been born when I was still working."

She said, "If I had photos of you, I think you would have been in jail twenty years ago."

"The passports."

She said, "The passports were produced through an unwritten request of WITSEC to the State Department. They don't officially exist. For practical purposes I wouldn't even consider them real."

He was silent, so she added, "There are things that are separate from anything else. You understand? After what Pete Stohler did that day, I lost all memory of how he looked, and I've never been able to get the photos back from the State Department. They were the only copies. Nobody else had a chance to leak them."

"Okay," he said. "Thank you."

She said, "I'm sure you're right that there are photographs of you, but I don't know where they came from. There are more cameras around every day, watching us wherever we go."

He closed his eyes. She was right. The UK was the first place in the world to put CCTV cameras on all the streets so the Brits could catch each other littering. There were a million ways he could have been spotted and photographed.

Elizabeth said, "I've asked my people to find out who has been trying to kill you. I don't know what we'll learn. If you would tell me anything about where they —"

"I'll be in touch."

Elizabeth waited for more, but it didn't come. He had hung up. It had not been a good first try. She didn't have anything to offer him yet. No bait.

20

Schaeffer stayed in Virginia, but moved every two or three days. Hotel employees started to wonder about people who stayed too long, and he didn't like having people wonder about him.

He spent several hours each day working out in hotel gyms and pools to bring himself back to his best level of conditioning. He had trained and kept himself fit all the years in England, but it was no longer the training of a man who fought for his life. Now that the bruises and strains from the fights in Manchester and Australia were disappearing, he worked on his strength, stamina, flexibility, and speed.

He hoped that Elizabeth Waring would learn who was after him, but he wasn't counting on her. He believed she would tell him if she thought it would serve her purposes, but she was essentially a cop. She had spent his last trip to the United States trying to get him into custody so that he would be locked up for the rest of his life telling stories.

The last trip he had avoided letting her trap him, so she had shut down any real information from her side. But the night when he came to her house and found the three killers there with her and her children had changed everything. He had killed her assailant, and then together they had killed the ones who were guarding her kids.

In gratitude, she'd obtained passports to get him out of the country safely — an enormous risk for her. The relationship should have been over then, along with the communication. The fact that he had gotten attacked now, years later, had made him think of asking for one more favor. He knew that for her, nothing she did would ever pay him back for saving her children. Every day brought Bala's parole hearing closer, and whatever was going to happen to Schaeffer was going to happen by then. She had come up with nothing. But this was his fight, and he had to act now.

He remembered the route from the old days. It was I-95 north and I-76 west. His phone said it would take five hours and thirty-three minutes in traffic. He checked out of his hotel and drove.

It took most of the day to reach Pitts-burgh, but when he got there, he felt strong and optimistic. He had come because he'd had a valuable realization. If someone was determined enough to send people to kill him in the UK, and then hire others in Australia to find and ambush him, they were probably serious enough to have learned details about him. There must still be older men who remembered that the reason people called him "the Butcher's Boy" was that he'd been raised by Eddie "the Butcher" Mastrewski — that Eddie really was a butcher and had a shop in the South Side Flats of Pittsburgh.

In those days the South Flats had been a real neighborhood inhabited by the families of factory workers, shopkeepers, store clerks, and salesmen, some of them living in big old houses divided into apartments and others in small single-family homes. Their roofs were covered with snow, like frosting, for most of the winter, and when spring came, the houses emerged dripping wet and a little derelict, with scraggly dead or dormant plants and piles of whitened dog shit in the yard that had been frozen under the snow all winter. The last days of winter were dangerous, as the warmth released big stalactites of ice along the gutters that speared down to stick in the last snowdrifts. It was only a week or two after that when the first crocuses would bloom, and then fresh paint would begin to appear on doors, porches, railings, and window frames.

The people in those houses were Eddie's neighbors and the customers who bought his steaks, chops, hams, sausages, turkeys, and chickens. As Schaeffer drove, he wondered about them. Were any of those families still here? They were mostly descendants of European immigrants — Poles, Irish, Italians, Germans, and Ukrainians. He remembered Eddie saying, "The toughest people in the world are Pennsylvania Polacks from the coal-mining country." The boy said, "Like you?" Eddie replied, "I'm Ukrainian. We didn't come this far west until we smelled cabbage cooking."

Schaeffer made a turn and then turned again at the sign that said "E. Carson St." The whole street was a long row of restaurants, boutiques, and places that sold pretty things to decorators. He tried to remember how long it had been since he'd been on this street, and realized his last visit must have been right after Eddie died.

Nothing on East Carson looked the way it once had, and so nothing triggered a memory. He turned right and down into the parts that hadn't been gentrified.

Schaeffer knew he had chosen the right destination. He had been the hunter many times, and the place to look for a lone man who was out of chances and marked for death was wherever he had started. There was a mostly foolish urge in fugitives to return to their home ground. Maybe they assumed that they would know the place better than the pursuers because they had played there as children and found all the hiding places. Maybe they had the illusion that all the people they had known in the old neighborhood would still be there, ready to help fight the final battle. Maybe when a person knew he was out of options, he tried to run backward through time.

Schaeffer wasn't one of those people, but he had seen the theory work a few times. Tonight, if Schaeffer had been one of the hunters instead of the prey, he would have found a comfortable place to stay right in the vicinity of Eddie Mastrewski's old butcher shop, or maybe within sight of Eddie's old house, and waited and watched. It would need to be a place where a hunter could fire a well-aimed rifle shot and kill him. An experienced killer would be too smart to go out looking for a man like

Schaeffer or risk meeting him on even ground. The reason a killer got to be the one to go home every time was that he didn't fight with his prey. He just took him.

Schaeffer didn't drive past the corner where the old shop had stood, or cruise up the street where Eddie's house used to be. If he was right, people would be watching for him in those places. Instead he parked and walked toward the old restaurant where Eddie used to take him sometimes on Sundays for minestrone or *pasta e fagioli*. Eddie could get better meat than a restaurant could, so they tended to order dishes that didn't involve much meat. The room next to the bar was where the boy had learned to play pool.

Eddie had taught him pool because there were times when a shooter needed to hang around in a place that was warm and dimly lit, except for the bright lights right above the table. It was a necessity of their profession to be comfortable in places like pool halls and bars.

As he was walking in the direction of the Italian restaurant, he realized that one reason the route felt so familiar was that it went right past the Whittaker house. He began to look ahead for the house, and when he spotted it, he could see the house looked almost exactly as it had when he was sixteen. He could barely take his eyes off it.

When he reached the offshoot of the sidewalk leading to the steps, the front door opened. A woman came out, closed the door behind her, and locked it with a key. She was wearing what looked like a jogging outfit — black yoga pants, a powder-blue pullover that fit her tightly, and thick-soled sneakers with chartreuse laces. She descended the steps and glanced in his direction, her face set in the sort of half-smile women gave to strangers, really a cover for the once-over that would tell her if he was a threat. She froze and her mouth opened.

He recognized her instantly. She didn't look anywhere near as old as she must be. Her long hair was in a ponytail, the same blond color as it had been so long ago, and her eyes were the same bright blue. She still stood upright with her shoulders back.

The blue eyes widened. "Michael? Oh my God, Michael!" She lunged to him and wrapped her arms around his neck. "I can't believe it."

"Diane?" he said. "You look wonderful."

"I was going to say the same to you," she said. "And I knew you would, and be in shape too. You always worked so hard. Eddie sure got his money's worth out of your keep. But that's why people stay healthy." She grasped his arm. "You've got to come in."

"I don't want to interrupt anything if you're —"

"No, you're not interrupting anything. And I don't think there's anybody I'd rather see." She ran up the steps and unlocked the door. "Come on."

"Are you sure?"

"I'm sure. The kids are all grown up, and Dan died, but I'm still here. I love company."

"But you seemed to be on your way somewhere."

"Just out for a run. It's a beautiful day, and it's early, so I'll go later." She charged in through the foyer and down the hall toward the kitchen. "Do you like tea?"

He was slightly off balance, as though he'd been asked an incriminating question. He had lived in England for over thirty years, and tea was everywhere. "I do like tea, yes," he said.

"I'll heat some water," she said, and put a pot on the stove. "Sit down."

They sat at the kitchen table, which appeared to be the same one where they'd sat the last time, when he was twenty and she was telling him his visits had to stop. He didn't realize he was smiling at her until she smiled too. "I'll bet I know what you're thinking about."

"I'm afraid you're right," he said. "I'm sorry to be so simpleminded and transparent. I should be old enough to keep from embarrassing myself by now, but I guess I'm not."

"It's all right," she said. "I started remembering the old days as soon as you popped out of nowhere. How could I not? I've felt guilty since those days. I've wanted to apologize to you. I was the adult, and you were, like, six years younger. If it happened now, they'd put me in jail. Aside from committing adultery, I was taking advantage of a minor."

He shook his head. "If you've been feeling that way, I'm even more glad we ran into each other. I want you to know that you did me no harm at all. For a lot of reasons, that was one of the things I desperately needed to have happen in my life. I was kind of a lonely kid. I had no parents or siblings, and the softer, kinder side of the universe never showed up. Knowing a beautiful woman was an incredible gift."

"You're still such a sweet person," she said. "I'm amazed you feel that way. Throwing myself at you was wrong of me. I was selfish and spoiled and careless about what it would do to you. I guess I didn't realize how bad I was being until I had kids."

He shook his head. "I always wondered what made you think of me. Did you know about Eddie's home-delivery customers?"

"Sure. I think most of the neighborhood knew — the women, anyway. People talked. Of course that was what made me think of asking you. I didn't think anybody would suspect what we were doing. Dan and I looked like the ideal couple, the handsome athlete and the cheerleader who had gone together in high school. Who would think I wasn't perfectly happy and satisfied with my life? And who would think that I'd pick out somebody so much younger to play with?"

"As far as I know, nobody ever suspected," he said.

"Except my best friend, Linda."

"Of course, Linda."

"Was she fun?"

"Honestly?" he asked.

She nodded.

"Yes. Wonderful, terrific fun."

Diane laughed, and he laughed too.

"Was she more fun than I was?"

"Of course not," he said. "That's not to take anything away from her. She was absolutely beautiful, and had a really alluring way about her. But you were the one — any man, any age, would have loved you."

"Thanks," she said. She smiled again and took his hand. "It was the worst thing I ever did in my life, but you make it seem as though it wasn't so terrible."

He said, "You made my life better. Not just then. Ever since."

Diane said, "Oh, God. I'm so happy to hear you say that. I've been so ashamed of what I might have done to your life that I hated to think about it." She got up and poured the tea, then put some cookies from a canister on a plate. They sipped the tea and nibbled cookies. She said, "What sort of life have you had? What have you done for a living?"

"People probably didn't guess this, but after Eddie died, when I was about twenty, he left more money than I ever suspected. He had no relatives, and his will left everything to me."

Diane shrugged. "Not married, with a good business. And with his special home-delivery customers, I guess he didn't waste money flying to Vegas to have fun."

"Right. No dependents but me, and we spent most of our time working. He never owned more than one car, and all our vacations were three-day holiday weekends. At the end, after he died, I considered going to college, but I was used to working in a small business. I invested Eddie's money in stocks and bonds and went to Detroit to work in the auto industry. Over the years I started a couple of businesses and let them grow until I could sell them. I've done pretty well."

"I see from your ring that you're married. Any kids?"

"No," he said. "That's one of my few regrets." He had done so much lying in the past thirty seconds that he had made himself uncomfortable. He had never even considered children.

"Where are you living now?" she said. "Can you give me an email or Facebook or something?"

"We've been living in Europe, but we're starting the process of moving back. Give me yours and I'll send you mine when I've got the new ones."

She wrote the addresses and her name on a pad and gave the paper to him. With the mention of his marriage, she seemed to sense that he was feeling ready to leave. "You were on your way someplace. I don't want to hold you up any longer, and I guess I should get my run in before I get too comfortable. I hope you really haven't been harmed by decisions I had no business making years ago."

"As I told you, I was — and still am — happier and better off because you called and asked for me that day. I hope you feel the same."

"Thank you," she said. "But we did the right thing to end our afternoon visits. My kids never knew. The rest of my life with Dan was good. He died without ever suspecting. Maybe I tried to make it up to him too, and that helped."

"Can I ask an unrelated question?" he said. "Has anybody around here ever asked about me? Maybe a stranger trying to find out where I was living or anything like that? I don't mean they asked you, but asked anybody you know?"

"Not that I ever heard. Except Linda. She or I would mention you once in a while over the years, but only to each other."

"Well," he said. "It's time to go. Thanks for the talk, the tea, and the cookies." He stood up, kissed her cheek, and walked to the front door. When he got there, he stopped and looked up the stairway leading to the guest room. Then he stepped out into the street.

He headed for Sforza's. In the old days when he and Eddie had gone for Sunday lunch, they had sometimes seen local mob soldiers there too. A few of them knew Eddie, and the boy could remember these men taking a table in the middle of the day to sit and talk endlessly. When one of them saw Eddie, he would give his head a little nod to acknowledge him and then turn his attention back to his friends. The boy took their presence the way lots of older people in the Flats did — as a guarantee that the restaurant served authentic Italian food. Now he thought that certainly when these men had seen Eddie, they had seen his boy too. The men looking for him might think of Sforza's as one of his old haunts, a place he might return to.

He had seen the old sign when he'd driven in to the neighborhood. It was tall and vertical, protruding into the sky with neon tubes bent and twisted to say "Sforza's." He approached the block from the other side of the street so he could see if anybody was standing around watching the door or the parking lot, the way they used to in the old days. There was nobody. He trotted across to the front door and went in.

The place was stripped. The old darkwood paneling on the walls was gone, and the red leather booths had disappeared, as had the bad local stained-glass that had covered the windows with pictures of the Bay of Naples and Mount Vesuvius, the Tower of Pisa, and the docks of Venice with the gondolas tied up. What had replaced them were plain tables and chairs that could have been in any restaurant. The wall with the swinging doors to the kitchen had been knocked out, and the stoves and vents and hardware were now exposed and polished behind glass.

He glanced at the customers in the brightly lit restaurant and saw nobody who would have come here years ago. The old-fashioned Italian food had been replaced by some kind of Latin-Asian fusion. He glanced at the bar and saw only wine bottles, no hard liquor. He spun on his heel and went back outside. He was not going to surprise his enemies there. He walked back to his car and drove to the downtown hotel district to have dinner and wait for dark.

Schaeffer would have to go into the areas where the killers would be expecting him, and that was best done at night. It was better to park during the hours of darkness and walk the South Side Flats neighborhood to spot the watchers first.

He hoped there would be someone. The men who would be burdened with ambushing and killing him would probably be young. The men his age or older would be home late at night, falling asleep in front of their television sets.

He was careful when he explored the South Side Flats, studying his surroundings for signs that someone was watching. Now and then he would recognize other old buildings he had forgotten about. He gradually moved closer to the place where Eddie's shop had been. The streets where he walked began to look familiar, and something in his memory was nagging him to look more closely. Then he passed another house and recognized it.

The house was tall and narrow, two stories and an attic. It had an old-fashioned door with a segmented glass window that was rounded on top and a brass doorknob in the center. It was Linda Casey's house, the place where his other special customer had lived.

He continued studying the neighborhood, looking for the men he believed would be there to hunt him. He searched systematically, clearing one block of a street and then moving to the next. On some blocks, the process was fast because none of the buildings offered a good vantage point for spotting a victim. On others, he would spend time standing still with his eyes on a row of houses, searching to see if there was one with a head visible in an upper window or a bit of light that might be a reflection off a lens. If he couldn't be sure during the night, he would return during the day and watch until he saw something that eliminated the house — a child leaving for school or coming home, an elderly woman weeding the front garden.

After a few days he had whole swaths of the South Flats cleared, but he was certain a team of killers was stationed there. He was almost sure of it, because there were few places in the country that the LCN could connect with him. They had to hope his hometown mattered to him, because they had to look somewhere.

Schaeffer studied the neighborhood carefully for three more days before he ventured close to the places where he'd spent his childhood. He began by making a visit to the old butcher shop. When he walked nearby in the middle of the night, he could see that the building had been remodeled and modernized during the decades since Eddie had died. The first floor was now a bar. From outside, the space looked as though it had been a bar for so long that it couldn't be the same building, but it was. The bar closed at 2:00 a.m., so he could see inside only by the dim light of some plug-in beer signs on the walls. He moved along the windows, peering in.

The old refrigerator room was still in back, probably because tearing it out would have been expensive, and it still could be used to keep the beer cold and the food fresh. They had divided the spacious room where he and Eddie had done the cutting. The stainless-steel tables and sinks and counters were now part of a kitchen, and the overhead tracks where sides of beef had been brought out and butchered were long gone.

He went to the parking lot behind the building and saw the old fire escape was still there. He closed the dumpster beside the wall, climbed onto it, reached up to drag down the fire escape ladder, and climbed up to the window. The upper floor was a storeroom, as it had been for the butcher shop. Now he saw glasses and chairs and trays of silverware, a couple of large wine racks, a few kegs, and many cases. This wasn't a place where anyone had been stationed to watch for him. He climbed down.

As he walked across the parking lot toward the sidewalk, he thought about the old house where he and Eddie lived. He studied the images of the house's interior in his memory. The best window for an ambush would be the second-floor front one in the big bedroom where Eddie had slept before the troubles. It certainly had the best view of the street and much of the rest of the neighborhood. This thought made him turn and walk the other way, around the block toward the backyard. The windows there were smaller and higher, and only gave a view of the house behind Eddie's.

He came through the yard of the house on the next street and went to stand behind Eddie's house. He picked a spot half hidden by a tree and saw that there were a couple of lights on in the back of the house. They were small bulbs, yellowish, the way old-fashioned forty-watt bulbs used to be. Now people used something like eight watts to make that kind of light. The rooms he was looking at had been the two regular bedrooms. The one on the right had been the boy's room, empty most of the time because he never slept there during the Mafia War.

The other had been a room he and Eddie both used for storage and closet space. They'd kept various kinds of clothes there — sport coats and suits worn as disguises, winter coats stored during the summer, the bleached and starched white aprons and hats they'd worn in the shop to wait on customers. Eddie had looked like a doctor when he was behind the counter. Early in the morning when they were butchering, they both looked like surgeons.

Schaeffer stared at the back of the house. The clapboards showed some cracking and peeling paint. He wondered who had been living in the house since he'd sold it. He remembered that the old stained-glass window that provided sunlight for the first landing on the interior staircase had always been defective. He looked to see if it was still there. Whatever subsequent owners had done to the house, they had left the colored window — green, blue, and white.

He stepped to the rear of the house and climbed up on an old oak tree with a thick, low branch that he'd always used as a bridge to the stained-glass window. He reached out and touched the glass with the back of his hand. The window was on a horizontal steel spindle, so if it was pushed at the top and pulled outward at the bottom, it would open. He had done this many times when he was young, slithering in over the sill.

He ducked and eased the upper part of his body in, slid in after it until both his hands reached the floor, and walked the rest of his body in on his hands. He shut the window.

The stairway looked almost the same as it had when Eddie had first taken the boy in, except that nobody had been caring for it the way Eddie did. He and the boy polished it frequently and varnished it at least once a year. He supposed that the whole place would be more worn and dilapidated than it had been the last time he had seen it. He crouched on the stairs and listened.

Schaeffer expected that there would be three men in Eddie's house tonight. That way they could station one of them in the front window at all times. If the lookout spotted Schaeffer on the street, there would suddenly be three shooters, at least one of them fresh from sleep.

He assumed that right now the man on duty would be sitting in the darkened front window in the big bedroom that was Eddie's old room. The door would be closed behind him, so that whatever the other two might be doing wouldn't throw any light that could be seen from the street.

Schaeffer climbed the last few stairs to the second floor, as always placing each foot only on the inner edge, because stairs usually creaked in the middle.

His first objective was to find the man who

was on watch at the front of the house. That man would be wide awake at this hour. He would have a loaded weapon inches from his hand. When Schaeffer reached the second floor, he turned his steps toward the front of the house.

He held his pistol in his right hand, crouched, reached up to the doorknob with his left, turned it, moved into the room, and closed it again. In those seconds of motion, he had spotted the head and shoulders of the lookout in silhouette against the dim lights from the street.

The man gave a little jump, as though he had been trying to stay awake and had dozed off for a second. Schaeffer was still crouching. When he saw the man's head and shoulders tilt forward as if he was about to stand, Schaeffer sprang against the man's back and knocked the wind out of him. His forearm hooked around the man's neck and tightened. He squeezed the man's throat as hard as he could, fighting against the man's attempts to throw his head back against Schaeffer's face, kick, and wrench the arm off his neck. Finally the man was unconscious, and Schaeffer twisted his neck to break it.

Schaeffer felt around on the floor in the dark until his hand touched the smooth, hard surface of a rifle's stock. He lifted it so he could see its silhouette against the indirect light through the window. It had a short profile, and he recognized it as an H&K MP5 or a close copy. It would have been a good weapon for the dead man, because he could swing it around in the closed space of the house without banging it against anything. It was a good weapon for Schaeffer because of the thirty-round magazine.

A second man in the house must have heard some of the scuffling because he gave Schaeffer little time. He strode down the hall to the front room and flung the door open. Schaeffer could only whirl and pound the rifle's steel butt into the side of the man's head until he fell unconscious, then drag him far enough into the room so that he could shut the door again. He touched the man's head, and his hand came back wet. He cracked open the door to let a little light inside and confirmed his suspicion. The blow had caved in the side of the man's skull. The blood was pooling on the floor under his head. Schaeffer patted the man's pockets and felt a familiar shape, reached in, and came back with a folding knife. Schaeffer opened it and cut the man's throat.

One more. Schaeffer wiped the knife and his hand on the man's shirt, sidestepped out the door, and moved along the hallway. He could see an open door at the end of the hall where the man he'd just killed must have been. He took a moment to be sure that the rifle's magazine was still properly seated after the hard blow and that the safety was off.

Schaeffer stepped in the doorway of his old bedroom and pivoted with the rifle at his shoulder, but nobody was there. He moved into the room and made sure nobody was hiding in the closet, under the bed, or in the bathroom. He checked the other room too. The lights were on in both, and the bed was unmade, so there must be a third man. Why wasn't the third man coming for him?

He heard a cell phone ring, and instantly the sound changed his view of what was going on. The third man wasn't in the house. He was somewhere else, calling in.

Schaeffer ran up the hall to the front room where the two bodies lay, and as he pushed the door open, he heard the ringing coming from the pocket of the man he had killed first. He reached into the man's pants pocket, took the phone out, pressed "Accept" and said, "Yeah?"

"What the fuck?" said the voice on the phone. "You said you'd call me when the food came. Did it come, or do I have to go get it?"

"No. Get it."

"Who is this?"

Schaeffer turned off the phone and pocketed it. He took the two men's wallets and keys, then went through the second floor turning off lights. He hurried down the stairs and out the back door, set the lock, and closed the door firmly so the plunger would be well seated in the jamb. He hoped the locks and darkness would delay the third man's attempts to figure out what had happened.

Schaeffer went down the street at a fast walk to keep from attracting attention, but he wanted to get to his car before the third man arrived. He had no way to know if the third man had been calling from ten minutes away or a hundred yards. He turned the first corner and walked faster.

He heard a squeal of tires — the sound of someone taking a corner too fast. Then he heard engines. He stepped into the dark passageway between the house where Bobby Moran had lived and the old Czimanski house. It sounded as though three cars were

arriving at Eddie's from different directions.
He began to run.

21

He moved his two stolen wallets to the pockets of his jacket so that they wouldn't fall out while he was running. He knew that he would probably be the only man running across the Flats at the moment. He had been prowling around at night for over a week, and he had seen few men out this late. There had been a couple of them leaving their houses or their girlfriends' houses and driving off, but no walkers. He tossed the men's keys into a storm drain and kept going.

He stayed off the sidewalks and instead moved along between the buildings. He emerged from the yards and driveways near Diane Whittaker's house and kept running toward the apartment building where he had parked his car. It had seemed safest to leave it parked at the curb in front of an apartment building, where there would be several other cars parked every night, so people wouldn't notice it.

He turned right at the next corner and saw a car turn onto the same street from the far end and come toward him. He took the few brisk steps necessary to get to the end of the next house and disappear up the driveway between it and the house beyond. As soon as he was out of sight in the shadowy backyards of the houses, he ran again, this time hoping to be past this block before the car on the street reached the driveway he had taken.

He ran along behind the next house and the next, making his way down the block in the direction he'd come the day he'd had tea at Diane's house. He had parked only about two hundred yards from her door. As he went, he heard the sound of an engine idling. He sped up, trotted to the next wooden fence, and leapt over it.

Then he heard voices. A man called out, "You go around and watch the other end of the block."

Schaeffer was as aware of where each man was from the sounds as he would have been if he could see them. He had ranged these blocks from the time when he was a kid playing hide-and-seek until the days when he was making deliveries to Diane Whittaker.

He knew that he was running toward the place where the men in one car would be waiting for him and another was moving up behind him. He might be able to slip out from between them onto the parallel street to his right if he moved fast. As he ran, he saw Diane in her kitchen window, pulling aside the curtain and craning her neck to see what was going on. She must have heard the men outside shouting directions to each other.

He ran toward her window. She saw him and opened the kitchen door, and he dashed forward, reaching the top of the concrete steps in two strides. He put his left arm around her waist and pulled her with him into the kitchen, then shut the door and turned off the light.

Her face was right beside his ear. "What's happening? Are they chasing you?"

"Yes," he said.

"Why? Who are they?"

"I think they're members of the local Mafia, or working for them. I seem to have convinced somebody they'd be safer with me dead. I don't want to put you in danger. If I can make it to where my car is parked, I'll just drive away and this will be over."

"How do they even know you?"

"It's complicated. I asked around about

245

buying Eddie's old house and shop back after all these years. The property was registered in the name of a company, and when I went to the state department of corporations to find out who owned the company, that set them off. They wanted to meet at the house to negotiate. That's where I was going when I left here. But when I got there, they made it pretty clear that they weren't interested in selling. They put me in the room that used to be Eddie's office with two men. They each had a pistol. They wouldn't let me leave. They were making jokes about how I was going to disappear and never be found — that kind of thing. One of them got a phone call, and the other went to listen in, so I ran."

"Oh my God," Diane said. "I thought the whole Mafia was dead or in prison years and years ago."

"The police seem to have missed a few of them."

She moved toward the telephone on the kitchen counter. "I'll call the police and tell them if they surround the block, they can arrest them."

"Hold on," he said. "Let's not do anything we're going to regret. I don't want to set up a firefight where some young cop loses his life just because I remembered the old shop

246

and thought I could make a quick profit on a turnover."

"That's crazy, Michael. They threatened your life. They're criminals."

"Real estate is a crazy business, and it draws money from surprising sources. Once you start looking into deeds and tax rolls, sometimes you turn up people you don't expect. And there's no question these guys would find out who called the cops. You would be in danger, and have no way to get out of it."

"What can we do then?"

"Wait them out."

"How?"

"Let's go upstairs so I can see what they're doing and when it's safe to leave."

They climbed the stairs and stepped into the guest room at the top, where they used to go on the afternoons of the home deliveries. For Schaeffer it was like revisiting a place from a dream.

When they were young and he would follow Diane up these stairs, she would often have her left hand on the railing and her right hand at the neck of her dress or blouse, already getting a start on the unzipping or unbuttoning. When they were at the upper landing, she would guide him into the guest room and close the door, then shrug off that garment, continue the process until she was naked, and then start on the boy's buttons and zipper.

They reached the upper landing, and she stopped and stepped aside. "I guess you know your way from here." She leaned against the wall.

"Yes," he said. "Thanks." He moved past her into the room and went to the front window, but remained at its side, where the curtains hid him, and looked down.

Three cars were in the street with their lights out. He could see the drivers waiting with their motors running. If he ran, they would catch up with him in seconds. If the others caught and killed him, they would pick them up for the getaway.

The men he was most concerned about were the ones on foot — at least three men who would be walking slowly and quietly around the houses trying to find him. Judging from the yelling he'd heard tonight, they weren't too concerned about making noise. They were here looking for which window to fire through or which door to kick down.

Schaeffer walked from the guest room toward the rooms at the back of the second floor. He passed a bathroom with smoked-glass windows. He kept going to the room in the left corner and stepped in to look out the window.

The men were walking through the yards in a line. There were four of them, all carrying pistols pointed down at the ground, each trying to stay abreast of the others as they stared into the darkness.

Diane moved beside him and whispered, "What are they going to do?"

"I'm hoping they'll move through here, find nothing, and move on to search somewhere else. Then I'll get in my car and go."

She said, "You can stay as long as you want, you know."

"Thanks," he said. "But it would be best if I disappear as soon as they do. I don't want to give them a chance to figure out that there was a right house and come back to find it."

He watched them move along the row of backyards. They were using their only advantage, numbers. If one of them saw him or was fired upon, all four guns would answer. He kept his eyes on them until the four reached the end of the block, then turned to the left and walked single file beside the last house to return to the street where their companions in the cars were waiting.

Schaeffer moved back up the hall to the spare room, where he stepped to the window and watched the men get into the cars and buckle up. Then the three cars drove off.

"That was sudden," Diane said.

"They probably got a call from someone who thought he'd spotted me somewhere else. I'd better go while I can," he said. "When they find out it was mistaken identity, they might come back. Thank you for taking me in tonight. You may have saved my life."

"Maybe I'll choose to believe that, because it will make me feel better. Goodbye, Michael," she said. "Be safe." She kissed his cheek, and he went down the stairs and out.

22

Schaeffer hurried to the spot where he had parked his car in front of the apartment building. But it was now between two others, one nosed up nearly to its trunk and the other just ahead of its headlights. He knelt and used the flashlight app on his phone to look at the wiring and the underside to be sure there was nothing attached to the car that would explode or transmit a locator signal.

He got in, started the engine, and listened to it. The engine sounded fine — still smooth and quiet. He looked up and down the street to verify that the hunting party had really moved on. Then he inched his car forward and back, until he was able to pull out of the parking spot.

He drove the twenty miles to his hotel, checked out, drove another hundred miles, and checked into another hotel. He went into his new room, bringing with him the bag containing the wallets and handguns of the men he had killed.

Schaeffer sat at the small table in the corner of the room and opened the bag. He took out the first of the wallets. The driver's license had the name James Joseph Pastore, age thirty. The second one was John Vincent Sarcone, age forty-one. Their license addresses should have been in or near Pittsburgh, but they weren't. They didn't even live in Pennsylvania. They had both lived in towns on Long Island and had New York licenses.

The two men had quite a bit of cash in their wallets, all of it in hundred-dollar bills. He supposed that they hadn't wanted to make any credit card purchases or other transactions that might place them in Pittsburgh. If they had managed to kill Schaeffer, it could have gotten them convicted. He set the cash aside. It would help keep him from being traced too.

He needed to know who was really behind the attempts to kill him. The men who had attacked him in York and Manchester didn't have names he could connect to an American crime family. The names in York were Morgan, Kaiser, Olanski, and Holmes. Probably they were just shooters who had been hired in America and sent off to do the work. The ones in Manchester had been English, and the ones in Sydney were certainly Australian. The two men he had killed tonight were the first he'd seen who might belong to La Cosa Nostra.

He couldn't call Elizabeth Waring from this far north. It practically placed him at the scene of the murders he'd just committed. And it would give her the number of the cell phone he had been carrying around for several days with its battery in it. The FBI would be able to tell her every cell tower it had pinged off for all that time.

He used this moment to take apart his phone, break the small parts of it, and cut up the SIM card. Then he showered and slept. In the morning, he packed and checked out, then drove south toward Washington, DC. He didn't assemble and activate his remaining cell phone until he was in Virginia.

He sat in his car in the shade at the curb and called the cell number she had given him the night of his visit to her house. He heard her phone ringing. It rang eight times and then went to voicemail — a recorded male voice that said the customer could not answer now, but if he wanted to leave a message, he should wait for the tone. He didn't. He took the battery out of the phone.

She knew that he would use a cell phone to call, and that her phone would record the number of his phone even though the call went answered. Her people at the Justice Department could have the phone company locate the cell phone that had just called her if he hadn't disabled it. He started the car and drove.

He wondered whether she hadn't been able to answer the phone or whether this was an intentional attempt to trap him. If trapping him like a wild animal had been her plan, then he had better know it now. The idea of trapping animals made him think of the zoo, so he drove into the city, got on Connecticut, turned on 14th, and found a place where he could park near the Columbia Heights metro station. He paid the charge at the station entrance and took the train to the station near the zoo.

He walked to the zoo, bought a ticket, picked up a map at the entrance, and then followed it to a place called Lion and Tiger Hill. He found a men's room, reassembled the cell phone, and turned it on. If she was having his GPS signal tracked, her people would be able to do it now. He left it in a trash can full of crumpled paper towels near the men's room exit.

He didn't know how much time he would

have, but he was going to need to cover the distance back to the zoo entrance quickly. By now the FBI could have identified his number as the one that had called Elizabeth Waring and located his phone, and they would be on their way.

He took a shortcut directly across the zoo. When he made it back to the entrance, he went out with a large group of tourists who were filing onto buses outside the gate. He knew he wouldn't have time to get out of the zoo if he waited his turn, so he slipped away from them and walked faster. If the FBI arrived and thought he was inside the zoo, they would shut the gates and begin hunting for him. They would take over the entrance and keep sending more and more cops until they had him.

He took quick strides away from the gate and managed to travel a few hundred yards on the sidewalk before he saw the first pack of black SUVs roar past him. He saw them turn into the entrance gate without coming to a full stop, and stream past it and onto the zoo's interior roads. After they had entered, the exit side of the gate closed and a vehicle moved in front of it.

Schaeffer walked to the subway entrance, descended to the platforms, and took the next train to the 14th Street station. When he got there, he retrieved his car from the nearby parking lot, drove to a hotel in Bethesda, and checked in. He went up to his room, turned on the television set, and watched the afternoon news. The first thing he saw was a helicopter shot of a green hillside inside the zoo with winding driveways around it, most of them still crowded with tourists, groups of schoolchildren, and families.

The screen changed to show an anchorwoman in the studio looking mildly concerned and disapproving. "We're going live now to Caitlyn Franklin on the scene at the National Zoo."

The shot changed again, this time to a spot he recognized outside the zoo entrance. "Yes, Tara," said a young woman in a windbreaker holding a microphone. "The police here say there was a phone call to the FBI warning that a bomb had been placed inside a building on Lion and Tiger Hill at the National Zoo. DC police and a contingent of FBI agents responded and are in the process of making sure that the men, women, and children already in the park get evacuated safely before the authorities enter the building to discover whether there is indeed an explosive device of some kind."

"Is there any indication whether we're

dealing with a real bomb or a hoax?"

"Minutes ago I spoke to Lieutenant Jerry Xavier of the DC PD." In a second she was shown holding the microphone in front of a man about a foot taller than she was. He said, "We always hope that every threat is an empty threat. But it's our job to find out. We're checking the cars, buses, and shuttle vans that leave the zoo to see if we spot any suspects, and keeping the entrances closed to keep more visitors from entering."

The young woman turned to the camera and said, "All we can report at the moment is that the police have not yet found anything dangerous, but they're going to systematically and thoroughly make sure things stay that way. Back to you, Tara."

Schaeffer had to admit the imaginary bomb call was a pretty good cover story. It even ensured that if civilians overheard them talking about a cell phone, it wouldn't sound like a lie. A bomb story added just the right level of fear, enough so that the people in the zoo would do what they were told to do. If the FBI arrested a lone man — Schaeffer — during the operation, or even shot him, their actions were explained and justified in advance. And if nothing at all happened, that was half expected too, and would be welcome news.

Schaeffer drove to a large chain drugstore and used cash to buy four more disposable cell phones and more minutes of talk time. He used the early evening to do his laundry at a small strip mall, then take it to the hotel and hang it in the closet of his room.

He watched the local news at eleven to see the zoo footage again. When it ended, he drove out toward Richmond for a half hour, so it was after midnight when he put the first of his new phones together and called Elizabeth Waring's number. He let it ring.

When the phone went to voice mail, he said, "You tried to play tricks on me today, and now it seems you're trying to do it again. I want to know about James Pastore, age thirty, and John Sarcone, age forty-one, both from Long Island. I want to know who they work for. If you want to tell me, then cut out the bullshit and answer my next call. If you don't answer, there won't be another one."

23

Elizabeth Waring was in Deputy Assistant AG Holstra's office, watching his expressions as he listened to her phone playing on speaker on his desk. "If you don't answer, there won't be another one."

They both heard the click as he hung up. Holstra said, "Do we know where this call came from?"

"Yes. He was along I-95 approximately at Falmouth, Virginia. We've got people looking along that stretch of highway for any pieces of the phone. They can figure out where he bought it, but I don't have that yet. And the next call will be from a different number. He's been changing them after one call."

"I guess you're right. He is good at this kind of thing."

"Yes," she said. "And at every other thing that makes a person scary. I thought he wouldn't let us get a cell phone number and use it to find his location. It's actually kind of a relief that he hasn't retaliated."

"Would he do that? How?"

"He could have turned on the cell phone and left it anywhere, and then from a distance killed the first five or six FBI agents who came to find it. Or he could have just killed me. He knows where I live, and he said on the recording that he believes I set him up."

"Are you still safe to be his contact?"

She hid her frustration behind her facade of professional calm. "I never was. Nobody is safe being his contact. He's a killer. He thinks I was playing tricks on him to capture him."

Holstra said, "You know, maybe we have no business even trying this kind of operation. We might be better off trying to narrow his location to a manageable area, surround it with SWAT teams and tighten the circle until he surrenders or gets shot."

"I think we can do this," she said. "He's not grandiose or delusional or permanently enraged. He's not fulfilling fantasies about killing people. He has none. He's protecting himself from people trying to destroy him. He's rational."

"So you think we can make some reasonable deal with him for information in exchange for safety?"

"I think it's worth a try. I can't pretend we didn't just lose a lot of ground with him on this phone thing. If I'd known it was happening, I would have tried to stop it. I might be able to convince some criminals that I personally had nothing to do with it, but not him. The question is whether he thinks of me now as a fed doing my job or as his enemy. If I can't get back some of his trust, we're done. He'll break contact forever."

"How does a person regain his trust?"

"I plan to give him what he asked for — tell him who those two men were."

"Were?"

She shrugged. "If he knows their names, ages, and addresses but not who they work for, I think he must be reading that information off their driver's licenses." She saw Holstra's troubled expression. "That tells me he already killed them."

It was after 3:00 a.m. when his next call came. She went instantly from a sound sleep to full alertness before the second ring. She picked it up. "Yes?"

"Sorry, it's not your boyfriend this time," Schaeffer said.

"I'm sorry he's not my boyfriend too," she

said. "He's just a nice man who likes me."

"Is he around?"

"Not tonight. Neither is anybody else."

"So what happened on my last two calls?"

She knew he was far too experienced and aware to believe that she had simply not been able to answer because she was in a meeting or something. It had been after midnight. She had to try a version that contained a bit of truth. "I told my boss I'd been talking to you, and he decided to take a bigger role. He had the tech people intercept your call and use your phone's location to throw a net over you. He thought you might not bother to change phones after not reaching me."

"So he's an idiot?"

"No. He wants what I want. Information. It's his job and my job."

"Is he listening now?"

"He told me he wouldn't."

"Have you got any information for me?"

"Yes. Your two names are both members of the Balacontano family. Sarcone is married to Frank Tosca's sister Janine. You remember Tosca, I'm sure."

"I do." He knew that Waring knew he had killed Frank Tosca on his last visit to the United States. "I'll call you in half an hour."

"Why?"

He had already hung up. She knew that right now he was disabling the phone he'd just used and driving fast so he would be far away before he called again. She knew he was less trusting than he had been the first night in her house, and that from now on every time their orbits overlapped for even an instant, he would think first about evading any traps she had set. All she could do was wait.

About thirty minutes later, he called again. She assumed he must be in a new location. He said, "I want to tell you about a killing."

"Of whom?"

"His name was Boccio. Rocco Paglia shot him to death in Newark in front of twenty or thirty witnesses."

"Go ahead. I'll be recording you."

He spoke rapidly, and she could tell that he must have been there at the murder because of the vivid details. Paglia had hired him and an older and wiser hit man to find Boccio, who had headed a crew, a part of Paglia's little empire. He recalled sitting in a car for hours waiting for Boccio, watching him come out of the front door of an apartment building, grabbing him and cuffing him, throwing a bag over his head, and closing the trunk lid on him.

"We didn't usually take jobs like that. We were strictly killers. But Paglia wanted to scare the hell out of this guy Boccio, and having the two of us pick him up was a big part of the scare. The work wasn't hard, and the job paid well. We pulled up in the parking lot of this bar that Paglia owned. We dragged Boccio in and let Paglia snatch the bag off his head. What does Paglia do next? He pulls a gun out of his coat and shoots Boccio. This takes place in front of at least twenty, maybe thirty of Paglia's men, who are sitting around in the bar that they used as a hangout. Paglia didn't know what he was doing."

"What do you mean?" she said.

"When you shoot somebody, the first bullet might kill the guy instantly if it's in the right place, but it usually isn't. To pull out a gun and be sure to kill a guy, you have to hit his head, heart, or a major artery. What Paglia did is not that. He waved his pistol around and started shooting. He missed on his first shot, and it hit one of his own guys in the head. Another shot went through an arm of Boccio's suit and hit somebody else, who probably lived. But Paglia kept shooting at Boccio, who kept taking the shots and not dying. Finally Paglia knew he was going to run out of bullets. If he had to stand there and reload to kill Boccio, he'd look like an idiot. He stepped up so close to him to shoot him in the head that blowback from the shot threw spots on his own face, shirt, and suit. He looked like he had the measles. We left after that, just to get out of there."

She said, "What am I supposed to do with that?"

"Do what you do. It was in Newark. Rocco Paglia was the capo. The victim's name was Boccio. Paglia made such a spectacle of himself that any of the people there that day will remember it. Not to mention that he also killed at least one of his loyal men by accident. That would make them remember it even more. You have, somewhere in the federal prison system, at least a couple of old guys from Newark who were there. Offer them a century or two off their three-hundred-year sentences to testify against Rocco Paglia, and they'll take it. He's living in luxury somewhere in the West — I think it's Palm Springs. Or don't. I don't care if Rocco Paglia goes to prison or not."

"Will you testify?"

"Turn the old Newark guys, who will hate him by now. If they won't turn on him, use the information to make Paglia turn on somebody else."

"You must know that I'm also going to put the two men you asked about on surveillance. I have to, now that I know you're interested."

"Knock yourself out," he said. "I've got to go break this phone now."

24

The way that Eddie described it, he and the boy were combatants in the Mafia War, even though they had no stake in it. If the two sides and their ever-subdividing factions killed each other off entirely, or one side took over the other or killed the other, it would mean nothing to them. He and Eddie were not among the five thousand or so Mafiosi, were not related to them, and could never really be friends with them, since they had to remain free to accept contracts from any of them to kill any of the others. The "made" members of La Cosa Nostra were tribal. Even during the boy's time they still held all other members — even enemies — above any of the many people, like Eddie and the boy, who merely provided services.

Eddie maintained his neutrality except when there was a specific reason for favoritism or enmity. He distrusted the five New York families the most because they were in a position to be more ambitious and grasping than the others. They were also the primary source of the men who showed up in Pittsburgh during those years to kill Eddie and the boy.

During that period, Eddie and the boy killed at least fifteen men for money, but they also killed more men defending themselves. A contract was still out to punish someone for shooting the two men outside Yankee Stadium in the early weeks of the war, and now and then somebody new would figure out who had done it.

As the next year began, the boy noticed that their part in the bloodshed had changed. They were more expensive to hire now, but they needed to travel farther and hunt for more important men. It was the end of the 1960s, and the boy had grown his hair long. He wore what other males his age wore — jeans, work shirts or T-shirts, boots, aviator sunglasses. Sometimes during those months he and Eddie would travel by airplane or train and pretend not to know each other. On those occasions they would choose seats ten to twenty feet apart and watch each other's back.

During this phase, the boy did more and more killing. Eddie would step into a New York bar and distract the people who were guarding some important man. Eddie was big and formidable, and in cold weather he often wore an overcoat that might be hiding a weapon. People looked where their attention was directed, and not where they would have seen something. Bodyguards were so sure a long-haired college student would do no harm that they didn't seem to see him. He was a distraction to be looked past to detect any real threats in the vicinity.

When the victim was on a street, the boy would approach as part of the passing crowd, a small fraction of the foot traffic. He would detach himself for only a second or two, lift a hand, fire without stopping, and drift back into the stream of people. If enemies noticed him at all, they lost track of him immediately, never sure which one he had been. As the crowd passed a doorway or an alley or turned a corner, he would be there with them and then gone.

They already had a reputation from Eddie's early killings, when the boy had just started working with him. After they had taken down a few important men through speed and misdirection, their reputation started to grow among the class of people who hired hit men.

Summoning a skilled pair like Eddie and the boy was like conjuring lightning. For that reason, the bosses who knew them, like old Victor Castiglione, did not share information about them widely or often. It was not wise for anyone to talk openly or specifically about who had been hired to kill this man or that man, so it wasn't done. That information was only whispered between men of a certain age and status, because the ability to call in a high-end killer was a big part of a boss's power.

The lower-level men who knew didn't speak openly about them either. That would violate omertà. Telling such secrets would weaken a man's leader and protector, a mistake that could be fatal.

When Schaeffer looked back on those years, he knew he should have been able to see the rest of it from the start. Eddie had taught him to think ahead. He tried to get him to make plans for a day when everything would change for the worse. "If nothing bad ever happens and we live forever, then great. You'll just have an extra plan or two taking up space in your brain that you never use. But if you're around long enough, things will wear out, break apart, and disintegrate."

Late at night on the way home from a hit in Chicago, Eddie took the boy through Buffalo. They drove beside the dark Niagara

River for a while and then along Grant Street. They reached an area where half the street lamps were broken and most of the businesses had steel cages locked down over their front entrances. He stopped the car by the curb at the end of a block of stores, where a narrow sidewalk led back through an overgrown garden to a brown two-story house with windows covered by wooden shutters.

"See the house back there?" Eddie said. "Memorize the sight of it. Never forget it or where it is. On the first day when you find that your time is up and you need to disappear, come here. Wait for night, then go up on the porch and knock on the door. When he opens it, tell him you're Eddie Mastrewski's boy."

"Tell who?"

"The man who lives there. He's black, a little taller than I am. When everything else has fallen through and you know they're looking hard for you, he can still help you. People have gone through that door who were as good as dead, and nobody ever saw them come out. I've run into a couple of them years later in other places, but they'll never say how he does it."

"What does he charge?"

"He'll tell you, but don't worry about that.

If you get to the point where you need him, I'll be dead. There will always be enough money in the freezer in the shop to pay him and set yourself up in a nice business somewhere else — one of those big white shops that have rows and rows of wine, and big cheese displays, and cooking equipment, not just meat."

Fifteen years later, after everything had gone wrong and he was being hunted, he had made his way across the country to the old brown house on Grant Street in Buffalo. Eddie was long dead, but he had been right. The man was still there in the brown house. The man was old by then, but he still knew who Eddie was and knew about the boy that Eddie had raised. Schaeffer's life had continued past that night because the old man had decided to help him.

Schaeffer stood in the bathroom of his hotel suite and looked in the mirror. His hair was once again sandy brown. He looked a bit younger, partly because this visit to the United States had deepened his tan. His face had some wrinkles, but his body was still trim and strong. His mind was quicker than ever, partly because he had long ago made most of the decisions about things that other men wasted whole seconds thinking about.

He knew that staying in the United States and hiding from the Balacontano organization would only work for a while. The word was already out that finding him and killing him was worth serious money. Even though La Cosa Nostra had become much less visible since the old days, their wealth and power had greatly increased.

Schaeffer felt a sudden wave of hatred for them rise along the back of his neck like heat. The arrogant bastards had spent over a century infesting the country like parasites, taking a little share of this, a rake-off on that. And he had helped them. He had added teeth to the notion that they were too strong to be defeated, or even resisted. He had killed more Mafiosi than he had civilians, but even that internal fighting had added to the families' reputation for violence.

He needed to evade the forces that were arrayed against him and find ways to divide them. The families were more afraid of each other than of anything else. The others didn't care that Carl Bala had been framed and sent to prison, or that he was still locked up three decades later. They didn't care who had done it or how it had happened.

What would be of interest to them was

that after all this time, Carlo Balacontano was getting a parole hearing. If Bala got out of prison, he could be an important problem to them. As a middle-aged capo, he had been alarmingly aggressive, a cunning manipulator and a tireless, implacable enemy. Because of the decisions he had made in his prison cell, the Balacontano family was richer, stronger, and more deeply entrenched in its strongholds than ever. There was no reason to assume that if he went free, he would be any weaker or less aggressive. Schaeffer was sure there were plenty of rivals who would like his parole hearing to fail.

Schaeffer took out his iPad, signed into the hotel Wi-Fi, and began searching current news stories about the five New York families. After a few hours he knew that in their present state, the Balacontanos were doing very well. Carl Bala had spent no money, only directed the businesses and encouraged younger ambitious caretakers to work hard to impress him. Other families had changed over time.

He already knew the Piscata family had been in decline since Angelo "the Fish" Piscata, his two sons, and the underboss Nick Fontana were all caught in a Justice Department sting five years ago. Nothing had changed.

The Vintoretti family had been spinning off their traditional New York operations to other families. Now they were so heavily invested in finance — drowning the world in embezzled securities, smart-sounding blockchain currencies, laundered money, and Ponzi-scheme investment accounts — that they were less a New York crime family than a European fraud empire. They had no reason to care what happened to Carlo Balacontano.

The Catrones had moved most of their money and people west thirty years ago. They owned resorts, casinos, cattle, timber, mines, and millions of acres of land. They were another extended American family that made enormous contributions to politicians who were most protective of wealth and its privileges.

The only family still heavily involved in the old businesses — theft, gambling, drugs, prostitution, and extortion — were the Scarpis, who were throwbacks. They had built power over five generations by having all their sons and sons-in-law join the business. The brothers had sons named Scarpi, and the sisters had sons named Catania and Calabrese and Pucci, but they were all the same. Many of them even looked the same

— broad-shouldered men with wide faces, black wavy hair, and craggy, immobile expressions that were like masks of toughness.

The drugs they sold now were mostly painkillers diverted from commercial sources. Their extortions and kidnappings were still often crude and bloody, but the payments were sometimes in shares of stock or free goods and services. The prostitutes were now escorts who were advertised, scheduled, and protected while they dated rich men. The head of the family at the moment was a man named Dominic Santangelo. His picture could as easily have been a picture of any one of his uncountable cousins. The Scarpi family had very strong reasons to hope Carlo Balacontano didn't get out of prison. Schaeffer decided that made them ideal for his purposes.

Schaeffer researched his plan. He looked at the pages of instructions for prisoners' families posted by the Federal Bureau of Prisons. They had stopped letting people send gift packages directly to prisoners. And while it was possible to order packages full of things that prisoners needed and have them delivered to the prisoner a certain number of times per year, that wasn't what he wanted.

Next he looked for news articles about Carl Bala's parole hearing and the recent appeals and complaints produced and submitted by his lawyers. Schaeffer now knew that the Balacontano family were the ones trying to have him killed. He supposed they thought he planned to stop Bala's parole somehow. They were wrong. He had wanted nothing, and he hadn't even known that Balacontano was going to have a parole hearing. But their course was set, and so his had to be too.

He kept reading articles that might tell him what was going on in Balacontano's crime family. He read an account that consisted almost entirely of things he already knew. Then came the part he was searching for: "Amid the discussion and speculation about the parole hearing, there is no indication of how John Cocella, the reigning caretaker don, feels about the prospect of the old lion's return."

He noticed a line in small italic at the bottom of the story: *This is Part 1 of a three-part series called 'Family Matters.'*"

Schaeffer went to the same section of the newspaper and found Part 2, printed the next day, which covered the legal aspects of the story.

The article quoted Balacontano's lead

counsel, Andrew Wain Herren, who said that parole was the least his client could expect. He said it was possible his client would get a new trial that exonerated him and awarded him damages for false arrest, an unfair trial, and an improper conviction.

Schaeffer now had the names of the acting capo of the Balacontano family and Bala's lead attorney. He looked up some addresses, and then packed and flew to New York.

The next day he took the subway and walked to the business address of Dominic Santangelo, the head of the Scarpi family. Schaeffer was not surprised when he saw the building. It was the old Bellissimo Products building, much remodeled. They had removed the old scrollwork at the top of the facade, covered the red brick with a sand-colored substance, and put in big windows on the upper floors. If he squinted his eyes, he could still see the exterior of the old building.

He walked around the back and saw a big white truck parked near a loading dock with its ramp down. The painted sign on the truck said "DOCU-SAFE SECURITY," with the words "archiving and shredding" in small print beneath. A pair of workmen were loading the truck with rectangular cardboard cartons while four other workers from inside the building were busy bringing out identical cartons and leaving them by the ramp for loading. The cartons by the ramp were all labeled in black marker — 1A, 2E, 4G, and so on. He looked at the building. There were eight stories. The bosses would have their offices on the eighth floor on the side with the best view. The big new windows were at the front, overlooking the street. That would probably put them at the beginning of the alphabet.

He waited until some boxes with the label 8A on them appeared. Then he watched for the moment when the faster workers would catch up with the slower workers and they would all be inside at once. That would also give the two-man truck crew a few minutes when they weren't loading.

At last, the workers doing the loading were indoors, the driver was sitting in the cab behind the wheel, writing something on a clipboard, and the other man was in the bay arranging boxes. Schaeffer put on one latex glove, stepped to the box labeled 8A, slashed the tape seal, and pulled out a thick sheaf of papers, all in a plastic wastebasket liner. He put the plastic bag under his coat and walked down the street to the subway entrance.

He kept the papers under his coat for the length of his subway ride. In his hotel room, he dropped the papers and envelopes that he had stolen on the bed, put another latex glove on his other hand, and sorted them, searching for any blank sheets of paper that might have been used to cover a check or a bill, a business envelope, and a smaller letter envelope. When he found them, he put them in a folder and then into an empty drawer of the dresser.

He began the next phase of his research on his iPad. He learned that of all the active ingredients in rat poison, four stood out. Cholecalciferol caused kidney failure. Bromethalin caused a swelling of the brain. Phosphides produced a poison gas when mixed with stomach acid. And anticoagulants prevented blood from clotting. Over the next few days he bought four different rat poisons, each of which relied on a different formula. He put on his surgical gloves and used a small mortar and pestle to break the pellets of rat poison into a fine powder, mixed them together, and stored them in a paper cup in the drawer.

Next he prepared his letter to the Metropolitan Correctional Center. The outer envelope said it was for Carlo Balacontano and was from his attorney, Andrew Wain

Herren of the firm Pfoel, Grebell & Herren. It said, "Special Mail — Open only in the presence of the inmate." The *Inmate Information Handbook* of the Federal Bureau of Prisons stated that a counselor would open and inspect the letter and then hand it over to the inmate.

Schaeffer wasn't sure whose fingerprints would be on the envelope and the sheets of paper in the letter, but it would be someone in the Scarpis' building, and he was sure many people there would have their fingerprints on file with the federal government. Inside his letter was a fresh return envelope addressed to Andrew Wain Herren, the attorney. The letter asked Balacontano to write down the names of any friendly witnesses he hadn't mentioned earlier, put the list in the stamped return envelope, and send it out in that day's mail. The glue strip on the return envelope was coated with the fine rat poison, and there was a small amount of it stuck to various interior parts of the outer envelope.

Schaeffer finished his letter and mailed it on his way out to dinner. When he reached the restaurant, he devoted more care and time to washing his hands than usual, and then had an excellent dinner.

25

Schaeffer estimated that it would take three days for the letter to arrive and be routed through the prison mail system to Carlo Balacontano and then another five for the FBI to identify the rat poison, run the fingerprints on the paper and envelopes, and figure out their owner's role in the Scarpi organization. When the eight days had passed, he called Elizabeth Waring's phone at 2:00 a.m.

"Yes?" she said.

"It's me."

"How was Pittsburgh?"

"I don't know what you mean."

"The two men you asked me about, Sarcone and Pastore. Tell me you killed them *before* you talked to me about them."

"Men have been trying to kill me, but these two failed. I don't expect you to be as happy as I am."

"I'm trying to solve your problem in the

best way I can. You still have information that could be of use to the Justice Department. If you're willing, I can introduce you to some people who are very good at making sure that men like Sarcone and Pastore don't get close enough to you to become a nuisance. You would be kept in absolute safety and relative comfort in return for occasional testimony about how you spent your twenties and thirties."

"Thank you, but I'm not interested in that kind of offer. Being inside a prison isn't an option for me, even a comfortable prison."

"I didn't say it was a prison."

"No, I did."

"The alternative isn't better."

"No, but if I'm outside, at least I can fight back."

She could tell that he was about to hang up, so she said, "Things are heating up out there in the underworld."

"Oh?"

"A few days ago Carlo Balacontano got a letter in federal prison that was supposed to be from his lawyer. It was laced with rat poison, and had fingerprints and DNA on it that came from someone in the Scarpi family, a girl who works in the office of Dominic Santangelo."

"That's the best the Scarpi organization

can do these days? Try to poison him by mail?"

"A poisoned letter could be something besides an attempt to kill him. It might be an insult or a warning. They might think the reason he's getting a parole hearing is because he's giving us information."

"Is he?"

"No. He would if he were smart, but he's not."

"On that I'll wish you a good night." He disconnected the call and broke down his telephone. He put the pieces in a bag so he could throw them away next time he was out. It was now ten after two. He went to bed.

When he woke the next morning, he went back to work on the trouble he was making. Balacontano knew that he had been sent a poisoned letter in an envelope with a Scarpi's fingerprints on it. Now it was time for the Balacontano family to retaliate against the Scarpis for the rat poison.

Schaeffer couldn't assume it would happen naturally. Was Bala's surrogate boss, John Cocella, able to see Bala in prison to get orders? In preparation for his parole hearing, Balacontano had been moved to Metropolitan Correctional Center at 150 Park Row, New York City. This was a much smaller prison than the one Balacontano was used to, with only eight hundred inmates. He was at Metropolitan because the court for the Southern District of New York was where Balacontano had been convicted of Arthur Fieldston's murder.

Schaeffer bought a seat on a train from DC to New York, which took under four hours. He was careful not to draw the interest of other passengers. He dressed well and kept to himself, spending most of the time looking out the window at the greenery and studying small towns near the tracks. He judged the train's speed by the frequency of the utility poles that drifted backward past his window. He had brought a copy of the *New York Times,* so he opened it and pretended to read.

He thought about death. He remembered Eddie saying, "Everybody dies. It's a question of timing, and whether the pay for it goes to you or a bunch of doctors. It might as well be you." The pay in the killing trade had been extremely good, but pay stopped being an issue to Schaeffer the day he had left for England thirty years ago. By then he had enough money and didn't need anybody to pay him again. It had often seemed ironic to him that after all the killing he'd done to get rich, he had then accidentally fallen for a woman who had a fortune that made his money irrelevant.

He arrived at Penn Station a bit after 1:00 p.m. and took a cab to the hotel he had selected. The Hotel Mulberry was thirteen stories high and overlooked the prison. He walked to City Hall Park, where he could still see the prison. It didn't look like much, a nearly featureless block of dark brown brick. Whenever a car passed into or out of the parking lot, a row of stanchions would sink under the pavement and then rise up again to block the next car.

He had read about people who had been incarcerated in this prison. The drug boss El Chapo was there now, and at one point Bernard Madoff had been here. The blind sheik who had ordered the first attempt on the World Trade Center had been here. Jeffrey Epstein had killed himself there while awaiting trial for sex trafficking. Like those people, Bala had probably been held in this prison for the convenience of the courts. But it was reputed to be an awful place.

Schaeffer walked back to his hotel and stepped out on his balcony to watch the prison. The people who came and went were divisible into groups: lawyers and prosecutors, police detectives, doctors and therapists, and visitors. He had managed to find

286

seven photos of John Cocella on the Internet, but he saw nobody who looked like him.

Schaeffer gave up at five o'clock, when the traffic into the prison stopped. He got up in the morning to watch the prison entrance again. This time he saw more visitors. There were far more women than men. It made sense. When a family got dysfunctional and fragmented, the ones left were usually the women and children. It was the men who got put in a cell or got shot.

Just before ten o'clock, he saw a man he thought might be John Cocella. A big black Mercedes pulled up at the curb, and two large men got out, one from the right side of the back seat and the other from the front passenger side. They stood together looking around, and then another man emerged from the back seat, moving quickly so that when his first step touched the pavement, he was already launched toward the front entrance of the prison. He wore an expensive, well-fitted gray summer suit and a pair of brown shoes that glinted in the sunlight.

The two men walked on either side of him, staying with him all the way to the front entrance. One of the men pushed open the door so that Cocella could step inside without slowing down.

The two big men stayed outside. They

were a very professional pair of bodyguards. The big black Mercedes drove off, but the two men remained, scanning the area they could see — the cars on the street, the foot traffic, the people leaving the building.

Schaeffer left his balcony and went inside his hotel room, turned on his iPad, and typed in the name Dominic Santangelo. In a few seconds he had photographs of the man, his address, and directions to his house on Staten Island. He found street-view photographs of the house and studied them. Then he looked at aerial photographs, studying the images for accessibility, hiding places, lines of fire, choke points, places to leave a car.

Schaeffer went back out on the balcony, spotted the two bodyguards, and watched them some more. A short time later, the front door of the prison opened, and the man Schaeffer had identified as John Cocella emerged. He was instantly flanked by his two men, and the three walked quickly toward the curb. The black car was not visible at first, but then Schaeffer saw it about a block off. Cocella and his men didn't slow down or make a visible attempt to match their speed to the car's. They simply kept moving and the car sped up to meet them. The two bodyguards reached for the door handles before the car even stopped and flung the doors open. Cocella sat, the bodyguards slipped inside, the doors slammed, and the car was off again. Schaeffer counted seconds, and didn't get to five before the car was a block away and moving into the left lane.

Immediately, Schaeffer packed and checked out of the Mulberry Hotel. He knew that completing the next step could take two or three days, possibly even longer. He took a cab to the nearest car rental, which was at Battery Park, rented a small, dark gray Toyota. He locked his suitcase in the trunk and drove to Staten Island.

He ate dinner at a local restaurant and walked the commercial streets for a while. When he saw that the parking space he had selected in advance on the aerial pictures was now available, he moved his rental car into it. At 11:20 p.m., he went to the trunk of the rental car, opened his suitcase, took out the disassembled AR-15 rifle with the telescopic sight, wrapped his coat around it, and brought it with him. He stopped in Dominic Santangelo's backyard, assembled the rifle on the grass, inserted a loaded magazine, and sighted it in on the rear window of Santangelo's living room.

He waited about forty-five minutes, sitting comfortably in the dark while Santangelo finished walking his dog, a fat cocker spaniel he addressed as Polly. Then Santangelo came into the house, sat down on the couch, and turned on a flat-screen television that was about six feet across.

Schaeffer placed the crosshairs on the center of the bald spot on the back of Santangelo's head. He squeezed the trigger, felt the recoil, saw the red mist, and laid the rifle on the ground. As he had learned while working with Eddie, a single shot seldom spurred people to action. They waited and listened for a second shot, and if it never came, then they figured that the first shot must have been a backfire or a firecracker. Nobody came out of the house or appeared nearby, so Schaeffer removed the magazine, disassembled the rifle, and left.

He drove the rental car to a hotel along West 38th Street, checked in, and resumed his research and scouting on the Internet. He found out that John Cocella was officially the president of a Balacontano-owned restaurant supply business called Trans-Matic Supply, which Schaeffer remembered from about forty years ago. It used to be one of those businesses that forced lots of small restaurants to buy their packaged food, liquor, and linens, and then used the deliveries to transport contraband and pick up money. The current headquarters was in a big modern building on the east side of the city, and seen from the outside, the company might have been in any business or no business.

The next morning Schaeffer went to take a look at the building, walked the neighborhood, and became familiar with his surroundings. He looked for ways into Cocella's offices and studied nearby buildings for vantage points that provided good views of the office windows.

Unless the Scarpi family had changed a great deal since the old days, they would hold the wake, funeral, and burial of Dominic Santangelo and then start working actively on their revenge.

26

Schaeffer stayed in New York to watch the next phase of his plan take place. A quiet older man who dressed well and didn't talk to the other guests could expect not to be bothered much in a good hotel.

Every day he thought about Meg. He wondered where she was and who she was staying with, and if she was completely safe. Sometimes he wondered whether she was thinking about him at the same moment. But he had no doubt that what he was doing in America was the best action he could take. He had made progress since he'd arrived. He had found killers who had been sent out to ambush him. He had learned they belonged to the Balacontano crime family. Now he was making sure that life got a bit more dangerous for the Balacontano organization.

Summers in the northeast could be hot and humid, but he needed clothes that would hide weapons and ammunition. He found some good lighter-than-summer-weight sport coats made of a synthetic fabric with labels that promised it was both "wicking" and "breathable." He chose light gray and dark gray, the equivalent of camouflage in the middle of a big city. The human eye always caught motion, and it usually caught color. He intended to mask them both.

He studied the online versions of the New York papers so he wouldn't miss any small mention of Carlo Balacontano's parole hearing or other news about the Mafia. He read the reports of the death of Dominic Santangelo to be sure there was no detail that might lead to him.

One of the articles that caught his attention had a section on the famous old hits on Mafia figures. It struck him that most of them had happened in daylight. Albert Anastasia had been killed in his barber's chair. Paul Castellano had been shot to death as he was getting out of his car in the daytime. The Valentine's Day massacre had involved the killing of seven men in the morning.

But there had been some night killings too. He had done quite a few himself, and it wasn't always easy. At night the target could be sleeping in a different room or even a different house. It was hard to approach a sleeping man in complete silence, and bosses often had somebody awake and standing guard. That kind of killing was usually done by a specialist like him, not a typical Mafia guy who made his living fixing games or scaring shopkeepers.

Schaeffer's best bet was that the Scarpis would go after John Cocella themselves and they'd do it in the daytime. Schaeffer began to spend early mornings at a café with a few outdoor tables on the same large paved area where the Trans-Matic Supply building was located. After he'd eaten breakfast and read the *New York Times*, he would walk through the neighborhood where Cocella's office was, looking for signs that today would be the day.

He looked for men with the Scarpi family's wide shoulders and craggy faces, and for cars that kept driving past the same spot or stayed in one too long. Manhattan was a place where people were busy most of the time. If they weren't on their way somewhere, they would be indoors doing whatever they got paid for. He didn't want to be seen as somebody who had too much time on his hands, so he kept moving.

He walked to a second restaurant just

before noon each day so he would have an early choice of the tables arranged inside a row of potted trees off the dining room, favoring the tables that gave him a good view of the Trans-Matic building and the street in front of it. On this particular morning he had seen a couple of signs that this might be the day. There had been a pair of men on the street across from his café. Their bodies told him they were impatient, waiting for something and killing time. They didn't kill time by going into a building or walking around the block. They walked about a block north and then two blocks south together, as though they didn't dare move to a place where they might not see or hear what was happening or be able to get back in time.

Ten minutes later, three men took seats at the small, black steel tables near Schaeffer's. Not one of them ordered the kind of food that a man might order if he was hungry enough to go to lunch early — just coffee and a pastry. Two sat on either side of Schaeffer, and one behind him.

Schaeffer didn't know any of these men, but they looked about right. They were all in their thirties or early forties, wore suits or sport coats that would hide weapons, and sat outside with him, even though the sky was cloudy and it looked as though it might rain.

When the moment came, things happened in several places at once. A vehicle that looked like John Cocella's black limo separated itself from the river of yellow taxicabs and dark limos. Cocella and his two bodyguards appeared inside the wall of windows in the front foyer of the building, prepared to come out onto the broad apron of concrete, presumably to duck into the car as they usually did. Schaeffer watched, but they just stood there.

Something was off. Schaeffer could feel it. He had a sensation that the flow of humanity on the street had changed. As the black car pulled up to the curb in front of the building, two men came trotting across the busy street at opposite angles. At the same time, a man on the sidewalk near the car did a stutter-step, as though he had been surprised by the two men, and changed something he was intending to do.

Cocella and his two bodyguards stayed inside the building, staring out through the glass front of the lobby at the car. The two men who had run toward the car now both pulled out semiautomatic pistols and began to fire at the black limousine. The car suddenly did a hook-turn and bumped up over the curb.

As it did, the three men who had been sitting at tables near Schaeffer stood and fired at the two who had attacked the limousine. They fired rapidly, hitting one of the men, who fell on the street, and then the second, who turned and limped a few yards, and then collapsed.

The three men beside Schaeffer came under fire from someone Schaeffer couldn't see at first. Schaeffer kicked over his steel table for cover and crouched behind it. When the two men closest to him were hit, Schaeffer scrambled on his hands and knees to the nearest man. A few shots pounded into the pavement near him, and another rang his steel table like a bell. He looked up and saw a man in a third-floor window with a rifle. Schaeffer tugged the pistol from the dead man's hand, then patted him to find a spare magazine. He fired four shots at the sniper in the third-floor window, ejected his magazine, and replaced it with the fresh one.

Schaeffer kept his head down beneath the nearest steel table. He heard an engine accelerate, took a glance over the table's edge, and saw the car. The limo gained speed as it roared across the concrete forecourt of the office building toward the glass front, where Cocella and his men were visible.

Schaeffer appraised the effort. The Scarpi plan to kill Cocella had been inventive, but it was not succeeding. Cocella was too well protected, and the Scarpis had already lost the benefit of surprise. Schaeffer judged that the only way for the plan to work was if he took it over. He shifted to his toes, pushed off, and dashed across the forecourt toward the glass front of the building just as the black limousine driven by one of the Scarpis crashed into the glass.

Glittering glass fragments flew in front of the limousine and to both sides, showering Cocella, his bodyguards, and the two security guards at the front desk. The car kept going for forty feet until it crashed into a large overstuffed couch and the wall behind it. Cocella's bodyguards produced pistols and started firing at the car, the shots pounding the safety glass and leaving big, round impact spots, like splashes, but not penetrating. Schaeffer stepped in over the empty window frame and across piles of glass, fired two rounds into the chest of one of the bodyguards, snapped his aim to the second, fired, and dropped him to the marble floor. Cocella turned on his heel and started to run, but Schaeffer aimed carefully and fired twice. The first shot hit Cocella in the back of his skull, so the second

298

in his back didn't matter. He was already dead before his legs gave out and his body fell and slid to a stop on the marble floor.

Schaeffer pocketed the pistol as he pivoted, stepped out over the glass, and became one of the many people running. He dashed the hundred feet past the overturned table on the patio where he had been sitting, through the patio door of the restaurant, and into the dining room. The customers seemed to be gone, and the staff must have been crouching in the kitchen to stay below the line of fire, so he was unimpeded all the way through the restaurant until he emerged at the building's front door. He walked quickly around the next corner, stuck up his hand to hail a taxi, got in, and said, "Columbia University, please." The car was already headed north, and the driver accelerated, because it was a long ride to 116th Street.

27

Elizabeth Waring arrived in New York City in a plain black car driven by an FBI agent named Anna Holcomb, accompanied by an agent named Edward O'Connell. The two agents sat in the front like a couple while Elizabeth and her briefcase took up the back. Her overhead dome light was on so she could work.

She studied the reports she had received over the past few hours. She was beginning to reach near certainty that she knew what was going on, because she had seen something like it happen a couple of times before.

Carlo Balacontano's parole hearing was in just a few days. He would have to establish that he had served his time honorably and been a good prisoner, that he had changed, that he had accepted his guilt and truly repented. He actually had caused no provable trouble, and for the real crime he'd committed — having people murdered by a pro and then deciding it was better to avoid paying a professional killer by trying to ambush and murder him, he was probably truly sorry.

She thought about the lawyer Balacontano had hired, the one whose name had been on the envelope of the poisoned letter: Andrew Wain Herren of Pfoel, Gebell & Herren. She had been surprised, because she knew him by reputation. He was lead attorney at the firm, the big litigator. It didn't fit. An inmate could have a lawyer attend a parole hearing, but not this inmate or this lawyer from this firm. The lawyers Pfoel, Gebell, and Herren were famous in a special way. Other lawyers knew their names and talked about them because they argued precedent-setting cases and made enormous business deals, but few ordinary people had heard of them. They wouldn't appear on television any more than they would join a carnival. They were the kind of help that ordinary people couldn't conceive of, and the cost would have struck most people as impossible. Elizabeth knew something odd was happening. She couldn't know what the plan was, but she knew there must be one.

And now the situation had become more complicated. The Scarpi family had sent a poisoned letter to Balacontano in prison.

Then someone, probably a member of the Balacontano family, had shot and killed Dominic Santangelo, the boss of the Scarpi family. Once the Balacontano family had done that, John Cocella, the Balacontano boss, was the only possible next target, and now he was dead too.

There was one player she hadn't heard from in a few days. He was the one she was most curious about, but she had no way to reach him, could only wait for his occasional calls. On this trip he had seemed marginally well disposed toward her, but he was so dangerous that he might kill her in a reflex, or out of the long habit of solving complications by cutting them off. But she still couldn't help wondering, *Where had he been, where was he now, and what was he planning to do?*

The enmity between the Scarpi and the Balacontano families might have erupted spontaneously. They had reasons to hate each other, and would have more reasons if the real boss, Carlo Balacontano, were to get out of prison. But having this fight now weakened both families. And that made the retired hit man stronger and safer.

The car pulled up the side street to the back of the prison, where a uniformed federal officer was waiting. He saw the car,

spoke into a phone, put it away, and then stepped close to the car to look inside. "Ms. Waring?" he said. "I'm Lieutenant Parnell."

Elizabeth stepped out of the car and pointed to the others. "This is Agent Holcomb and Agent O'Connell. Where would you like us to park?"

He pointed. "Over there, where the sign says 'Visitors.' Take any space. There are no visitors at this hour."

Elizabeth waited with Parnell while the two FBI agents parked and walked back. The group went around to the front of the building and in a main entrance. Elizabeth stopped and said, "I'll be seeing him alone. Is there a comfortable place where the agents can wait for me?"

"Yes," said Parnell. He turned to the two agents. "Just show your identification at the desk over there, and they'll take you to the waiting area."

She went with Parnell to another corridor, where they were met by guards. She went through the routine of giving the guards her purse to rifle through and holding out her arms while they ran a metal-detector wand up and down her body.

Parnell took her to a small interrogation room to wait. The room was bare except for a table and chairs. She sat across from the ring in the table that was supposed to hold the prisoner's handcuffs.

She waited a few minutes, and then the door opened to admit Carlo Balacontano and two guards. He was short — about five feet seven — but he seemed even shorter this time because the two guards were so tall. She supposed the old man had been placed on the list of prisoners who needed special protection after the poisoned letter.

The ritual of bringing him in and locking him to the table gave her a chance to study him. Seven years ago when she had gone to visit him at his prison in Illinois, he had seemed like an old man who had been forced to live under healthy conditions on a nutritious diet for so long that he was physically younger than his age. She had interrupted him when he was goofing off in the middle of his morning chores, and he had jumped right up and begun working. Now he seemed stronger, heavier, and more robust.

The guard finished locking him to the table and nodded to Elizabeth. She smiled at the guards and said, "Thank you." They opened the door and left.

Carlo Balacontano sat still across from her and waited.

She said, "Mr. Balacontano, my name is

Elizabeth Waring. I work for the Justice Department."

"I remember you. Do you think these places have an endless parade of chicks coming through?"

"No, I don't," she said. "Half the inmates in this prison are female, but I don't imagine you see them."

"Not a one since I've been here," he said. "What do you want this time?"

"You can consider this a kind of welfare check, like the police do when nobody's seen some old person for a while. I understand you have a parole hearing coming up."

"Yeah. Three more days. The federal prosecutors as good as framed me. You know it, and I know it, and my lawyers know it, and pretty soon everybody else will too. And then I'll be out and free. I'll take whatever standard buy-off the courts give for being locked up illegally — a million a year or whatever."

"You're dreaming."

"I don't care about the money. I already had enough money before I got sent to prison, and I don't have that many years left to spend it." He smiled. "So if the money is why you're here, you can tell your bosses to breathe easy."

"What do you think is going on out

there?" she asked, indicating the small, high window with a nod.

"Probably what always went on out there. People take charge and then you find out what they wanted power for. Some people like it and some don't, so they fight over it."

"Is that what happened to Dominic Santangelo?"

"I don't know what happened to him. I heard he got shot while he was watching television."

She smirked. "It's got nothing to do with you, right?"

He stared at her for a couple of seconds. "You haven't mentioned John Cocella yet. Are you going to?"

"I heard he was murdered too. Know anything about that?"

"Obviously I wasn't present when he was attacked and murdered. It seems like some people are unhappy that I'm getting out."

"Really? You're getting out?"

He smiled. "You know what part of this place I'm in, right? It's the place where they keep the people they think are in danger. When all the court proceedings are done, they'll keep me here for a while because the Justice Department will delay things and ask for do-overs and all that. I'm going to get out. People — smart, knowledgeable people — are working on it. See how the guards treat me? They talk to me like a person. They make sure the cuffs aren't too tight and I don't trip over my ankle chains. They know that before long I'm going to be outside. Outside means the place where they and their wives and kids live. Someday very soon I'm going to be a free man with a lot of money and a lot of men who like and respect me and want to do me favors."

"You seem very sure of the outcome of your hearing," she said.

"I have very good lawyers, and they assure me that I'm not getting my hopes up for nothing."

"Want to tell me how they know that?" she asked.

"I told you. They're good lawyers."

"Then I guess all I can do to help you is to remind you that if you do get out on parole, you're still subject to the laws that got you in here. You won't be able to hang around with people convicted of felonies or miss an appointment with your parole officer. People will be watching to be sure you don't make a mistake."

"Okay, honey," he said. "I promise I won't. Can I go now? There's something I want to see on television."

"Sure," she said. "I'll tell the guards." She

got up, opened the door, and beckoned for the two guards, who were waiting down the hall, to come back in before she stepped out.

She collected the two FBI agents and got into the back seat of the car while they prepared to drive out. She dialed the office of the deputy assistant, but changed her mind and hung up. Then she called her colleague John, who was assigned to the Balacontano hearing. The phone rang four times and offered to record a message.

She said, "It's me. I just talked to Carl Bala. He sincerely thinks he's getting out. He's always been very cynical and, I think, realistic before. I'm wondering whether he's confident because he has a great lawyer, or whether his great lawyer actually told him he's getting out. In this case, there could be a big difference."

28

Schaeffer picked up his car and drove south again, this time to Maryland, where he was far away from the dangers of New York. He was alive, and John Cocella, the acting boss of the Balacontano family, was dead, along with his bodyguards. Some Scarpis were dead too, and that would add to the general climate of anger and hatred he had needed to create.

The training Eddie had given him was what had made the difference yesterday. The instant Schaeffer had seen the Scarpi soldiers were going to lose, he had started to move, and kept moving until he had killed Cocella and gotten away. He could still hear Eddie's voice from long ago: "Plan a job for a month if you have to, but do it in seconds. Once it starts, you're an egg in a frying pan. If you take too much time, you heat up and burn."

He fell asleep and woke only when the

service people started rattling carts full of china and silverware in the morning. As he lay in bed, he soon heard guests walking along the hallway outside his door, some of them talking to companions. He was just outside DC now, partly because he wanted to mask his travels from the Justice Department.

He would have to go back to New York to check on the struggle at some point, if only to keep the two families angry and fearful. What he would like best was for the Scarpis to acquire some allies among the other New York families, because that would keep the pressure on the Balacontanos. But he was sure that what he'd done already would keep Bala's men thinking about the Scarpis for a few days instead of going out to search for him.

The next night he activated one of the new cell phones and called Elizabeth Waring.

When she answered, he said, "I read in the paper that you arrested Rocco Paglia for the Boccio killing."

"I saw that too," she said. "You called me at two a.m. to read me the newspaper?"

"To give you a chance to thank me."

"You told me a story, and I passed that on to other people. And you were right that there were still a few eyewitnesses who were

310

willing to testify in exchange for a couple of years off the sentences they were serving."

"Doesn't that buy me a thank-you?"

"Thank you. It also keeps you on the list of people I could convince my bosses to make a deal with. For the moment you're a reliable source of information. Would you like to take the department up on the offer before some young hit man collects on you?"

"No, thank you," he said. "I just called to see if you had any information for me about Carl Bala's parole hearing."

"It's scheduled for two days from now, on August 1, as you know. It's at the federal prison where he's locked up. If you're considering going in the hope that he sees you and has a heart attack, forget it. Only his victims or their immediate families can attend the hearing. A hearing examiner asks the questions and puts together the report and sends his recommendation to one of the US parole commissioners, who makes the decision. If the parole is not granted, Bala could get another shot at it in two years."

"What do you think is going to happen on August 1?"

"I don't know," she said. "A couple of months ago I would have said his chances were nil. Now I'm not so sure. He's got a very good lawyer. Most of the time, inmates aren't represented by counsel, because these hearings are not adversarial proceedings. These prisoners have already been convicted and served their sentences. The hearing officer looks at the written record, reads comments from victims, asks a few questions, says no or maybe, and sends it on. This time Bala clearly thinks he's getting out. The people from our office who are submitting their own statement to the hearing officer think otherwise."

"Okay."

"You're positive he was the one who hired you to do a couple of killings, right?"

"Right."

"If he hired you, then you're both guilty."

"I know. I apologize."

She suddenly changed directions. "Do you know that there was a big shootout in New York this week?"

"I read about it."

"I have to take an interest in these things," she said. "First Dominic Santangelo gets shot through the back of the head at his house, and then John Cocella and four of his men and four Scarpi soldiers all get shot down around a Balacontano office building. You know what stood out for me?"

312

"No," he said.

"There were lots of bullets fired from lots of handguns. I know the police picked up at least seventy-five brass casings. But it turns out that all of the bullets that hit John Cocella and his bodyguards came from one gun."

"So?"

"It reminded me of something."

"What was that?"

"A long time ago I was on a case. First there was a machinist killed when his truck exploded outside a California union hall, and then there was the murder of a US senator in Colorado, and then a series of killings of LCN bosses all over the country. The killings caused maximum confusion and chaos and violence, and it also seemed that there was only one person who benefited from the chaos."

"Interesting story," he said. "To me this one just sounds like the usual fighting these people used to get into once in a while."

She was hoping she'd succeeded in making him lose track of the time. The Justice Department's technicians would be frantically narrowing down his location.

"Well, anyway, I've got to go." The line went dead. She knew he was already taking the battery out of his phone. She waited for her phone to ring so someone could tell her they'd found him. After a few more minutes, the silence told her that they had not.

A few minutes after hanging up, he walked up to the front desk at his hotel, turned in his key card, and took the receipt the night clerk printed for him. He got into his car and drove. The hotel where he had stopped was one of about fifteen large ones in the surrounding mile, as well as twenty or more smaller ones that weren't tall enough to dominate the horizon. Every one of them was close enough so that a cell phone call would ping off the same repeater towers.

As he drove, he took apart the cell phone he had used. For the next few miles he threw parts of the phone into any sewer grate he passed on his drive north. When he reached the outskirts of Philadelphia, he checked into his next hotel. He liked it immediately because it had an underground garage with an elevator, so he would be able to come and go without being seen. He could deal with the late-night-shift people tonight and then never see them again. For now he had to wait. Waiting had kept Eddie and the boy alive a few times.

He remembered one job they'd taken in the dead of winter. He and Eddie had spent days finding a man named Barzoni, who was the head of a crew of thieves. The boy hadn't retained the list of the man's crimes after all these years. All he remembered was that Barzoni and his crew had somehow betrayed the trust of the Draco family, a central New York State tributary group reporting to the boss in Buffalo. The Buffalo underboss, Bobby Moscato, had put out an open contract, a promise to pay $100,000 to anyone who killed Barzoni. For each of Barzoni's men he would pay $20,000.

It was a cold winter, and Eddie and the boy were driving along the southern shore of Lake Ontario, a part of upstate New York where a man's ears would freeze while he was walking from his house to his car and it hurt to breathe too deeply. The wind was arctic air that screamed across Canada and the lakes with the intention of making human life unbearable and dangerous.

It was after dark when Eddie and the boy passed a small town outside Oswego and came upon a row of cottages that had been built along the lake side of the road. The boy spotted a car that matched the description of Barzoni's parked in the garage of a cottage, nose outward. Eddie stopped his car and turned it around while the boy got out, touched the parked car's hood, and felt no heat. That meant the car had been there a while. They drove back the way they had come to get indoors and plan the hit.

The only sheltered place for a stranger on this stretch of shoreline was a small hotel that rented rooms to ice fishermen in the winter and tourists in summer. When they walked into the foyer, they saw coats on the rack and realized they weren't the only visitors.

A big table in the dining room and bar was occupied by seven men in their thirties. At a seat with his back to the wall sat a man who appeared to be their leader, a professional killer and competitor of Eddie Mastrewski's nicknamed Cat-head Malone.

Eddie stepped up to the table and said, "Hello, Cat-head. I'm surprised to see you here."

"Likewise," Malone said. The boy could see the origin of the nickname. While Malone was a tall and athletic-looking man, he had a head that was small and round, and ears that protruded from a spot slightly higher than most people's ears. "We've been here since morning, waiting for all of them to get here. This one is ours."

Eddie's hand gave a slow sweep to indicate the many empty beer bottles that had collected on the table. "I can see there's no denying you've been here a while. And I

316

know he's down there in one of the cottages, but he's not alone. Are you sure you want to try to take him by yourselves?"

"Nice try, Eddie," Cat-head said. "There are seven of us. There are two of you, and I'm being generous there, since that kid can't be more than half your weight. You'd better tie a beer keg to his ass or the wind out there will pick him up and blow him to Florida."

The boy glanced at Eddie for a signal. Eddie didn't look at him but gave his head an almost imperceptible shake. The boy had both hands in his parka pockets with his fingers wrapped around a pair of .45 Model 1911 pistols, his favorites. He let the muscles relax but didn't move his hands.

A moment later, a tall, stocky blond woman wearing a waitress's dress and apron with a pair of jeans underneath because of the cold came by with a tray to clear the empty bottles. Eddie took this moment to order another round of drinks for Malone and his friends. This seemed to make them more at ease, and the boy saw a couple of them take their hands out of their pockets without bringing anything up with them. After the next round had been delivered and consumed, they seemed more affable.

A bit later Cat-head told Eddie, "Now all

we have to do is kill some time, wait for the night to get really dark. Around midnight, before the last quarter moon rises, we'll get the work done."

Eddie shrugged. "The moon can be pretty bright when it's reflected off the snow."

"I got a way to fix that, too," Cat-head said.

"Are you going to paint the snow?"

"When the time comes, you'll see. It's been five degrees or less around here for the past month, and nearly that cold for the month before. The lake is frozen solid for at least two miles out from shore. Some of the ice fishermen have been driving cars out to their fishing huts."

"More balls than brains," said Eddie.

"They've been doing it for a hundred years around here."

"Not them," said Eddie. "You."

"What are you talking about?" Cat-head said. "If the guys in that cottage are watching for anybody, they're watching the road. They'll never expect us to come sneaking across the ice to come up behind them."

Eddie surveyed the seven men. Then he said, "Cat-head, I'd let it go for tonight. I'd think it all through one more time in daylight before I went out there."

Cat-head grinned. "You just know we're

318

going to collect on this, and you think if you undermine my confidence we'll let you join us. But then it would be the same money divided by nine instead of seven."

"Not interested in a ninth of anything," said Eddie. "I'm just giving you my best advice. If you go out there on the ice, you've got no place to fall back to if something goes wrong. There's nothing to hide behind. You'll die out there on the lake. What can it hurt to go get a night's sleep and start fresh? Maybe then you can make a sensible plan."

Cat-head said, "No. It happens tonight."

Eddie stood up. "Well then, good luck. I hope you get through this and collect." He turned and walked to the foyer. The boy tugged down his watch cap and zipped his parka, followed Eddie to the car, waited for him to unlock it, and got in. Eddie didn't drive in the direction the boy expected. Instead he headed toward the cottages along the lake.

"What are we doing?" the boy said.

"We're going to get the best seats for the show. They're going to walk across the ice. If we don't see that, we'll always wonder what it looked like."

The boy wasn't sure he would but said, "I guess so."

Eddie drove along the lake road, past the

cottage and the two other cars parked on the far side of it. He made the curves carefully to avoid sliding off the road into a snowbank. When they were a distance away, he slid to a full stop, turned, and drove his car into a pinewood lot where the exposed roots of old trees alternated with dry needles and the dusting of snow that had made it through the evergreen boughs above. The car bumped along, bouncing Eddie and the boy out of their seats toward the ceiling.

"A little rough," the boy said.

"That's good," Eddie said. "If it gets soft, it'll mean we're stuck." He turned off the headlights and drove by the dim glow that came from city lights reflecting off the clouds from Oswego and maybe even Syracuse.

When they reached a break in the trees, he stopped where they could look through the windshield and see the cottage. Eddie let the engine idle and kept the heater and the defroster fan running. "This will do," he said. "We should see fine from here."

He looked at his watch, couldn't see it, then held it close to the faint greenish glow of the dashboard. "Eleven forty-five. It won't be long."

Twenty minutes later Eddie and the boy saw the first dark figures walking carefully on the snow-dusted ice about three hundred feet from shore. The boy watched, counting them as they appeared, one through seven. They were carrying long guns. One of the men took a careless step and his feet flew up in front of him and he landed on his back. After a few seconds the man rolled onto his belly and then got on his hands and knees, crawled a few feet to pick up his rifle, and used it as a crutch as he stood unsteadily on the ice.

"Slippery," said Eddie.

"For a second I thought he got shot," the boy said.

"He will. Give them time."

The seven kept stepping along, moving each foot only a few inches at a time. Gradually the wind grew stronger and concentrated into gusts that rocked Eddie's car a little. The wind blew the snow up from the ice in what looked like clouds. The men turned their faces away from the onslaught, pulled their coats tighter across their throats, and tugged down their wool caps.

Finally the seven made it to the stretch of ice in front of the cottage. They arranged themselves in a row about fifteen feet apart. Then they lay prone on the ice to aim their rifles at the cottage.

The boy surveyed the scene. It was late

and there were no lights on in the cottage. It seemed likely that the Barzoni crew of enemies were asleep, not standing up in windows where they could be seen and shot.

As he watched, a switch was thrown somewhere inside the cottage, and the scene changed in that instant. A row of floodlights mounted along the eaves of the house all went on at once. Their beams lit up the ice so that it looked like an empty snow-covered parking lot. The glaring white headlights of the two cars parked along the side of the cottage flared on too, and the firing began.

The men on the ice were clearly visible, planted on the white frozen surface of the lake. The lights were blinding them. Behind them, their own dark shadows lay like pointers to show exactly where each of them was. All the men who were lit up on the ice could do was pour rifle fire into the lakeside wall of the cottage.

Their shots were punching holes in the wooden clapboards, and a couple of well-placed or lucky shots hit floodlight bulbs. The front ends of the two parked cars were hit many times, and eventually their headlights blinked out.

The defenders in the cottage were invisible except for the muzzle flash when one of them got his rifle sights lined up on one of the men on the ice. The muzzle flashes drew fire, but one by one the bullets found the men on the ice.

The boy counted four men lying prone on the ice who were not moving or firing, and then one more. Two others got to their feet with difficulty and tried to run, but their short, awkward footsteps took them only a few yards before a ferocious barrage cut them down. Then all the boy could hear was the wind blowing across the ice, covering the seven bodies with powdery flakes.

"Everything was just like you told Cat-head," the boy muttered.

"Yeah," said Eddie. "But what now?"

"What do you mean? It's over."

"Cat-head and his friends are dead, but Vic Barzoni is not dead. And there are still people who are willing to pay good money for him to get that way."

"Could we do it?"

"Well, they used their two cars well in that fight. Their brights blinded the ice boys and made them easy to see. But those two cars got popped a lot of times. The headlights, radiators, windshields, and at least one front tire all got hit. If we were to drive past the cottage and put a few rounds into the front of the car that's backed into the garage, they'd be stuck here or have to walk out."

"But they would have enough guns to turn our car into a pile of scrap."

"I'm not sure. Look at the ice now."

The seven corpses lay wherever they were when the bullets had found them. But now there were new figures on the ice. "What are they doing?"

"What I'd be doing is taking wallets, watches, and keys. They're going to want to know who attacked them, and to take a car or two from the lot by the hotel to get them out of here. But I've seen Barzoni, and I know his face. He's a big guy, about two sixty and tall. I don't see him out on the ice. Maybe he's afraid he'll fall through."

"So what do we do?"

"You take the wheel. Keep the lights off. Put the car in low gear and drive slowly and carefully toward the cottage. Try not to step on the brake pedal, because that will make the taillights go on. It's hard as hell to sneak up on anybody in a three-thousand-pound car, but the wind will help muffle the sound. We head for the garage. I'll try to mess up their car. If Barzoni is the one to come see what's up, we kill him. If not, we just keep going."

The boy reached for the door handle, but Eddie said, "Don't. It'll light up the dome light. Just climb into the backseat so I can slide to trade places. Then you climb forward over the driver's seat and take the wheel."

"Okay."

When they had traded seats, Eddie reached into the back seat and picked up the rifle and its two magazines he'd hidden under the floor mat. He loaded the rifle, put the second magazine in his breast pocket, and switched off the safety. The boy took one of his .45 pistols out of his coat and stuck it in his belt.

Eddie said, "Okay, let's go. Don't back up. Swing around so the backup lights don't go on."

The boy made a wide turn between trees and then found the shallow ruts that Eddie had made driving onto the lot. When he reached the edge of the road, he had to let the car coast and simply steer it between the snowdrifts. Even in the short time they'd been parked to watch the slaughter, the configuration of drifts and the depth of snow had changed, but he kept the car moving and got through.

The slow progress made it feel as though the trip along the lake road was taking forever, but his fears about who and how many would be at the cottage when they arrived made him want to make time stop.

When he swung around the last turn before the cottage, the boy could see the lights on the ice, and some of the crew of defenders struggling to keep their footing while dragging the corpses to shore. It had not occurred to him before that they would do that, but he supposed it would delay their discovery.

Three men were up on the road near the cottage, watching the others work. He knew that as soon as one of these men turned his head, he would see the car rolling toward them. They would produce guns and start shooting.

"There. The big one," Eddie said. "That's Barzoni." He opened his window, leaned to the side, and stuck out his rifle.

The three men turned in unison. They reached into their heavy coats to free pistols from belts and pockets.

Eddie shot the big man, who fell backward. He fired at the others and clearly missed, because they ran to hide on the lake side behind the cottage. The boy stopped the car next to the open garage, and Eddie fired about ten rounds rapidly into the radiator, windshield, and front tires, and then swung the rifle forward again. He ejected the magazine and clicked the spare into place.

The boy began to move ahead, but Eddie said, "Stop."

He braked but slid a couple of feet, and Eddie got out. He went to the corner of the cottage and stepped one pace past it. Eddie fired another rapid series of shots in that direction. The boy saw Eddie kneel by the big man's body, reach into his pocket, and fiddle with the man's hand before running back to the car.

The boy shifted into drive and accelerated gradually, trying to keep the car from fishtailing. He was aware of when he passed the hotel where they had spent the evening, but he was looking straight ahead. He just kept on the road, adding every bit of speed he dared. "What were you doing back there?"

"Taking his ring."

"What for?"

"So I could give it to Bobby Moscato to collect our money. Be sure to watch for the blind curve up there about a mile. By now it must be smooth as a mirror."

Eddie was wrapping something in his handkerchief while the boy drove, and the boy didn't need to see it to know what it was. After he thought about it for a few seconds, he conceded it had been the thing to do. That thickening at the knuckle was easy for a butcher to find in the dark.

29

Eddie died alone. It was six months later, the next summer. Eddie had received a couple of phone calls that week from a man named Pirizelli who wanted to arrange a hit. The boy had been working with Eddie for about five years by then, but Eddie still did certain jobs alone. There were times and places where it was easiest for one man to get in and out. Eddie was good at working alone, and sometimes the boy wondered if Eddie just asked him to come along to give him experience.

That night one man was not enough. Afterward the boy knew that he had no right to be surprised. Nobody who made a living discharging firearms into the bodies of other men could be ignorant of the damage bullets caused, or how easy it was to hit an opponent who wasn't expecting to be a target. He was even aware that reacting by hunting down the ones who had killed Eddie would be an empty gesture, but he occupied himself with plans to accomplish it because it made him feel less alone and helpless.

He knew that Eddie wouldn't have wanted him to avenge his death. He would have said he had spent too much time and effort teaching the boy about the world to have it all bleed out of him now. Eddie was a mercenary, and mercenaries knew revenge was for the deluded. There was no such thing as getting even for being dead.

The boy arranged a funeral. Eddie's religion had not been part of his adult life. The boy guessed he had probably been raised Catholic, so he lied to the parish priest and said he was, then had the priest do the service. The event drew a healthy crowd, partly because Eddie had been a familiar and popular figure in the neighborhood, and partly because his death was surprising and notorious. The boy heard a number of people marveling that such a nice, ordinary guy should end up dying of gunshot wounds on a simple weekend trip to New York. The boy also noticed that several — and maybe all — of Eddie's special home-delivery customers attended.

A few days after the funeral, the boy sat in the office of the butcher shop and called numbers that Eddie had written down on the strip of white butcher paper he always had taped to his desk for messages and orders. Only a few had area codes, and some of them the boy recognized. There was a 212 number that had a time of day written beside it: 10:15 p.m., after Eddie's shop was closed. The boy waited until that time of the evening and called the number. After a couple of rings, a woman answered. "Hello?" He recognized a New York accent.

He said, "Hello. Is this Nora?" He didn't know where that name came from.

"No. This is a phone booth. I was just walking past. I don't see anybody near here that could be a Nora. Sorry."

"Wait. Don't hang up yet. Can you tell me where the booth is?"

"Twenty-fourth and Lexington."

"Thank you," he said. "You're a good person and I'm glad you answered." He had already put the "Closed" sign in the window of the shop the day he'd learned of Eddie's death. Now he put tape around it and over the clock face so it was permanent. He packed and got into Eddie's car to drive to New York City. He checked into a hotel and left Eddie's car parked in its underground lot. He took a cab to Twenty-Fourth and Lexington and found the phone booth.

It was outside a large office building that

held a few shops and two restaurants at street level. He walked, coming back to that corner now and then to see whether anyone was using the phone. Most of the time nobody was. Only once did he see anyone in the booth, a girl about his own age whose talk was animated, her happy face breaking into sincere laughter now and then. After a few minutes a young man who appeared to be her boyfriend stopped and waved through the window. She hung up the phone, came out of the booth, and put her arm through his as they walked away.

He spent hours floating around the neighborhood like a ghost, watching everything, seeing so much that he had no way to decipher or even remember for long. He made sure to be in sight of the booth at 10:00 p.m. Soon he saw a man about fifty years old, wearing a golf shirt and a windbreaker with pants that looked like they came from a suit. He walked along Lexington at a quick, businesslike pace, the soft fabric of the pants flapping a little as he went. He sidestepped into the phone booth, looked at his watch, and then slid the door shut. The boy noted that it was now 10:15 p.m. The man took a small spiral pad and a pen from his jacket, dialed the phone, put money in, and talked. He wrote some things while he was talking and after he'd hung up. He made four calls and then left.

The boy followed him, staying on the other side of the street and a hundred feet behind. Only a couple of blocks down the street and around the corner, the man went into a door on the side of a building. The boy walked past it. Above the door was an inscription that looked like the engraving on a tombstone, reading "Napolitano Social Club, est. 1921."

The boy left and then came back about an hour later. This time four men were outside the building, two older men smoking cigars and two younger companions hanging around to listen to their conversation. It was a calm night, and he could tell why they'd come outside. The smell of the cigars was still pungent and strong more than two hundred feet away. He watched them for a while, picked up a few words and phrases, but couldn't assemble the words into a topic, let alone a conversation. Occasionally others would come outside to smoke or would arrive from the street. There were men from twenty years old to about eighty, but he saw no women. What he'd seen was enough.

Pirizelli was probably a false name, but the club was real enough. These were likely to be people who still held a grudge over the Opening Day shootings or wanted to collect for them, but that didn't matter to him. What mattered was that the phone booth was just over a block from their club, and somebody had used the phone to get Eddie to New York to kill him.

He went back to his hotel, walked down the ramp to the underground garage where he'd parked Eddie's car, and selected his equipment.

Eddie and Don Sarkassian had taught him to break down, clean, and reassemble most common weapons in the dark. He put on surgical gloves, partially assembled the AR-15 rifle he had brought from Eddie's house into four pieces — the upper and lower receivers, buttstock, and barrel assembly. He had Eddie's razor-sharp folding knife and both of his .45 pistols with spare magazines in case he needed to discard the rifle. He also brought a device he had made for an earlier job. It consisted of about twenty feet of hundred-pound-test fishing line with a lead sinker firmly tied on each end. He put them all in a backpack.

He took a cab to Lexington and walked to the place he had chosen on his earlier visit, a fire escape a half block away from the Napolitano Social Club. The fire escape consisted of a flat platform at each floor level and beside it a window from the end of that floor's hallway. So the fire escape couldn't be used to enter the building, the fire escape ladder extended from the second floor down to about twelve feet from the ground. It was attached to a counterweight, so if a person on the second floor stepped on the nearest rung, the person's weight would make the ladder slide downward almost to the ground, but not quickly enough to cause injuries.

The boy stepped below the end of the raised ladder, took out his coiled fishing line, and tossed the sinker up twelve feet and over the bottom rung. Then he let out enough weighted fishing line so that he could reach both ends of the line. He wrapped them around his sleeve, gripped them tightly, and pulled the ladder down to the ground. He stepped onto the ladder, freed his fishing line from the bottom rung, and put it in his coat pocket. He climbed the ladder up to the second-floor level.

The second-floor level of the fire escape was an iron grating about twenty feet above-ground. He assembled the four pieces of his rifle, loaded it, sat on the fire escape, and sighted the rifle on the front door of the Napolitano Social Club. His own position was above the street lamps and the light that spilled from ground-floor windows onto the sidewalks, and was in the shadow of the building's wall.

At around midnight, a group of five men came out of the Napolitano Social Club. One of them lit a cigar, then gave one to another man and lit it with the high yellow flame of a Zippo lighter. Soon they were in the middle of a heated discussion, puffing and gesturing with their cigars as they talked. One by one, the three younger men left, but the two older men stayed.

The boy chose one of the two older men. He was wearing a good gray suit with a silk tie and a matching pocket square, while the other man had a dark blue jacket that looked like the kind baseball pitchers put on when their team was at bat. The boy watched until the man in the suit made a gesture with both arms wide, so he could easily see where his heart was, then squeezed the trigger. The round made a loud pop, and the man fell dead. The second man was dumbstruck, looking around in all directions. It occurred to the boy that he would gain time if the man didn't run back inside to raise the alarm. He aimed at the door, and when the man reached for the knob, he shot him through the back of the head.

The boy stepped on the fire escape, rode the ladder down, dropped the last couple of feet, and then walked swiftly around the first corner into an alcove at the entrance to a dark building. He knelt there long enough to divide the rifle into four pieces again and put them into his backpack. Then he ran to the end of the block and came out on Lexington. He went to the 23rd Street subway station and descended the steps. It took only a few minutes before the first train appeared, and he took it.

Then he drove Eddie's car to Philadelphia and checked into a hotel. He bought the New York newspapers the next afternoon. The papers were full of photographs and descriptions of the victims, the scene of the crime, and gang assassinations of the past. He noticed that many people in New York had begun to think of LCN as faintly antiquated, dying out, and unrelated to honest people's lives, even though everything in New York — from the cost of a dinner to where the napkins came from to who picked up the garbage afterward — was determined by agreements among five bosses. What people knew or didn't wasn't his problem. He was just looking for obituaries.

The obituaries were delayed, probably because the bodies were part of the evidence against the killer and were at the medical examiner's, so the decisions about the wakes and the funerals were held up. Then, after about a week, the two obituaries appeared in the same edition. The two older men had been cousins, both named Tronzoni. The viewings would be held for two days in the Florellio Funeral Home, and then the bodies would be buried at Saint John's Cemetery, 80-01 Metropolitan Avenue, Middle Village, in Queens.

He looked at city maps, drove to the cemetery and looked around, and then drove back to his hotel in Philadelphia. On the night before the funerals, he left Eddie's car in the underground lot and packed his weapons in his backpack. He took a cab to the train station and then rode the train to New York. When night came, he took a couple of buses and got off near the Florellio Funeral Home.

He visited the funeral home long after it had closed. There were a dozen hearses and even more black limousines parked inside a high fence with four strands of barbed wire along the top. He could see that there was a coiled hose with a high-pressure nozzle for washing hearses and limousines, and a carport to provide shade for waxing and detailing them. Twenty feet farther along the building was a large steel door, and across from it was a second steel door to the big garage.

He walked around the garage. There were no windows, and the front had a large metal door. He saw that on one side was an air-conditioning unit mounted on a concrete pad. He stepped closer to hear if it was running, and it was. The way in and out of the yard where the hearses were parked was through the back garage door, out the front garage door, and down the driveway.

He went over to look at the big metal garage door. A bolt with a hasp and a padlock anchored the door to the building. The boy looked closely at the padlock. It was a popular brand in a very common size. He knew that on Eddie's key ring were a few bump keys for getting into houses, but also at least a couple of filed-down padlock keys. He looked and listened for a couple of minutes before testing the key on Eddie's ring that looked closest to the right size. He turned it just until he felt resistance, then pushed it a little farther, tugged the lock tight, and turned it. The lock opened.

He removed the lock, withdrew the bolt, opened the garage door, stepped in, and saw the sets of car keys hanging on a board with hooks. There were even keys for the padlock on the second garage door. He went out, looked in the back of the first hearse, saw there was no coffin inside, looked at the license plate, and took a set of keys with a tag that matched the license plate. He drove the hearse into the garage, loaded a couple of rolls of fake grass and some folding chairs into the back, stopped to pull the doors back down, and drove off.

When he arrived the next morning at the cemetery, workmen were riding lawn mowers up and down the long rows of bronze plaques, while others sat along the sides of a stake truck with shovels. There were a couple of power shovels for digging graves.

He drove his stolen hearse to the kiosk at the entrance, where the guard leaned out and said, "Can I help you?"

"The boy said, "Yes, please. Where is the Tronzoni service going to be?"

"You from Floriello's?"

The boy said, "Yes. I'm new."

"I thought I recognized the hearse." The guard looked in and saw the rolls of grass and chairs, then reached into the kiosk and handed him a printed map of the big cemetery. He took out a pen and put an X on a gravesite.

"Thanks." It took the boy a short time to find the section where the two men would be buried. He scanned the area and found a good spot to park the hearse, on a curve up a slight rise a few hundred feet away, near a freshly covered grave.

He watched from a distance as the cemetery employees made preparations for the funeral. The two graves had been dug sometime before he'd arrived, a blue tent roof had been put up to shade the mourners, and about a hundred small white folding chairs had been opened and arranged in ranks.

The boy got into the hearse and pulled it forward around a bend so that it was facing away from the site of the two-man funeral of the Tronzoni cousins. He left it idling and turned the air-conditioning up. Then he climbed over the seat into the back bay, where a coffin would normally be carried, and reassembled the AR-15 rifle he had used to kill the two men. He lay it flat beside him and set out the stack of loaded twenty-round magazines where he could reach them with his left hand.

He watched four policemen on motorcycles pull up the gently rising road that led from the kiosk, followed by two black hearses. Next came six black limousines, and then a long procession snaking up the hill composed of at least a hundred cars full of mourners. The boy could tell that more people had come than the family had prepared for. That seemed good to him, because it would add to the confusion when the time came.

He watched the cops dismount from their motorcycles to direct traffic on foot, getting the long line of cars pulled over along the shoulders of both sides of the road and waving the next ones on to the next hundred-yard stretch. When all the cars had parked and begun to empty men in suits, women in spike heels that would sink deep into the soft grass, and bored, cranky children onto the road, the cops remounted their motorcycles and puttered down the hill, out the gate, and into the regular traffic, probably to escort the next funeral procession to the cemetery.

The pallbearers gathered near the backs of the two hearses. They stood around, most of them looking solemnly down at their shoes with their hands clasped behind their backs, or looking at each other side-eyed.

The boy knew the sight to watch was the pair of hearses, and the man to watch wasn't the priest. It was the funeral director. He made his way to the first hearse, opened the rear door, reached in, and slid the coffin back on rollers while the two sets of wheels swung down to the ground to lock.

The eight pallbearers arranged themselves on both sides of the coffin.

The boy slid the first magazine into the rifle until it clicked, pulled the charging handle of the rifle, set the safety lever to Semi, and aimed. He put his eye to the scope and settled the crosshairs on the pallbearer nearest to the front.

The second team of pallbearers waited at the back of the second hearse. Apparently, they planned to carry both caskets to the graves in a procession. As he watched, he saw that female relatives were beginning to react to the sight of the caskets coming out of the hearses. Handkerchiefs appeared from purses and dabbed at eyes, a couple of women dressed in black hunched over and shook as they sobbed. The boy stared through the rifle scope at other faces.

The two caskets were lifted off the gurneys onto the shoulders of the pallbearers, who began to move toward the grassy slope and the graves. The boy rested his rifle on the door of the hearse and placed the crosshairs on the head of the first man on the near side, blew the air out of his lungs to get rid of the carbon dioxide, and fired. The man collapsed, and the boy moved his aim back along the line of pallbearers, firing three more rapid shots.

The pallbearers on the far side of the casket had no way to hold up the heavy object. The casket fell so quickly that it looked as though they'd thrown it down on the grass. They had seen the blood from their companions in the air, and the red mist had sprayed most of them. They all turned and ran toward the crowd near the graves, trying to slip in among them.

The boy moved his aim to the second casket, but the second set of pallbearers dropped the casket on the ground and joined the others running into the crowd. Some of the mourners at the edges ran too, and others were knocked down. The priest dissolved into the immediate family and knelt to hide behind a large woman in a black dress.

The boy knew he had little time, but he looked for one more target. An old man in a black suit stood still, and people were converging on him as if to ask him what to do. The boy aimed, fired, and watched the old man collapse, then scrambled forward over the driver's seat, threw the hearse into drive, and headed up the hillside to merge onto the cemetery road.

He drove fast, but not fast enough to risk losing control of the long vehicle. He drove straight to the next exit from the big cemetery, at Woodhaven Boulevard. He could see the gate was closed and chained, but he pulled up to it and parked the hearse beside it. He took the rifle apart and slipped the pieces into the backpack he'd brought, stowed the loaded magazines with them, climbed onto the hearse's roof, went over the gate, and began to walk.

When he came to a bus stop two hundred yards on, there were a half-dozen people waiting. He waited with them and took the bus a few miles into Brooklyn. Then he took a cab into Manhattan. By nightfall he was driving Eddie's car on the Pennsylvania Turnpike heading for Pittsburgh.

The boy knew what he needed to do next. He put the house and Eddie's butcher shop up for sale with a local realtor named Foster who used to buy meat from Eddie. Foster's wife, Karen, had been one of Eddie's special home-delivery customers. She had cried at his funeral in spite of the fact that her account had gone inactive when the boy was about twelve.

Mr. Foster told the boy that the house was valuable and would sell quickly, but warned him that it would be hard to find a buyer for the butcher shop, with its huge refrigerator room, or its expensive equipment — Eddie's industrial-level meat slicers, his bone saws, and the overhead track for hanging sides of beef.

If the boy wanted a job in the trade Eddie had taught him, he would likely have to go to work as a meat cutter at the A&P. In spite of his skepticism, Mr. Foster arranged a sale at the shop, and was pleased and surprised when many of the expensive items did attract buyers, including the manager of the A&P.

The boy was already feeling rich before the sales. He had followed Eddie's instructions about thawing the freezers before he left for New York and had found about forty brick-shaped ice-covered packages at the bottoms of the two freezers. All of them were tightly wrapped packets of hundred-dollar bills.

There were also another group of items he'd had to move quietly at night. Eddie had about twenty firearms of different calibers and configurations, all of them with supplies of ammunition. The boy kept only a few of the most practical ones. He also kept knives — a Ka-Bar marine fighting knife with a black blade, a six-inch switchblade, a high-quality lock-blade folding knife — and an artisan-made strangling cord with polished wood handles that were exceptionally comfortable to hold.

The day the boy drove Eddie's car away from the house, the Mafia War was over for him. After a few months came a peace that was not imposed or negotiated. The war died of fatigue. Later, some people identified the last, most convincing proof of its pointless cost as the killing of the Tronzoni cousins, done so that the rest of the family would be brought together in the open cemetery where they could be shot down too. During the 1980s, there was another set of killings that reporters called the "Second Mafia War." But Schaeffer and many other people who had carried guns for a living in the 1960s knew that the name didn't make sense. The second war had happened over ten years earlier.

30

Andrew Wain Herren had stayed at the dinner party later than he usually would have, given the array of friends and colleagues that he'd been glad to see. He had escorted Camilla Sealey, the widow of a former governor of Virginia. Austin Sealey had married Camilla because she was an heiress who held vast tracts of land in Tennessee and Kentucky, had gone to the right schools, and knew how to host and carry on fluent but unquotable conversation with anyone at any time. These qualifications were essential for a politician's wife, which was what her mother and grandmother had been too. Governor Sealey had died young enough not to be a burden to his wife's social ambitions.

For events like tonight's, Herren would occasionally invite her as his guest. She was still beautiful in exactly the right middle-age patrician way, enjoyed any event where she could wear her jewelry and fashionable clothes, and expected little actual attention from him during the evening. They both conversed with the people seated to their right and left at the table, and when they were moving around, she placed her hand on his arm but spoke to everyone but him.

Camilla probably thought she was his beard, but she was wrong. She probably suspected he had realized he was gay late in life, but he had not. He was a straight older man whose sexual interest in women was unchanged. He loved the same kind of women he'd loved when he was twenty-five and they were too. The ones he loved were still twenty-five, only he wasn't. These relationships had become increasingly difficult and complex, not only because the current young women had to be paid, but also because his clients, colleagues, and the world expected him to behave like the statue of a great lawyer and statesman.

Tonight he'd had a few conversations that had required him to skirt topics and listen carefully to questions. Most of the questions had been about the Carlo Balacontano matter. His old law-school classmate Calvin Rialto, now a justice on the Ninth Circuit Court of Appeals, came out and said it: "Why are you working on the Balacontano thing? You never took on that kind of client. Are you planning to buy a yacht or a country estate?"

Herren shrugged. "It's a case that somebody needs to take. It's a murder conviction that people should have looked at more closely thirty years ago. The federal court took the lazy way. The defendant was bad, so they got careless about what they used to put him away."

"Is that any different from Al Capone's case?"

"Yes," said Herren. "It was too hard to prove Capone had committed any of his violent crimes, but they could convict him of tax evasion. They gave him such a long sentence that time would execute him. We've heard a million times how clever that was. Maybe it was. At least he was guilty of the tax evasion."

"And Balacontano is innocent?"

"Carlo Balacontano is a different story. He was a crime boss too — a racketeer, certainly a tax evader, and probably a murderer. But he wasn't guilty of the particular murder he was charged with. The average person hears that and says, 'So what?' "

Rialto nodded. "And of course there's plenty wrong with that."

"There is. We — our profession — have

gotten too good at the machinery of the law without clinging tightly enough to the purpose of the law. Thirty years ago a federal court convicted Carlo Balacontano of being a bad man. He was certainly guilty of that. He just didn't happen to kill Arthur Fieldston."

"And what are you doing? What's your strategy? Are you trying to get him a new trial?"

"He was convicted so long ago, he's about to have a federal parole hearing. To start with, I'm going to help him at the hearing. After that, we'll see."

"I wish you luck, Andrew. It's always right to correct the system when it gets sloppy. Even if nobody else ever thanks you, I will."

Herren and Camilla Sealey left the party almost two hours after that conversation. His driver took Camillla home, and then Herren. The doorman opened the big glass door with a remote control before Herren could reach it, and then closed it as soon as he was in. Then he pressed the button to summon the private elevator that went to the upper floors, where Herren's New York apartment was. "Thanks, Ray," Herren said. The elevator doors closed and the elevator rose, moving faster until it had nearly reached the twenty-third floor, decelerated, and stopped at Herren's private hallway.

He stepped out of the elevator into his foyer, walked to his door, and opened it with a key. Much of the time he left the apartment door unlocked. But a few weeks ago the maid and the cook asked him not to. They had read an article in the *New York Times* that mentioned he was representing the boss of one of the five New York crime families, and once a lawyer dealt with clients like that, he just might get a visit from other people from that world.

He locked his door again and pressed a button on the console by the door to turn on the pattern of lights for late evening. It was lighting his decorator had designed for romantic encounters, but it was also good for times like these, when it was late and he was simply going to go to sleep.

He went to the kitchen to get a chilled bottle of water from the refrigerator and then entered his master suite.

He stood paralyzed in the doorway with a glass in one hand and the bottle of water in the other. The man sitting on the couch in his suite didn't look like a burglar or anything like that. He looked like the sort of man he might have seen in the locker room of his club after a round of golf — late middle age, well dressed. "Hello?" Herren said.

The man said, "Relax, Mr. Herren. If you don't do anything suicidal, we can talk, and then I'll leave. I've read that you're Carlo Balacontano's lawyer. Is that right?"

"Yes," said Herren. He set the glass and the bottle on the bureau beside him and then instantly regretted it. If this man was another gangster or a madman, he could have thrown them at him and made a dash for the elevator or stairwell. Not now.

"How much is Balacontano paying you?" the man asked.

"Nothing."

"Nothing?"

"Most of the time in a parole hearing, the prisoner isn't represented by a lawyer. His guilt isn't in doubt, legally. I'm only advising him, so I'm doing it pro bono." He took a breath. "I think I've said enough. Your turn. Are you going to tell me your name?"

"No."

"Are you here to intimidate me?"

"I don't do that."

"Then what?" asked Herren. "What is your profession?"

"I'm retired."

"From what?"

"Killing people."

353

"For money?"

"Yes. Usually because the customers were afraid of somebody."

"Weren't you afraid of them too?"

"No."

"Why not?"

"Because it's not a duel, challenging somebody to a fight to the death. It's more like a hunt. I'm the wolf. They were all deer. No matter how things go, the deer doesn't get to eat the wolf."

"Why should I believe you about any of this?"

"You can or not. If you don't, just don't make me prove it."

The man opened his coat and took out the loaded pistol that Herren kept in the built-in compartment of his bed's headboard. He held it up and then put it back.

Herren's knees felt weak. He tried to look casual as he raised his left arm to rest his elbow on the bureau and keep himself from toppling over. He said, "How did you get into my apartment?"

"It doesn't matter. There are tricks and bits of knowledge about how things work that people like me rely on. But mostly I observe other people coming and going."

Herren's hands were shaking, so he put them in his pockets and concentrated on controlling his voice. "Before we get any further, I think it's important that you know something. Killing me will make no difference. Whatever is going to happen will happen whether I'm advising him or one of twenty other attorneys from my firm is. He should get out because he's served the minimum sentence he was given in 1982, and is now, under the statute in effect at the time, entitled to parole because he hasn't gotten any other infractions on his record during his time in prison and meets the other criteria."

"Do you think he will?"

"No. In public I've been bluffing, acting as though he will, but he won't."

"If you can't win, why are you involved?"

"For one thing, I'm making it clear to the authorities that someone is watching them to be sure they follow the rules."

"What rules?"

"No misplaced paperwork. No charging him with mysterious new capital crimes on evidence that they've had forever but didn't notice until now. That kind of thing."

"You know he's a really bad man, right?"

"Yes. But the integrity of the system is more important than he is. If we preserve that, including correcting the system when it fails, it will protect people after we're long

355

gone. I'm playing the long game. I'm building public discussion about the fact that he was wrongfully convicted. I want him to get a new trial. For the system to work, he needs to be either convicted of something he actually did or be set free."

"All right," said the man. "I'm going to tell you some things that may help you, and I'm going to let you record my voice. One warning though. If a picture of me ever surfaces after this conversation, it won't matter what high-minded motives you had. You'll be dead within a week. Do you understand?"

"Yes."

"Then get your recorder ready."

An hour and a half later, the man who had been waiting for Andrew Wain Herren in his twenty-third-floor apartment appeared at the reception desk in the foyer. "Hey, Ray," he said. "Miss Zoellner said to give you this." He handed the man at the desk a hundred-dollar bill.

"Thank you, sir."

"Don't thank me. It's from her for making sure she didn't miss her old uncle's visit. Have a good night."

"You too, sir."

He walked out of the building and down

the street, and then the night enveloped
him.

the street and then the right approached
him.

31

Elizabeth Waring was in her office reading
the reports of agents in the field. "The three
victims have been identified as Richard Pellagria, age 37, Michael Gonno, age 29,
known associates of the Balacontano crime
family, and Daniel Scarpi, age 30, a member
of the Scarpi crime family. At approximately
10:00 a.m. on July 30 Pellagria and Gonno
appear to have been making collections at
businesses in Queens, when they were
ambushed in Monty's One-Day Dry Cleaners. Scarpi, who is believed to have been
one of the men at the ambush, was killed
that evening in an apparent retaliation." She
looked away from her computer and rubbed
her eyes.

The fighting between the Balacontano and
the Scarpi families in New York was heating
up. The two reigning bosses were now dead,
as were an increasing number of the younger
men. There were going to be a lot of funer-

als before the fighting stopped.

It occurred to Elizabeth that this morning she was doing exactly what she had been doing in the basement of this building the year she'd graduated from college. She had been trying to keep track of the men on the list of bosses, and in every moment when she wasn't doing that, she was scanning the descriptions of deaths all over the country to find homicides that might have been the work of La Cosa Nostra members. She was still checking deaths, only now she did it in the corner office of the fourth floor.

The reports she evaluated were about the same — casualties of the squabbles between groups of greedy, violent men. Now the reports often included photographs or maps or diagrams, but other than technology, nothing much had changed. Crime bosses were usually older men. They were migratory, trying to be warm in the winter and cool in the summer, but they seldom left their own territories for long periods at a time, because they needed to keep an eye on business. They often traveled with women, some with their wives, and others with girls young enough to be their granddaughters.

The man she had been most concerned about lately, the one who had turned up again after seven years away, was not mentioned in any of the reports. He was not a member of LCN and had no business with them anymore. She was almost certain that the week's most notable activities had been his doing. He had every reason to want the Balacontano family weakened and without its acting boss and a few soldiers. Their main concern over the past couple of months had been finding and killing him. Now, at least for the moment, it wasn't.

If Balacontano had a chance of being released on parole, it would be good for everyone in the world of crime if his family was weakened in advance. Maybe the Scarpi family had figured that out too and acted on it. But over the years of her long career, she had developed a sense of how things happened. One thing she was sure of was that the solitary killer who used to be called the Butcher's Boy would not sit still and let somebody else solve his problem.

Her telephone rang, and she picked it up. "Waring."

It was her assistant. "Your car is ready to take you to the airport, Ms. Waring."

"Thanks." She got up, grabbed her travel bag, and headed out the door. She would be in New York in less than an hour, and at the Metropolitan Correctional Center in another hour.

She thought about Balacontano's parole hearing. Its exact time and place hadn't been announced to the public. She would be flying up with Bill and John, making a three-person delegation from Organized Crime. Usually the hearing was simply a review of the prisoner's post-conviction record, the details of his original crime, and listening to the statements of the victims of his crimes. That was a one-day job.

She met John and Bill at the airport in the waiting area for their departure gate. She could see they were anxious, standing a distance from the other travelers and whispering. She said, "Hello, gentlemen. What's up?"

"A new development," John said. "Andrew Wain Herren has submitted a request to provide additional evidence to the hearing officer. We were asked if we object, and the deputy assistant decided that we would not object. Herren swore that it came to his attention in the past twenty-four hours and that he believed that it had a bearing on the eventual decision."

Elizabeth sighed. "Why does this sound like we just got forced into playing somebody else's game?"

"I think that's a good description of

what's going on. He's been hinting for some time that he was going to try to get Bala's conviction thrown out after he was paroled. I thought it was a bluff, because I couldn't see how he could get a mob boss paroled or get a new trial for a man whose appeals are exhausted. I think we're being played by Andrew Wain Herren."

"Or somebody."

"What?"

"All lawyers lie," she said. "But all lies don't come from lawyers."

"I'll ignore the insult for now. But what are you talking about?"

"For the moment, I believe that Herren wouldn't manufacture evidence to set a man like Carl Bala free."

"How do you get to that conclusion?" Bill asked.

"I've never believed that Carl Bala killed Arthur Fieldston and buried his body parts on his own farm. He had no reason to do the killing, let alone to have the head and hands brought across the country just so he could hide them in the most incriminating place. Since he's innocent, there could easily be evidence of it that has come to Herren's attention."

"Like what?"

"Maybe somebody saw the real killer do

362

it, or cut up the body, or move it, or bury it."

"Why would they come forward now?"

"Who knows? Maybe a lab ran a DNA swab on something in the house where Fieldston was killed and it matches somebody. If Herren genuinely thinks it's enough, he's probably right."

"You believe the truth will always find its way into the sunlight?" said Bill.

"No," she said. "I'm not even naive enough to think that you and I will ever know what this new evidence is. This isn't a trial — it's barely an interview. It doesn't have to stand up in court or be shared with anybody. All it has to do is sway the hearing officer and possibly one of his bosses on the Federal Parole Commission."

Their flight left on time and landed at La Guardia ahead of schedule. The Justice Department in New York had an FBI man waiting to drive them to the Metropolitan prison, so they were in the hearing room twenty-five minutes ahead of schedule.

A few minutes later, the principal people came in. The hearing officer was a man named Donald O'Hara, a federal official who had been with the Bureau of Prisons for about as long as Elizabeth had been in Organized Crime. He had a thick briefcase she imagined must be full of files. Balacontano had been in prison for a long time and had been moved from prison to prison, prompting records to be added at each facility.

Then a court reporter came in and set up her transcription machine. There were a few other people whom Waring couldn't identify. Maybe they were relatives of victims who planned to speak or merely observe. They could be federal officers who were, like her, professionally interested in the fate of this prisoner.

Hearing Officer O'Hara took out a pile of file folders, a yellow legal pad and pen, and a single folder with several typed sheets clipped to it. He looked down, as though rereading the sheets to prepare.

Elizabeth and the others watched and waited, and finally the inmate, Carlo Balacontano, was escorted into the room by two guards who looked like the ones Elizabeth had seen the night she had come to the prison. Ten steps behind him, she recognized the lawyer Andrew Wain Herren from photographs of him she had found online. He was a tall, handsome man who looked about sixty. He wore a perfectly tailored gray suit, a luminous white shirt, and a navy-blue tie with a subdued pattern of tiny squares. He had a thin folder that wouldn't hold many sheets, and a tape recorder about five by eight inches in size. The machine was the only part of the scene that she had not expected, and she couldn't take her eyes off it.

O'Hara called the room to order in a calm, quiet voice. As soon as it was silent, he identified himself, and the court stenographer began to type. He announced that this was the first parole hearing for federal inmate 95762, Carlo Antonio Balacontano, and rattled off a long case number that Elizabeth didn't listen to. She was staring at the tape recorder that Herren had placed beside his left hand, away from Balacontano. What was that for? Why was it an audio recorder, and not a video ? Even if whatever it contained had been from 1982, there had been video cameras available for years. Depositions had been videotaped even then. Was it a copy of a telephone wiretap recording? But the FBI used a big reel-to-reel recorder, not a portable cassette.

The hearing began. O'Hara asked for the people who were relatives of Balacontano's victim, Arthur Fieldston, to speak. Nobody spoke. He then went through his notes, summarizing Balacontano's record. He had been convicted on July 5, 1982, sentenced

365

immediately afterward, and had begun serving his sentence. He had not been charged with any crimes committed in prison, had not been disciplined for serious infractions, had a satisfactory work record, and had participated in educational and rehabilitative activities.

He asked Balacontano a few questions. Since he was over the normal retirement age, he could not be held to the requirement that he have gainful employment. But how did he plan to support himself?

Balacontano said, "I've been offered a consulting position with the Trans-Matic Supply Corporation. The corporation is located in my old neighborhood, and I worked there as a young man."

Elizabeth Waring looked down at her hands in her lap. Balacontano had owned the company for about fifty years, and had carried his own name on the payroll in those days to give himself an excuse for having money.

The rest of the hearing went according to the usual procedures. One by one, O'Hara asked him about each of the requirements for parole. Did he have a stable address? Balacontano said that his attorney's office had rented an apartment for him. Herren nodded and handed a sheet — presumably the receipt for a lease deposit — to the hearing officer.

After about an hour, O'Hara said, "I've reviewed all the records and read the submissions from Mr. Balacontano's attorney and the Justice Department's attorneys. All the information, as well as my recommendation, will be submitted to the parole commissioner tomorrow. This hearing is adjourned."

Elizabeth was on her feet before O'Hara, Balacontano, or Herren. She walked from the seats to the table and intercepted Herren. "Hello, Mr. Herren," she said. She showed him her identification. "I'm Elizabeth Waring from the Organized Crime Section of the Justice Department. I wonder if I could speak with you for a minute."

He looked at her, appeared to be about to refuse and walk away from her, but then seemed to be swayed by her identification and by the fact that her size, sex, and age made her unthreatening. "It's kind of irregular. You could reach me at my office," he looked at his watch. "But I've got a minute now."

O'Hara and the small crowd in the room had gone out one door, and Balacontano and his guards out the other, so they were alone.

Elizabeth said, "I couldn't help noticing your tape recorder. It wasn't turning during the hearing, so you weren't recording. You didn't use it to play a tape during the hearing. You played it for the hearing officer before you came in, didn't you?"

"I'm sorry. I can't —"

"I don't need to hear any of the words. I just need to hear the voice for two or three seconds to be sure."

"I'm sorry," he said.

Elizabeth said, "When he was young, they used to call him the Butcher's Boy. He is the most dangerous professional killer I ever saw, and I've been in the Organized Crime Section for over thirty years. Just let me hear the voice, and I'll leave you alone."

"I'm afraid I can't help you."

"If he made that tape to help you get Balacontano paroled, he plans to kill him. If you've seen his face, he may kill you too."

Herren stared at her for a moment. "Thank you for the warning." He turned and walked out the exit where his client had been taken.

Elizabeth took out her phone and called her colleague John. "It's Elizabeth. I'm positive he's getting out. We've got to be sure that we've got agents sitting in cars with their motors running before he steps out the door. Call the warden and ask for advance warning of his release. Call the New York FBI office to say we'll need him under surveillance. We need to have things set before we leave the city today."

John said, "Why the red alert?"

"If we don't protect him, he'll be dead."

"He's got hundreds of people to keep anybody from getting near him. He's safer than we are."

"Just do it," she said. "When we're home, we'll see if we can get WITSEC involved. Maybe Bala can be relocated and given a new identity."

"Balacontano isn't a witness."

"If we keep him alive, he might be."

Twenty-one days later, the Notice of Action for the parole hearing in the case of Carlo Balacontano was issued to the inmate. The time it took was about average, and the other concerned parties received the same information. Carlo Balacontano was granted parole. FBI agents were assigned to observe his release and to begin surveillance.

32

Michael Schaeffer drove his car up Route 9, the highway overlooking the Hudson River. Once he had passed the first few miles, the land leveled out, and dozens of small towns were laid out on flats that looked only inches above the wide, slow river. He passed places that seemed to have come from his childhood — parks with old bandstands, grassy expanses with wooden picnic tables and boat launches, baseball diamonds of Little League dimensions, and one full-size field near a high school.

The life he and Eddie the Butcher had lived in Pittsburgh didn't include much time for those things, but their secret work did. They drove through hundreds of little towns just like these, often staying at rustic motels.

Eddie liked these places. He said it was because he could watch everything that needed to be watched, and that was true. He liked the baseball fields, and what he

370

called "real hardware stores," where the tools and equipment were up to a workman's standards. He even liked the old churches. He liked eating in diners with booths and counters and big front windows.

Anybody could see he was glad to be there, so in spite of his size and the fact that his muscles were from heavy work instead of playing games, people glanced at him and felt comfortable. Eddie and the boy traveled through those towns, not past them, from Maine to Oregon, and Canada to Texas. As far as the boy knew, they never left a trail behind them, because little towns on big highways saw plenty of travelers, and he and Eddie were by no means the ones who stood out the most.

After he grew up and lost Eddie, he occasionally traveled that way, but it was mostly because he missed Eddie. A lot of the little towns had become suburbs and bedroom communities of bigger places. Other little towns simply died of weathering and obsolescence because the local economy didn't work anymore. After that, when something — a business, a building, a road — broke down, there was no practical reason to put more money into it. Eventually the size and anonymity of large chain hotels just outside the biggest cities kept him safer.

Once Schaeffer left the United States, he never missed it consciously while he was in England, only when he was back in the country. He would have stayed away forever except for the fact that those men from the United States who were visiting England had, in spite of his efforts to stay out of sight, recognized him and known that his death was worth a great deal of money. This trip back was his third; he had managed to make it back to England after his first two, and was hoping to do so one more time.

Driving along the east side of the river toward the north, he realized that Eddie was what he was missing. Eddie was what he'd had instead of a family. Those road trips they'd taken to murder someone were what he'd had instead of family vacations. This part of the world, the Northeast and the Midwest as far as Detroit, reminded him of his teenage years. After that, Eddie was dead and he was alone, and he had traveled where he needed to, gotten paid for many deaths, and had become rich. Even before his troubles hit, he had begun to think about where he could go if everything went wrong and he had to leave the country. The choices were limited because the only language he spoke was English, aside from a smattering of southern Italian slang and expletives. He had flown to England and taken a train to Bath because he'd seen pictures of it in a brochure.

This trip was different. He knew for certain that the one who had been sending killers out to get rid of him wasn't some enemy of Balacontano's who thought the Butcher's Boy was good bait to trap Balacontano, or an underling who wanted to impress Balacontano and become his heir apparent. It was Balacontano himself who didn't want him to do something to jeopardize his parole. And he knew that once Balacontano was out, he wouldn't stay at some apartment in New York City being watched by the FBI until he died.

Just outside Albany, Route 9 crossed the Hudson River, and he switched to Route 4, which took him into Saratoga Springs. The town was exactly as Schaeffer had remembered it — old brick buildings with carved wood flourishes at the eaves, a few green parks and ponds, and wooden Victorians along the major streets. He drove through town, stopping at only two traffic signals and using the time to study the place until the light turned green again.

And then he was out in the countryside, among the vast horse farms with their white fences and broad green fields. Each had a fancy gate with a name on it that opened onto a straight farm road, most of them wide enough for two trucks to pass. The roads led up to the highest spot on the property, where the house stood, and went on past it to the barns and stables. They all had lush pastures and dirt-covered paddocks for exercise and training.

There were dozens of these places, many of them founded in the 1860s, when the racetrack opened. Now and then he would see the shiny brown thoroughbred horses far up the incline near the stables.

His memory was his road map. He remembered the frigid winter night when he had driven along this road looking for the farm. That night the big trees along this stretch had been bare, black silhouettes, skeletal against the white snow and ice. Today the big trees — possibly the ones that had grown up to replace the old ones — were thick with bright green leaves that had been washed by last night's summer rain, so they shone in the sunlight. The fences of piled stones along the road looked about the same.

Saratoga Springs was founded in the 1690s, and the stones were the ones that farmers' plows turned up. The farmers carried them to the edge of their land and piled them up, artifacts of their small victories over the wild land's resistance.

When he saw the horse farm, he immediately recognized it from that night all those years ago. He remembered being worried that the ground would be so frozen that he wouldn't be able to bury the fragmentary remains of Arthur Fieldston. Most of the land had been frozen rock-hard, but he'd found the big manure pile up there not far from the stables. The manure was much warmer than the ground was, some fresh from the horses and the rest producing its own heat as it composted.

Today he saw no horses — the farm was as deserted as the scene of a plague.

33

"Ms. Waring?"

"Yes?"

"This is Agent McGuinn, FBI. I've been asked to let you know that we have a temporary glitch on the Balacontano matter."

"What is it?"

"Mr. Balacontano has been kept under remote surveillance, so that he and his associates would not be aware that he was being watched, and so that any of the people who may have been waiting for his release could be intercepted and arrested before they got close to him. The problem is that the elderly man who was being followed and protected was not the right one."

"Who is he?"

"His name is Mario Silva. He's a cousin of the subject."

"How did that happen?"

"When the subject was released, a large contingent of relatives and associates were waiting to greet him — men, women, and children. They surrounded him, patted him on the back, shook his hand, and hugged him. The subject and his cousin are both short, around five feet six, so the view of them was sometimes blocked by taller associates. The cousin had arrived wearing a raincoat and a hat. At one point, people slipped an overcoat and hat onto the subject, and at the same moment the cousin shrugged his off, and it seems to have disappeared into a baby carriage. The associates hustled the cousin into a limousine and drove off, while the subject left with Mario Silva's family."

"You've been briefed on who the subject is?"

"Well, yes, ma'am. His name is Carlo Balacontano. He was a Mafia boss."

"Yes. He's the boss of the biggest New York Mafia crime family."

"He was? Interesting."

"Not was. He *is.* When he was in prison, he had stand-in bosses on the outside watching the businesses — meaning the prostitution, extortion, drug sales, money laundering, kidnapping, and so on. But he still makes all the tough decisions, such as who should be killed. Now that he's out, I would say that would make him one of the twenty or thirty most powerful men in America."

The man sounded sick. "I see. We have several addresses for him. I'm forwarding them to Organized Crime right now."

"Send it to me personally. Elizabeth Waring."

"I will. Thank you for letting me know. Good-bye." He sounded as though he was embarrassed and in a hurry to escape this conversation.

She hung up the phone and walked out of her office and down the hall to the deputy assistant's office. The receptionist saw her and immediately called Holstra, who came to the door of his inner office. "Come in, Elizabeth," he said.

Elizabeth stepped in, and he shut the door. She said, "The FBI got faked out. They've been conducting the surveillance we requested on Balacontano's cousin."

"A double?"

She shrugged. "Close enough, apparently."

Holstra shuffled through some papers and held one up. "I see a notation here that his attorney, Mr. Herren, has filed a lawsuit to demand a new trial to clear him of the crime he's been convicted of. That means they'll be in touch."

Elizabeth said, "I can clear your mind of worry about the lawsuit. Carlo Balacontano is now free. He's a man who has committed hundreds of felonies and continues to every day. He is, conservatively, a multibillionaire. Now he doesn't care whether people think he's innocent or guilty. The potential appeal was just a way to get important legal talent interested. If the parole had been denied, he would have pursued the lawsuit. Now that he's free, he'll forget it. He'd be a fool to let federal prosecutors have another crack at him."

"What are you thinking of doing?"

"As of a few seconds ago, we have a list of his addresses. I'll get people started on checking those. But if he gave the authorities the addresses of the places where he actually intends to stay, he would be the first crime boss to do that."

"That sounds troublesome."

"Much less troublesome than finding him a few months from now will be. And right now his family is in a fight with the Scarpi family, which may keep him in or near New York, where he can command his forces."

"It's ironic, isn't it?" he said. "This is the convict you've always said hadn't done the crime he was in for."

"He's innocent of that murder, yes. But

he's not innocent of murder. He got into that mess in the first place because he thought it was a great idea to hire a first-rate killer to do some murders, and then hire some third-rate killers to ambush him instead of just paying him."

"I'll bet he's smarter than that now," said the deputy assistant.

"I'm pretty sure he is," she said.

34

Michael Schaeffer rented a suite in a good hotel in Lake George, only twenty-seven miles from the farm outside Saratoga Springs. Each morning and each evening after dark he would pass the farm on the highway. In the morning he looked for cars, farm vehicles, and people. In the evening he looked for lights.

On the third morning he parked his car in the woods at the edge of a nearby farm's fallow field a distance back from the road and then walked to visit Balacontano's farm. He had not seen any horses on the farm, and his nose told him no animals had been living there for a long time. He supposed that Carl Bala's horse business had been an expensive operation, one that must have involved fixing races.

Clearly Bala's stand-in dons hadn't sold the place. It still had the same sign at the gate, which had been repainted to keep it bright. Carl Bala hadn't needed any money in a federal prison, and a large parcel of land in a famous place was one of the few things that almost always gained more value the less the owner did to it.

It occurred to Schaeffer that there might have been other, secret reasons for Bala to keep it. The farm was big, at least a thousand acres. Bala had nothing to do with burying Arthur Fieldston's head and hands, but he might have buried almost anything else on the property. Or he may have kept the land because he hoped that someday, evidence would be found there that would exonerate him.

Schaeffer walked along the fence at the edge of the pasture to reach the house. He walked around the building searching for signs of an alarm system or surveillance cameras, but found none. Professional criminals, as a rule, didn't like alarm systems because a false alarm gave police probable cause to enter without a warrant, and surveillance cameras were most likely to record their owners doing something illegal. And Balacontano had last visited here years before cheap, modern alarms became available.

Schaeffer got into the kitchen by sliding the cover of a large dog door upward with his fingertips so that it opened from the bottom, lying on his side and reaching up to turn the small knob that unlocked the deadbolt, feeling to find another bolt that went into the floor, and then turning the inner knob. He supposed that in the old days the main security device had been the dog.

When he was inside, he opened the big Sub-Zero refrigerator and saw that the shelves were empty except for an open box of baking soda to keep the air inside smelling fresh. To him this meant that the current caretakers were not the live-in variety, and confirmed his belief that the place was not yet staffed with Bala's soldiers.

He wandered through the rooms. There was a collection of horse-themed table lamps, a glass case full of ribbons that his horses had won, and a wall of nineteenth-century prints with jockeys riding or standing and holding the reins of horses with backs that looked too long for a real horse.

The detail most important to Schaeffer was that all this clutter had been dusted, so somebody must have been hired for janitorial duty. He would need to be ready to meet them or sneak out if he saw them coming.

He searched drawers and cabinets for weapons, cell phones, hidden cameras, or any kind of defensive or communication system other than the telephones on some of the tables and counters.

He kept moving, trying to memorize the whole house. He was briefly tempted to sabotage a few of the locks and latches so that he could get in and out easily, but knew it was best to change only one that was unlikely to be noticed. If too many were tampered with, then someone doing even the most cursory check would find something. He chose one of the windows in the basement and unscrewed the latch without removing it, so it looked the same but would fall off if he tugged the window from the outside.

It was only a couple of hours later that he heard the sound of a car coming up the farm road toward the house. He looked out the front window and saw the white van of a cleaning crew. He went out the kitchen door as they approached, and hurried to the stables to watch. The crew consisted of four women who arrived with their own mops, brooms, and buckets of supplies, including an arsenal of commercial-grade cleaners. From time to time, he would see one or two of them washing windows or polishing furniture. Whenever one of them opened a door, he would hear the sound of a vacuum cleaner or a floor polisher from inside.

The four women from the cleaning service were a very encouraging sight to Schaeffer. Their presence might mean that the house was about to be occupied. They worked a very long day, roughly a double shift, and in the evening he still saw lighted windows in bedrooms and bathrooms upstairs. When they finished and drove off, he entered the house again. He saw that they had put sheets and pillowcases on the beds, and soap, towels, toilet paper, and facial tissues in the bathrooms.

Late at night, he walked to the farm where he had parked his car in the woods, drove it to Balacontano's horse farm and up to a large barn that held trucks, tractors, lawn mowers, and trailers. He opened the big barn door and drove the car inside, parked it among the other vehicles, covered it with a tarp, and then set some old paint cans on the roof and hood. He closed the door, climbed up into the loft, and slept until dawn.

Late in the morning, a pair of men arrived in a big black SUV with tinted windows. They drove to the gate and up the road to the house, then kept going the rest of the way up to the stable, got out, and began a walking inspection of the whole property. They went to the barn where grain and hay used to be stored when the horses were still on the farm, and then to the barn where Schaeffer was hiding. Schaeffer watched them enter, take short-barreled assault rifles out from under their coats, and walk around surveying the machines, but they showed no curiosity about what they were or whether they were as they should be. He decided the men were just looking for the presence of strangers or signs that any had been there recently. When they stepped out, covering their short rifles with their coats on their way to the next building, his theory seemed confirmed. Schaeffer waited a few minutes and then crawled to the closed hatch to the loft, put his eye to the crack where it met its frame, and watched.

They were checking the property to make sure it was safe and ready for Carlo Balacontano. When they had finished with the outbuildings and the general survey of the farm through binoculars, they got back in their black SUV and drove around the perimeter of the outer fence and then to the house. They parked with the front wheels aimed down the farm road toward the distant highway.

They opened the hatchback of the SUV,

took out a pair of suitcases and a large, heavy cooler, and carried them up on the porch and into the house. Schaeffer sat in the loft of the barn and watched them work. These two were scouts sent ahead to verify that the house was clean and in good repair, and that nobody had gotten to the farm first or posed a hazard. The next stage would be to call New York City or wherever Bala was and report that the farm was ready.

He could tell the Balacontano family had a pretty effective strategy. When the next SUV got to the area, maybe to the city of Saratoga Springs, someone would call the cell phone of one of the two men who had secured the farm. If nobody answered, it would mean that the two scouts were dead and the house was no longer secure.

Schaeffer prepared to wait, and the place he had picked was ideal. It was a spot where he and the two advance men wouldn't meet but from where he could easily see the house. He had the tactical advantage of altitude, and his space was one that the two men had already searched and found safe. He waited until after dark to retrieve from his car trunk the AR-15 rifle and three loaded magazines, a .45 semiautomatic pistol and two spare magazines for that, and some protein bars and water left over from

387

his long drive to Saratoga.

The next morning, another large black SUV appeared at the far end of the long farm road. Schaeffer saw a man get out of the passenger seat, take the spike out of the hasp at the latch, move the gate out of the way, watch the SUV drive past him, and then close the gate again. He climbed back into his seat for the ride up the hill to the house.

Schaeffer climbed down the ladder from the loft, walked briskly to the rear of the house, knelt to open the basement window, and then put his legs in, turned, and lowered himself into the basement. He pulled his weapons inside, closed the window, replaced the latch, and climbed the stairs to the kitchen. He walked through the kitchen to the dining room cradling his loaded AR-15 rifle. He stepped into the living room and then stopped near the front window to look out and be sure everyone was in place.

The new black SUV was climbing the gradual incline toward the house. The two advance men who had come to secure the house were standing on the front porch, now wearing the suits they had worn the day before instead of just shirts and pants. He knew they had neckties on too, because the one on the right hadn't properly tugged down the back of his collar, leaving a thin line of green silk showing beneath it.

Schaeffer had decided that he could not begin until the car came to a stop. If the two advance men did not remain where they stood, the car would wheel around and roar off. He studied the sight, making final decisions about the order of his shots and the ways he would need to move as it happened.

As the car moved closer and tilted upward slightly on the road's last incline, he could see the sun light the two men in the front seats, but got only a shadowy view of the important man in the back seat.

The car stopped fifteen feet from the front steps, and Schaeffer fired through the living-room window at the men standing on the front porch, placing a rifle bullet through the back of the head of the man on the left, then the one on the right.

As they fell out of the way, Schaeffer adjusted his aim a degree to the left and fired through the car's windshield into the driver's head, then moved his aim ten degrees to the left as the man in the passenger seat swung his door open. Schaeffer fired three rapid shots before he saw that the first shot had gone through the man's temple.

Schaeffer leaned the AR-15 against the

wall. The silence of the big farm returned, but this time it was more profound. His six rapid shots had scared off most of the birds and left the others still and voiceless, so the only sounds were the faint breeze moving through the leaves of the trees that shaded the house and a slow tick as the hot engine of the SUV cooled down.

He waited. The man alone in the back seat had not moved. Schaeffer wondered whether his rifle shot into one of the men in front had gone through and hit the one in back. The world remained still, as though holding its breath.

Then the lock of the left rear door clicked, a shoe kicked it open wide, and a crouching man dashed out, running hard.

Schaeffer walked out the door onto the porch, sidestepped past the bodies of the two scouts, then jumped off the porch and ran.

Schaeffer was surprised that Carl Bala could run so fast after all of those years in prison, but he supposed that Elizabeth Waring had been right. The forced regime of plain food and daily exercise had kept him fit.

Bala set off across a vast green pasture, a level expanse of grass surrounded by white wooden-rail fences. After a hundred yards,

Bala craned his neck to look over his shoulder.

What he saw was Michael Schaeffer, running steadily at a fast lope directly toward him. Instantly Bala seemed to feel the weight of regret at slowing his pace long enough to look back. He turned his face forward and ran as hard as he could to make up the lost time. Soon the extra effort began to tire him, and his steps slowed. He wasn't running straight anymore. He was weaving, pumping his arms too hard, and Schaeffer could see his back rising and falling with his labored breaths.

Schaeffer maintained the same speed, not following Bala's meandering path, but focusing on his back and heading straight for it. Every step brought Schaeffer closer to Bala's back, and he was gaining fast.

Bala began to have trouble lifting his knees high enough. Soon his left toe scraped the ground, and he sprawled on the grass. He pushed himself up with his arms and set off again, but Schaeffer caught up. He gave Bala a push and watched him fall again.

Bala gasped for air, his face contorted into an open-mouthed mask. "Wait," he said. "I'm Carlo Balacontano."

"You've been trying to kill me."

Bala's eyes focused on Schaeffer as though

he had just realized who he was. He rasped, "I can fix this. All of it. I have the money."

"You were safe in prison. You should have stayed."

"You think so?"

"Yes. That's why I made sure you got out." Bala's hand slithered toward the inner pocket of his jacket. Schaeffer waited until he could tell the hand had reached the weapon, then fired his .45 pistol through the old man's forehead.

Schaeffer picked up the brass casing his pistol had ejected, walked back across the pasture to the house, and went inside. He disassembled the AR-15 rifle and picked up the six brass casings that had been ejected onto the living room floor.

There was still quite a bit of work to do. He went to the barn where his car was parked, uncovered it, and threw the tarp over a lawn mower. He climbed to the loft, retrieved his remaining belongings, swept away his footprints, and climbed back down to put his weapons and belongings into the car.

Next, he looked closely at the backhoe that was parked with the other machinery. It was not so different from the one that Don Sarkassian had taught him to operate to sift the dirt and sand on the firing range when he was a kid. He saw the key hanging in the cab, sat in the seat and tried it, but the battery was dead. He looked at all the other machinery and found that the battery in one of the two tractors was strong, so he traded it for the battery of the backhoe.

He had to siphon some gasoline from the tractor's tank and pour it into the backhoe, then drain the tank of the second tractor to fill the backhoe's tank. In a few minutes he managed to get the machine started. He let it idle to warm up while he opened the big barn door and drove his car out. Then he drove the backhoe out and down the farm road as far as the pasture behind the stable. He began to dig.

He calculated that he would need a hole about ten feet wide, forty feet long, and seven feet deep, to do a proper job. He worked at the project for hours without stopping. He found that the backhoe Sarkassian had taught him to use about fifty years earlier had been much harder to operate than this one, which had a more powerful engine, more responsive controls, and a much better seat. He worked quickly once he got used to the backhoe, and his scoop dug deeper into soft, yielding levels of earth.

This part of the country had been forests since the last ice age, so the ground was a mixture of plant matter and ground-up minerals, and the bedrock was far below. He dumped each big shovelful of dirt he lifted out onto the ground, and when the glow of the sun looked as though it might soon be too weak to let him work any longer, he decided it meant that he was done.

He drove the backhoe out of the big trench, climbed down from the seat, walked to the front of the house where the two black SUVs were parked, and got into the first one. The key was still in it and so was the dead driver. He pushed the man into the passenger seat and drove the SUV into the field where Carlo Balacontano lay dead. He dragged and lifted the body into the back seat, drove to the big trench he had dug, lined the SUV up carefully, and drove it down the incline to the end. He found he had made the trench just about as narrow as it could be to still allow him to open the driver's side door far enough to get out.

He walked to the second vehicle but didn't see a key. He found it in the pants pocket of one of the two dead advance men. He drove their SUV close to the front porch, loaded the two bodies into the rear hatch, loaded in the remaining body, and then drove the SUV into the trench.

Because of the incline, he couldn't drive the second SUV down far enough to get the roof completely below ground level, but that was all right. He wanted the bodies to be found within a day or so, to be sure all the men who thought that killing Schaeffer would make them rich learned that it wouldn't anymore. The man who would have paid them was dead.

He got into the backhoe and then scraped and shoveled the mounds of dirt back into the trench on top of the cars. The volume of the two SUVs was great enough so that the dirt he'd dug out more than covered both vehicles when he was finished. The top of the second SUV rose a couple of feet above ground level in a small mound. When he was satisfied, he drove the backhoe back into its place in the barn.

Next he went to work on the final touches in the house. It took him about two hours to be sure he'd removed any sign that could have proved who the intruder had been. Then he drove from the farm toward the south, and in the dark he took all his own ammunition and disassembled weapons and disposed of them in bodies of water along the way.

He stopped at a hotel on Long Island and made reservations for his flight from JFK to

Paris, then showered and put on new clothes. He left the car he'd bought in a parking lot with the keys in it before he walked to the well-lit spot where the Lyft driver was to pick him up to take him to the airport.

35

Elizabeth Waring was in her friend David's apartment in Boca Raton, watching him bring the two plates to the table. He said, "I think you're going to like this. I was planning it for the next time you came to Florida, and here you are."

She looked down at her plate. "It smells wonderful. What is it?"

"It's chicken paprikash, a humble dish, but deservedly revered among bachelor chefs of Hungary and elsewhere."

"I thought that might be what it was. I can hardly wait."

David said, "Years ago when I was at the UN, a Hungarian diplomat told me that when he was young, his love life depended on this recipe, and that the women he served it to had made all the terrible things in his life bearable."

Elizabeth dipped the tip of her fork in and tasted the sauce. "I can see how you might impress a woman, particularly during a period when food was scarce and she was close to starving."

"Not the best compliment I've had. But I have many more recipes. I was in the State Department for years."

"No you weren't, you liar," she said. "You were in — and that means still are in — the CIA. State was just your cover."

"Believe that if you want," he said.

"Well, it helped you meet some great cooks."

"And now I dine with great women."

"Not too many, I hope."

"I meant you," he said. "When are you going to retire and travel with me?"

"Interesting coincidence," she said. "Just before I left for the airport this afternoon, I filed my notice of intention to retire in three months."

David grinned, knelt, and said, "Will you marry me?"

"What?"

"I'm unprepared right now, but I'll get you a ring with a diamond the size of a brussels sprout tomorrow."

"No, of course not," she laughed. "Get up and stop it."

He sat back at the table.

"I'm not marrying anybody," she said.

"I'm a grandmother."

"And I'm a grandfather."

"So you should know better. I'm perfectly pleased with my sinful ways and plan to keep them up. Now that I know you cook things besides fried eggs, I may visit more often, but I'll never marry again."

"Suit yourself," he said. "I guess all I can give you is dessert."

"Perfect," she said.

He got up and disappeared into the kitchen. Elizabeth reached into the purse at her feet and looked at her cell phone. The message began, "Carlo Balacontano has been murdered." She sighed. "Of course he has." She turned the phone off, slipped it into the purse, and pushed the purse away with her foot.

36

The man with the British passport that said "Charles Ackerman" spent five days in Paris walking and scanning the faces around him to be sure he had not brought anything unwanted back across the Atlantic behind him. It was a self-imposed quarantine.

At the end of the five days in Paris, he took a train from Gare du Nord to St. Pancras station in London. It arrived on schedule in two hours and twenty minutes, and he took the underground to Victoria Station and then another train to Bath.

He carried his well-traveled leather suitcase along the streets, walking past the familiar sights and enjoying the pleasant feel of the place in spite of the unusual number of college students and tourists.

He kept going to Holroyd House, Meg's family's favorite home, and the place where he and Meg had lived since their marriage. He went past the Royal Crescent and uphill for half a block on one of the next streets, climbed the stone steps, and unlocked the big creamy-white front door. He walked toward the rear of the house along the hallway, then turned and stepped into Meg's office.

He stood by her desk, facing the window, where she could look out at the bright flowers of the eighteenth-century garden, but she was not there. He walked the rest of the house, but there was no sign of her. The place looked as though everything had been dusted, polished, and cleaned, but he'd noticed the calendar on her desk still had the date 5 May on its top page.

He took a set of keys from a drawer of her desk, walked out the door and a few streets away to the house he had bought right after he had arrived in Bath over thirty years ago. At the time he had been suffering from the knowledge that he had implacable enemies, and his imagination had not yet been restrained by educated taste. He had remodeled the house to install an indoor pool, brick-and-steel reinforcements to the outer walls, and thick glass bricks where windows had been. He had turned it into a small fortress. Since his marriage, he hadn't lived in the place for more than a few days at a time, usually when Meg was away on a trip

401

or they were waiting out crews of painters or carpenters working at Holroyd House.

He unlocked the door of his house and walked through the living room to the den that he had designed years ago to find Meg sitting at his desk, looking at her laptop computer. She sensed she wasn't alone and looked up.

The tears welled in her green eyes and streaked down to her chin, and she smiled the smile that had caught him over thirty years ago. She called out, "Oh, there you are, Michael. It's been weeks and weeks. I've been planning your funeral. I guess all that work is wasted now."

He smiled. "Where were you going to bury me?"

"Well, I wasn't sure if I would get your body back. If I did, you would be in the family crypt with me, where our bones would intertwine. If I couldn't get your body, you'd still get a tastefully engraved plaque, like the ancestors who died at sea."

"Since I couldn't have a noble birth, a noble burial is nice."

"You wouldn't be the worst man in the family crypt by any means."

They stood face to face and then kissed in a long, gentle embrace while he felt her tears streaming on his cheek. After a while, she pushed him back a little. "I'll bet you would like a strong drink. Let me make you one."

"A little later, I think," he said. "I've been traveling most of the day. Right now I'd like to get these clothes off and take a bath. No, a swim, since we're here."

"An excellent idea," she said. "If you don't mind, I'll join you. I don't think either of us has a bathing suit here though. They're all in York."

He put his arm around her waist, and they walked across the foyer toward the steps that led to the dressing rooms and the pool below. He said, "I suggest we do without them."

"I was sure you would. Did things go well in Australia?"

"Not so bad. Practically a false alarm. Is all well here?"

"Now it is."

ABOUT THE AUTHOR

Thomas Perry is the bestselling author of over twenty novels, including the critically acclaimed Jane Whitefield series, Forty Thieves, and *The Butcher's Boy,* which won the Edgar Award. He lives in Southern California.

The employees of Thorndike Press hope you have enjoyed this Large Print book. All our Thorndike, Wheeler, and Kennebec Large Print titles are designed for easy reading, and all our books are made to last. Other Thorndike Press Large Print books are available at your library, through selected bookstores, or directly from us.

For information about titles, please call:
(800) 223-1244

or visit our website at:
gale.com/thorndike

To share your comments, please write:
Publisher
Thorndike Press
10 Water St., Suite 310
Waterville, ME 04901